RADIO SILENT

BOOK ONE: PAIGE TURNER MYSTERIES

T.E. ROBINS

1st edition, 2023 – ISBN 978-1-990802-32-4 (ebook) | ISBN 978-1-990802-33-1 (paperback) | ISBN 978-1-990802-34-8 (hardcover) | ISBN 978-1-990802-35-5 (dust-jacketed hardcover) | ISBN 978-1-990802-36-2 (audiobook)

Contents

Prologue

A CLEARING IN THE woods. Sun beams on a camp chair with a hoodie splayed over the back of it. A water bottle lists drunkenly out of the too-shallow cup holder.

In the dip of the canvas seat lies a walkie-talkie which crackles to life, "Rider seventy-seven, clear over jump three."

Several seconds later, "Rider seventy-seven, clear over jump four."

The birds keep twittering. They're used to the all-day-long white-noise chatter of the radio.

"One refusal at jump five. Over on the second attempt."

A distant thrumming builds to a drumming tattoo. Hard hooves striking a hollow sound from the earth.

The horse's breath ragged and throaty. His rider calling, "Steady! Steady!"

They pound through the clearing with the sun glinting off the horse's bright bay coat and the rider's satin helmet cover.

The horse's hooves cut the sod. He rocks back on his haunches and launches over the huge log — white flag on the left, red on the right — flying, landing, flicking his tail and carrying his rider forward.

The interruption ends on an enthusiastic, "Good boy!" and retreating hoof-beats. The birdsong resumes, along with the walkie-talkie's reports, "... clear over jump seven ..." all the way through to the finish.

Then, "Jump six? Radio check jump six. We didn't get your last report."

The feathered beating of a chickadee's wings, a breeze riffling the newly-leafed-out trees, the rustle of a squirrel in the underbrush.

The radio again, "Hold on the course, please, while Nate goes to check on jump six. All other jump judges hold position."

The next sound in the clearing is the rumble of a golf cart and the bump of its small tires over the grassy trail. It stops in the space between the big log and the camp chair. A man walks over, picks up the walkie-talkie, and says, "Control? I'm at jump six. There's nobody here."

One

I'm standing at the edge of a rugby pitch watching the demo of a robotic line-painting machine ... which has just lost a wheel and keeled over.

The guy in question, wearing a polo shirt emblazoned with **Grass Graffiti** is sprinting across the pitch.

The info sheet I'm clutching explains that the Grass Graffiti 2.0 will save the rugby club fifty percent on its paint costs. I lift my camera and zoom in on the glugging paint forming a white puddle around the capsized robot.

At least I didn't have to pay for the paint.

Next to me a man swears and turns to the woman standing beside him. "Kick-off for under-sixteen regionals is at 8:30 tomorrow morning."

At least I'm not organizing the under-sixteen regionals.

I'm trying to look on the bright side.

That was my editor's advice when she handed me the press release titled **Robo-Rugby Rumble: Line Painter Tackles Turf Trouble** and said, "Three-hundred words should do it. You'll get a photo credit, too," and I replied, "Fantastic. I'll wait for the Pulitzer committee to contact me."

"Pulitzers are about attitude." Maddy's voice was unusually sharp. It made me double-take. "What does that mean?"

She sighed. "Studies show people who look on the bright side live longer, Paige."

"Do they also win more Pulitzer Prizes?"

"I don't know. Why don't you research it and write me a story on it?"

I was tempted to point out no matter how good my attitude, nobody could expect to win a Pulitzer with the type of stories she'd been assigning me — **Party like it's $19.99** on how to host a barbecue on the cheap, and **Baking Bad** about a cannabis dispensary that helps people incorporate pot into their favourite family recipes — but there was something in her tone that made me cut my losses and head out to the rugby club.

Now I suspect the Grass Graffiti rep wishes he could cut his losses.

I send Maddy the photo of the incapacitated robot, with the press release headline rewritten "Rogue Rugby Robo: Line Painter Triggers Turf Trouble."

And that's when I receive the text that changes everything.

***

My sister doesn't text me in the middle of the day. She doesn't text me "just because." In fact, my sister rarely texts me at all.

So, when I read her message saying, **Any chance you could meet up soon?** my spidey senses tingle. Even more so when I reply, **I'm actually only fifteen minutes away. I could come now?** and she immediately types, **Yes, great. At the office.**

It's an even shorter drive to her office than to her house. I've never been there, but I know it's on the main street of the village close to our tiny hometown. Fortunately, that village is still small enough for me to easily find Faye's law firm.

As I start the car, my latest podcast starts auto-playing. After enjoying the first two episodes, it's grating on my nerves, so I fumble to switch to radio. On the local news, they're interviewing the owner of the cannabis dispensary I wrote about for my **Baking Bad** story. *You've got to be kidding ...*

Power off. Silence.

Which, of course, just provides a vacuum for my thoughts to slide over to why Faye wants to see me now.

Don't get me wrong. I love my sister, and she loves me. It's just that our love is polite, and somewhat restrained, the way it is with all my siblings who are just enough older than me that they sometimes feel more like aunts and uncles than brothers and sisters.

I see them regularly — for holidays, and milestone anniversaries, and the births of nieces and nephews — almost always organized by invitations from Faye.

Just never by text, and never at 2:00 p.m. on a Thursday.

***

When I step into the reception area of Faye's office, which was once the spacious front hall of one of the classic three-storey brick houses sprinkled along the main streets of most small Ontario towns, I don't expect the receptionist to recognize me.

Which is why it's disconcerting when a smile spreads across her face and she says, "You must be Faye's sister."

"Did she tell you I was coming?"

"No, but you look so much like her. And, of course, I've seen your photo in her office."

The woman rises from her chair. "She's just wrapping up with a client in the meeting room. I'll take you through to her office to wait."

I follow her, wondering, *Do I look like Faye?* I would have said no. From top to bottom, we're so different. Every hair in Faye's long bob turns under at all times. With her tasteful earrings, clean-framed glasses, and capsule wardrobe of Oxford shirts in a variety of tasteful colours, paired with chinos that look custom tailored to her slim frame, she's got the look of someone you'd trust to write your will or run your parent council.

I, on the other hand, call my hair tousled, and pretend it's a style. I can usually only ever find one earring at a time, and my wardrobe is a capsule of denim and jersey.

My sister and I are the same height, though. Our hair's the same shade — although she enhances hers with subtle highlights. I definitely have more freckles than her, but I suppose the bone structure underneath those freckles is quite similar.

It's a funny feeling to think I look so like my sister that this person I've never met pegged us as siblings. It's even funnier to walk into her office — cream walls, original trim around the windows and doors, Persian rug on the wood floor, and well-cared-for plants on a shelf by the window — and see a picture of me on her tidy desk.

Not just me — all five of us — Faye, Xander, Macy, and Rowan as well. I guess all the Turner siblings look alike. Especially when we're smiling for the camera.

"Can I bring you anything? Something to drink?" The receptionist snaps my attention away from the photo.

"No thanks." I say it less because I'm not thirsty and more because I have no idea if this strange midday, midweek summons is more of a cup-of-tea or whiskey-neat situation.

Besides, I have my water bottle with me. After the woman leaves, I pull it out of my canvas satchel. Its original fake-wood effect is mostly rubbed off and what's left is largely covered by stickers from my university radio station and newspaper, along with one that says, **That sounds like a you problem** and, taking pride of place, one wrapped around the entire bottle that reads, **Page Turners Pub – Books and Beers / Beers and Books.**

I hear Faye's hard-soles clicking behind me and shove the tatty water bottle back into my bag.

"Paige. I hope you weren't waiting long."

My sister's voice is just as calm and polite as it always is. Her clothes are wrinkle-free. Her nails are clean and neatly rounded. No visual hints as to why I'm sitting here.

She settles onto her tufted velvet chair upholstered in a rich yellow shade. I was one of many people who chipped in to buy it for her fortieth birthday. It's designer-gorgeous and ergonomic — form and function together. Perfect for my capable sister.

It's the slump of her shoulders that provides the first clue. Faye isn't a sloucher. Next, the sigh. Growing up in her house, I heard her chastise her kids, "A sigh says more than you think it does." The unspoken ending to that sentence was, *and what it says isn't good.*

Then she rises again, steps over to the floor-to-ceiling built-in unit which takes up one entire wall of her office and opens a door that turns out to hide a small refrigerator. She pulls out two cans, sets them on the desk, and sits down again.

Diet Coke. Jeepers creepers. This is worse than a whiskey-neat situation.

This is an aspartame-level emergency.

I lift my eyebrows and pick up one of the cans. "Is it that bad?" Back when I lived with her, the only fizz Faye allowed in the house was sparkling water. If I wanted a Diet Coke I had to hide it in my bedroom.

"What?" She rubs her temple. "Oh, I drink it when I'm stressed."

She pauses, then a grin steals across her face. "I drink it every day."

Although the grin is gone in an instant, its effect lingers. I've always been secure in my sister's love, but that love has been as her ward — a charge for her to protect. I sit a weird half-generation between herself and her own kids, making me neither child, nor equal.

For the first time, in our shared guilty pleasure, I feel like an adult in her presence.

The equal footing gives me the guts to ask, "What's ruffling your feathers, sis?"

For a second, I wonder if I've gone too far. If she's going to shut down, clam up, collect herself, and say, "Nothing at all."

Instead, she takes a big swig of her drink and says, "Oh, Paige. There's no good way to tell you this — a girl's gone missing."

***

I'm not sure if I'm more shaken by the news of the missing woman, or by Faye raising it with me.

We don't talk about this.

It's my first reaction, and I know it's wrong. *This isn't about you,* I tell myself. *Focus. Ask a semi-intelligent question.*

"Who?" I manage.

It's not great, but it's enough to get Faye talking.

"Her name's Wren. Wren Sheedy. She works at Oak Copse — you know, the stables where Charlotte rides. Charlotte's rattled. Wren teaches her sometimes and she really looks up to her."

"Oh!" I clap my hand to my breastbone. I know what it's like to be fourteen and to have someone you care about go missing. "I'm so sorry for Charlotte. And, of course, for Wren. And for you, Faye."

The only time I've ever seen my self-possessed sister cry was when she tripped on a pile of my nephew's Lego, landed on the coffee table, and broke her arm. Now, though, her eyes are suspiciously shiny.

She exhales so forcefully her hair lifts from around her face. "It's hit me hard, Paige. I'm finding it really upsetting." My gut twists. The pain in her voice hurts me more than I could have guessed.

"What happened?" Wow. There's my journalism degree showing. I'm up to two-word questions now.

Still, it's enough to prompt Faye to hand her phone to me. "It's probably easiest if you read this." She leans back in her chair. "Take your time. I'll just sit here and numb my stress with artificial sweetener."

Loaded on her screen is a Facebook post from a group called Eastern Ontario Eventing.

> To anyone who was at the Oak Copse Horse Trials today, or in
> the vicinity, please read this post. Wren Sheedy, a member of the
> Oak Copse staff, did not return from the cross-country jump

where she was judging. Wren's last walkie-talkie report was at approximately 2:15 p.m., after which she stopped answering her radio.

At the time of this post, we don't know where Wren is.

Wren lives at Oak Copse, and stables her beloved palomino, Shine, there. Her car is still in its parking spot at Oak Copse.

We hope Wren will soon be home, safe and sound, but in the meantime, if you attended the horse trials, please review any photos or video footage from today. If you live in the area, please check any trail or security cameras, or dash cam footage from this afternoon.

Wren is twenty-seven years old, approximately five-foot-five, slightly built, with pink-streaked brown hair. She has a butterfly tattoo on her right shoulder. Today Wren was wearing an Oak Copse baseball cap, large silver hoop earrings with multiple small studs, a red Oak Copse volunteer t-shirt, rust breeches, and dark brown paddock boots.

Please contact provincial police with any information.

The Facebook group has thousands of members. There are two or three pictures of Wren posted over and over again. In this world where so many people walk around with high-quality cameras built into their phones, it always amazes me how many of the photos I see of missing people are blurry or grainy, and Wren's are no exception.

In one she wears a baseball cap. A dog's snout is just visible pushing over her shoulder and she has a hand up to the dog's nose and is laughing. She looks casual, carefree, happy.

In another she's mounted on a gold-coloured horse, wearing dark green riding pants, a peach-coloured shirt and, of course, a riding helmet. Although it's a tight shot, the horse's mane suggests they're in motion, as do Wren's eyes, fixed clearly on something she's riding toward.

The third one makes me catch my breath. It's not only that the pink streaks in her hair are visible — just like the ones my sister Leila had — the lift of her chin and the glint in her eye also remind me of my sister on certain days, at certain times. Like she had something to prove and was just about pulling it off.

My eyes fly to Faye and she nods. "I know. The one with the pink hair, right?"

Along with the photos are many comments using lots of praying hands and broken heart emojis. I pray you come home soon, You are loved and missed, I don't know you, but you are in my prayers.

Reading the post has given me more questions than answers. "If it was a competition, weren't there a lot of people around? How could she just disappear?"

"Jump judging is strange," Faye says. "While there are nearly thirty people distributed along the course, most judges are alone at their stations, and they usually can't see one-another, which is why they use radios to communicate. There's about three or four minutes between each horse-rider combination. Wren radioed one rider in, and was gone by the time the next one came through."

She continues, "At the end of the competition, when she didn't check in and return her radio, the stable owner — Rose — asked all the volunteers to search the property. Nobody found anything."

"What do the police say?"

"Rose called them out after the search. One car showed. They didn't search that night and they haven't made any public statements since."

"But ... the press ... I haven't seen anything."

"Mmm-hmm." I'm relieved to see a revival of my sister's usual very strong (and rather opinionated) personality. "Ever since the OJJ closed ..."

I've heard my sister's thoughts on losing the Oak Junction Journal more than once. She likes to talk to me about them, waxing on about the value of local news and how it's the lifeblood of the community. Personally, I think she just misses the affordable full-page ads her law firm always ran.

I realize Faye's still talking but, with my mind wandering, miss the beginning of her sentence. "... should write about it."

"Excuse me?"

"You should write about it," she says. "It's an important story. Somebody needs to cover it."

"I ... no ... that's not what I do." An edge of panic shortens my breath until I realize she's not serious. When people say "should" they don't really mean it: *I should exercise more, I should get to bed early, I shouldn't drink Diet Coke.* "I write shitty stories about robotic line painters."

Faye gets those two little creases between her eyebrows which, in somebody else, might indicate confusion, but for her, often means her stubbornness is taking hold. "That's what you left home to do. To go to journalism school and write important stories."

"Well, we don't all get what we want." I snap it out, fast and flip, then bite my tongue to keep from adding, *Except for those of us who have offices that could feature in* Style *magazine, an adoring husband who's kind, a good earner, and easy on the eyes, and three kids who over-achieve at every turn.*

Faye leans forward, and it's the calm, cool, collected, and in-control version of my sister I'm used to seeing who says, "Don't I know it, Paige. Do you think I signed up for fifty hours a week of writing wills and pushing paper around to complete real estate transactions?" She shakes her head. "When I went to law school, it was to right wrongs, to correct injustices, to wear robes and make clever speeches that would captivate the courtroom."

"I'm not complaining," she says. "Not exactly, anyway. But you have a chance to actually do the thing you set out to do when you got into journalism. So, all I'm saying is, do it."

"Also." She sits back, and that unfamiliar flicker of softness crosses her face again. "Charlotte was stationed at the jump next to Wren's."

No wonder she's rattled.

Lightning may not have struck twice in the same place, but it's come far too close.

Two

There's the direct route home. Then there's the way I go.

I follow back roads, blacktopped at first — even if crumbling at the shoulder — then switching to gravel, raising billows of dust behind me as I go.

I descend from the escarpment to the valley-snugged settlement where I was born. Where I had one kind of life until my early teens, until everything changed, until Faye took me in. Where I left eight years ago, just as Faye said, to go to journalism school and write important stories.

I snort thinking about how that turned out.

I pass the high school, flags limp in the summer humidity, noticeboard out front reading, Happy summer, students! Pick up your report card from the main office. Or, that's what it said back at the end of June. Somebody's removed strategic letters to spell out penis at the bottom of the sign.

Leaders of tomorrow.

Every time I'm in this place, a heaviness settles deep in my gut. *Is it an anchor of stability or a boulder of anxiety?* I ask myself and can never come to an answer.

I think the truth is, it's both at the same time. Which is no surprise. Contradictions abound here. The roads are ruler-straight, but their orderly grid is laid over wild terrain — forests growing right up to the verge. In our valley lies a manicured golf course, enclaves of suburban houses featuring outdoor kitchens and custom pools, and a row of gated mansions with manicured landscaping owned by hockey players and high-tech whizzes ... each flanked by near-impassable, wildlife-filled bush. Oak Junction residents can sip Pinot Noir in their backyard hot tubs while coyotes stalk the family dog from the other side of their picket fences.

Just last year a sunny summer day gave way to a line of thunderstorm-fueled tornados in less than half-an-hour. And a place where young women can lead an active outdoor life is one where they can also disappear in a blink.

I continue along familiar roads and revisit vivid memories. This was the route our school bus took — the bus I used to ride with Leila, our unspoken sixth sibling, and the one closest in age to me. The one not featured in the photo on Faye's desk.

Because she was gone by the time that picture was taken. Long gone.

Here's the corner where the Atkinson triplets used to catch the bus — most girls in our school had a crush on football-playing Tommy, but Leila liked Anthony, who played the cello. "He has beautiful eyebrows, Paige." Once she pointed it out, I could see that he did. Leila always found good things other people missed.

Because Leila used to, I lift my feet when I cruise over the old railway crossing, even though it's long-since been converted to part of the Trans-National recreational trail. I also slow to a near crawl when I reach the big hill our bus once slid down during an ice storm. I close my eyes just long enough to remember the sensation of Leila's fingertips pressing into my arm.

It's a bit too early for the after-work rush (such as it is in Oak Junction) so, although I slow as I pass under the flashing four-way light at the main junction, there's no need to stop. Other than the café, on the southwest corner, there are fewer memories for me here, anyway. The post office and the Oak Junction Journal, on the northwest and southeast corners, have been closed for years. Following the tornado damage, businesses are just reopening in the mini strip mall on the northeast corner and most of them are new to me.

On the last stretch of long, straight road up to the turn-off to the city, there's one memory-bomb. The bungalow I grew up in with Leila and our mother. It was my home for fourteen years, then everything changed. That's when I went to live with Faye.

It doesn't stand out. It's just one of many 1960s bungalows you can see along any roadway in the country. I don't wish I still lived there. I don't begrudge its new occupants — they have it maintained and landscaped like it never was when my mother rented it.

I do, though, wish the circumstances that forced me to leave were different.

But, like I just told my sister, we don't all get what we want.

***

By the time I park behind the pub, I'm hungry. Hot, too. The city is a good three or four degrees warmer than Oak Junction and even though both flank the same wide river, there's a big difference between being surrounded by trees and fields versus buildings and buses. Big emotions are draining, too — or at least that's what someone I interviewed for a story once told me. That's why at family gatherings we talk about easy things, like the dogs Macy breeds, the outdoor adventure business Rowan runs, and the latest extracurricular activities of Xander and Faye's kids.

Until Faye texted me today.

It's not that I condemn her for that. It's just ... a *lot*.

I have a choice. Walk up the metal staircase to the apartment I share with Dave. He'll be in the pub, working. I'll have the apartment to myself. I can stream a mindless show and let the tetchiness leave my system.

But then I'd have to make my own dinner.

Or, I can open the door in front of me, walk through the pub kitchen, sit at the bar, and have Dave serve me a(nother) cold Diet Coke and a plateful of cheesy nachos.

Nachos are the quicker, less-work-for-me, and — let's face it — more delicious solution to my grumpiness.

I step into the pub.

***

It's busier than it has any right to be this early in the day. "What's going on?" I ask Rachel, Dave's right-hand helper, who's coming from the dining area with two empty trays.

"Bus tour." She points to a hulking bus blocking the sunlight in front of the pub. The decal on the side reads, **Chapter and Verse Voyagers**. "They're mostly ladies, mostly of a certain age. They think Dave's the bomb."

Sure enough, while all the tables look occupied with handbags and jackets draped over the back of chairs, most of the people in the place are clustered around the reading area that gives Page Turners Pub its name.

From where I stand, it's the back of a lot of heads adorned with hair in shades from steel grey to bright white and, facing me, one dark-haired head, bent over a book.

I have that feeling in my gut again, only this time it's easier to analyse. I love him and I'm afraid I'll never have him.

Or not the way I want to.

Because I'm lucky enough to be his best friend and his roommate. And I'm secure in the knowledge he'll always have my back. He proved that four years ago when I wandered in here halfway through my journalism degree, freshly evicted, and on the verge of both dropping out of school and moving back to Faye's basement. If she'd take me.

I was staring at the two coffees I'd ordered — that I couldn't afford — one for me and one for the woman I was supposed to be meeting. He said, "It looks like you're not having the best day."

I agreed, "Not the best. I was supposed to have a job interview for a live-in nanny position which would have kept me from being homeless, but ..." I shrugged, and put a ten-dollar bill on the table. "If someone comes in asking for Paige Turner, just tell her ..."

"To fuck right off?"

The first thing Dave ever did was make me laugh. Then he offered me the free room in his apartment at a stupidly low rent.

When people hear the story, he tells them, "It was because of her name — same as the pub — how could I not?"

I know, though, it was because of his insane kindness and generosity. I've told him so a hundred times. But just like with my family, we only talk about the easy things. "You're kind," "You're a great friend," "You make the best nachos in the city."

I've never said, "I lie in bed at night and listen for your breathing," "That time last month when you went on a date, I had to wash dishes in the pub kitchen all night to keep from spending every minute imagining you sleeping with her," or "Your eyebrows are even sexier than Anthony Atkinson's who I used to ride the school bus with."

Leila would love Dave.

If I'm honest, that's part of the reason I hit on him, that one time, back when I'd only lived here for a few months. Sure, there was the fact that I'd had a sangria on an empty stomach, predisposing me to be giggly and horny. And there was the undeniable physical attraction that flares in me every single time I lay eyes on Dave. I could have fought both of those, though, if it wasn't for how safe he made me feel. Other people loved me, and I loved them, but they didn't look after me, and I didn't let them. Dave was different. Dave was the first person since Leila disappeared who gave me the same feeling of security she did.

So, I did what anyone would do in that situation. With Rachel home sick and me helping close the pub, I gave a final wipe to the counters, flicked off the overhead lights, and with the satisfaction of a job well done — and a lingering sangria buzz — stood on my tiptoes, slid my hands up Dave's sides, and leaned in to kiss him.

He said no. He was nice about it. He took my hands in his, and held them still, and said, "This isn't why I offered you a place to live."

The sangria curdled in my stomach. My inner voice asked, *How stupid can you be?* And the fear rushed back in. The fear I hadn't noticed inching away since I moved into his spare bedroom. The fear I'd had for so long that nobody, ever again, would love me just because I was me.

I forced a laugh, and said, "I'm so sorry. I'm tipsy and so tired I can't think straight. Please forget this happened."

What I really meant was *Please don't ask me to move out, please don't stop being my friend, please don't make me pay for this dumb mistake.*

I never drank sangria again after that night, and I never crossed the line with Dave again.

And I never will. Even though I love him more every time I see him.

He lifts his eyes from the page, and he meets my gaze, and I blush as pink as the frosting on the cupcakes Rachel's carrying toward the bookish group. Then I immediately look away. He can't know how I feel about him. Not through words, not with a loving glance. Some days it's easier than others to stuff my feelings down. Today it's particularly hard, which doesn't help my mood.

I'm also hungrier than I was when I first came in, and the busload of geriatric bookworms means I'm going to have to wait for my food, if I can even find a place to sit.

I should just go upstairs.

"Paige!"

One of the tables previously reserved by a purse and a jacket-draped chair is now occupied by Maddy.

She points to a pint glass across from her. "I got you a drink!"

She doesn't need to tell me twice. I head her way, and when I reach the table, she says, "I also ordered nachos a while ago. They shouldn't be too long."

"OK, now I'm swamped with guilt for sending you the 'Rogue Rugby Robo' headline."

"Why?" She shrugs. "It's what happened. Your headline was very funny" — I relax and enjoy a moment of smugness. It *was* funny — "one of the best things you've written in ages."

Ouch. "Yeah, well, maybe if I got assigned to decent stories."

Maddy narrows her eyes. "The writer makes the story."

"Oh, right. I forgot. Sally Armstrong and Jesse Brown always get assigned to cover pet food store openings and daycare board meetings." My words aren't nice, but my tone is worse, containing all the frustration and anger I've accumulated through the day.

Maddy straightens her shoulders, fixes me with an even gaze, and takes a deep breath, in through her nose, out through her mouth.

I know exactly what she's doing because she told me this is the technique her therapist taught her to use when facing her often-racist future mother-in-law. *Great*, now I'm on par with the bigoted MIL.

When she speaks, Maddy's voice is calm and firm. "Paige. You get the stories you earn." She stands and puts her purse over her shoulder. "Bring me a decent story and let's see what you can do with it."

***

Rachel benefits from Maddy putting me in my place. I go find her at the bar and she wrinkles her nose. "Sorry, Paige. Your food — I know. It's just that we didn't have enough staff scheduled for this many customers, and nobody's available to come in, and ..."

"I can help out."

"You can?" Her face lifts, then she shakes her head. "You don't have to. And you must be hungry."

"It's fine. If you give me a tray, I'll bus tables. Before I start washing dishes, I'll make myself a PB and J sandwich."

"Right, well, I won't say no." She hands me a tray. "If you bus, I can help the kitchen get a bunch of meals plated up."

I move around the room, collecting empty plates and glasses. This place is a reflection of Dave — with dimmable overhead lights, an individual lamp on each table, the west wall wood paneled to match the floor, the front all windows, and the east wall built entirely of bookshelves, it's welcoming, safe, and comfortable.

I linger when I'm close to Dave, listening to the edge of gravel in his voice as he moderates the group. "Who else has a story to share about meeting a famous author?" he asks. The smiles say it all. They feel welcome. They'll post five-star reviews.

I finish with the two tables that aren't part of the bus tour. One is a young couple. I'm guessing they're on a first date, heading to the nearby cineplex. The other is a guy who's been coming in regularly for the last few months. He's writing his PhD dissertation, and it's become a running joke to ask him, "What's up, Doc?"

I lift away his empty coffee cup and ask, and he says, "Actually ..."

The twinkle in his eyes makes me stop. "No!"

He nods. "Oh, yes. Submitted this morning."

I wonder what that feels like — to see a meaningful piece of work through to submission. I bite down my jealousy and force a wide smile. "Congratulations!"

It must be convincing because he stands and gives me just enough time to rest my tray on the table before grabbing me in a hug, which turns into a twirl. "I'm so happy for you!" I say as he lowers me back to the ground.

But even if I hid my envy, it's there. Gnawing at my insides so hard, I find I can't eat after all. Instead, I run two sinks of scalding water and start the repetitive process of *wash, rinse, stack. Wash, rinse, stack.*

By the time I've let the dirty water drain away for the first time, I'm ready to think about what Maddy said. She's right. I've known it all along. There are great stories in every single assignment she's given me. The new pet store was opened by a seventy-six-year-old grandmother who always wanted a dog but can't own one because of severe allergies — "I finally figured out how to make my dream come true," she told me.

For the story about hosting parties on the cheap, I interviewed a family who fled war to immigrate to Canada, then had to figure out how to afford their daughter's wedding a year later.

I could have punched up the original stories. I could have pitched spin-off stories. I didn't do either.

There was a time when I would have. But that was before the twenty, or maybe thirty, false starts I made, turning to a fresh page in my notebook, writing the words, *I had a sister named Leila* … then — nothing.

Finding myself wanting in both talent and inspiration, but mostly courage.

If I couldn't write *that* story — the one I knew most intimately, the one that was most important to me — then pushing myself to make more of the other ones I was assigned seemed impossible.

Maddy's right. Maddy's right. The words cycle through my head in rhythm with the *wash, rinse, stack* of all the pub's vinegar dispensers. I'm washing everything I can get my hands on — letting the warm water, repetitive movements, and the solitude of facing the blank wall help me process the day's experiences.

"Hey," Dave's familiar voice spins me away from the sink to face him leaning against the wall, with a bar towel over his shoulder. "Rachel says you've washed everything that isn't nailed down. I thought you might need this." He holds out a clean dishcloth. He knows I like to switch cloths frequently, and he knows if I've washed this many dishes it's because I'm working something out. "Everything OK?"

Deflect. "Is the traveling grannies book club gone?"

He grins. "You bet. They had a booking to play glow-in-the-dark indoor mini-putt. The bus driver came in and rounded them up."

"You were a hit," I say.

"I reminded them of their grandsons."

I fish around in the sink, finding the inevitable items that escaped during washing. "I would have thought most of them would have been trying to set you up with their granddaughters."

Pathetically, I want him to tell me no. Even the thought of him potentially being set up with a fictitious granddaughter flares my jealousy.

Instead, though, he says, "What about you?"

"What about me, what?" With the water up to my elbows, I use my shoulder to push at a stray hair stuck to the side of my face.

"Old Doc there looked pretty happy to see you."

I shoot a look at him, but his eyes skitter away so I can't tell whether he's serious. "Oh that. He submitted his dissertation this morning. He'll probably hug you when you go back out there." The combination of summer heat and steam from the dishwater has my skin so sticky I can't dislodge the hair from my cheek.

Dave steps forward and lifts it away, tucking it behind my ear. I freeze. I want him to tuck my hair behind my other ear. I want him to do it while he kisses me. Instead, he says, "I think you're underestimating your appeal to the good doctor-to-be."

I don't want to appeal to him, I want to say. *I want to appeal to you*. And I certainly don't want Dave to fob me off on anyone else.

I tense, and he asks, "Are you OK? You didn't answer earlier."

I think of the rugby story fiasco, of my sister's summons and her request. Of my falling-out with Maddy. Of my record of journalistic under-achievement.

"I'm fine," I say. "Something was bothering me, but now I know what I have to do."

***

I'm as comfortable as I can be on a hot summer night in our non-air-conditioned apartment — lying under a light sheet with a fan keeping the bedroom air in motion — I'm tired but not ready to go to sleep.

I slide open the drawer of my bedside table and pull out a sheet of paper. It's a print-out of an old OJJ story — one of several I made after finding it on microfilm at the library, so I could keep one in my bag, one in the glove compartment of my car, and this one, here.

Even though I like having the story nearby, I don't look at it often. It's been so long that now, seeing my sister's smiling face, my heart gives a little bump.

When did she get so young?

Those freckles, and the sweep of her eyelashes.

In my memory I hold an image of lean midriff exposed between her ul-tra-low-rise jeans and her cropped vest, chandelier earrings sweeping her shoulders, and bright clip-on hair extensions because her own dark hair wouldn't hold the Manic Panic hues all her friends used.

Leila seemed cool, and capable, and the two years she had on me felt more like a decade.

But here, in this picture, it's clear. She was just a grade eleven student who collected beanie babies, who was the fifth child in our big family, older only than me.

In my mind, she was a big sister. A source of advice — "Shave your legs in the same direction as the hair grows," and of comfort — holding her duvet up to let me climb in after a nightmare, and of strength — "Come on, Paigey, we don't need to wait for Mom; we can make our own dinner."

I blink and look at my hands — at the indent worn into my index finger by my favourite ring. At my skin, showing signs of too much dishwashing, and not enough sunscreen. I suddenly realize if Leila's hands were next to mine, mine would mark me as the older sister — the one expected to comfort, care, and help.

The write-up accompanying the photo is pathetically short and factually questionable. I would never have written it and Maddy would never have let it go to press. Still, it's all I have.

Leila Turner, 16, a student at Oak Junction Secondary School, was last seen at school on Thursday and did not return home afterwards. She may be in the company of an older male.

She's described as 5'5", 115lbs with pink-streaked black hair and brown eyes. She was last seen wearing a denim jacket with black leggings. Her family is concerned for her well-being.

Leila was known to frequent The Crazy Mule on Highway 9.

If you have any information on her whereabouts, please call the Oak Junction police detachment at 123.456.7890, or submit information online at www.oa kjunctionpd.com.

Reading it again reminds me why I mostly leave the print-out in the drawer. It makes me want to find out who said Leila was with an older man, and that she hung out at The Mule. It makes me want to track down the person who combined some whispers of gossip with a hint of half-truth and came up with this distortion they called a news story.

It made me want to go to journalism school.

It makes me want to do better.

Three

A SHAG RUG AND bunting. Pink walls with cream trim.

In the same way as Faye's office reflects her personality, I feel like Maddy's childhood bedroom couldn't have looked much different from the place she now works.

When I knock on the frame of her open door, she looks up at me through her rose-gold framed eyeglasses. I happen to know the lenses are clear glass — she wears them so people will take her more seriously. "Yes?"

"Good morning."

She pushes the glasses to the top of her head. "Is it? Because I'm sitting here looking at the summer vacation schedule that tells me my two best reporters are on holiday for the next two weeks, which leaves me with a bunch of freelancers — many of whom are also taking summer vacation — and *you*."

The way she says "you" is not flattering. I'd like to refute it. I feel like I should refute it. But I don't know where to start.

"Paige, you know my mantra."

"Curiosity is the compass that leads us to the heart of journalism."

It might seem impressive that I know it by heart … except I don't. It's stenciled in rose-gold cursive font on the wall behind Maddy's desk.

It's a quote from Canadian poet, journalist, editor, and novelist, Brian Brett, and it was the mantra of our favourite journalism prof, who had it stenciled in bold black sans serif font·on the wall of *his* office.

"Right. I've been waiting for you to understand that. To embrace it. To write by it. Because, Paige, if you believe that quote, you'll find worthwhile stories everywhere. I've been waiting, and waiting, and waiting, and waiting ... and now I give up. You don't get it. You *won't* get it. Paige, the quality of your stories reflects on me — you're making me mediocre, and it can't keep happening."

I don't know if she expects me to protest or to argue. I'm positive what she doesn't expect is for me to say, "I have a story for you."

She arches her eyebrows and lowers her fake glasses to read the two print-outs I push across her desk.

One is the Facebook post Faye showed me yesterday. The second is an email Rose sent out to Faye — and all Oak Copse clients — addressing Wren's absence.

The email starts in a business-like manner — emphasizing that nobody will miss out because of Wren's absence, that Rose will cover her lessons — then it gets personal:

> Not only is Wren an amazing rider and horsewoman, she willingly shares her skills with anybody who wants to learn. She's an important member of our Oak Copse community and she deserves to be safe at home with Shine. Please do anything you can to help make that happen, including sharing any relevant information with the police.

I give Maddy a minute to skim the pages, then say, "She hasn't been found, and there hasn't been any press coverage."

Maddy looks up at me. She blinks once, twice, three times. "OK. This is a story. But why should you be the one to write it?"

The very fact that I'm not prepared for her question says something. I should have anticipated it. Should have a list of reasons ready for her.

Right. Think. If I was to make that list, what would be on it? What was the last story I wrote that I was proud of? My mind fuzzes with an interference pattern of nothingness.

There has to be something.

Then I think of the writer who used to have this office: Greg Thompson. He had his byline on an explosive series about city hall corruption. It got city staff members fired, got the entire city talking, and turned out to be largely fabricated. "You've never had to retract any story I've written," I say.

Maddy's perfectly (and not naturally) arched eyebrows lift again. "So, you're not Greg — that's your sales pitch? You haven't been fired for cause and investigated for defamation?"

"It's a baseline," I say.

Maddy frowns.

I bend over and brush the top of her fluffy area rug. "Like, an extremely low, very close to the floor line."

Maddy sighs. *Shit*. I'm about to lose this pitch without even putting up a decent fight. And if I lose this pitch, that's symbolic of something so much bigger. Losing Maddy's long-tested faith in me. Without Maddy backing me, I'll be assigned to a tiny desk in a cubicle to give cursory rewrites to formulaic press releases.

Must. Do. Better.

"Wait," I say.

I think of how everybody talked about Leila being missing for the first week she was gone, then Mary-Lynne Engelhardt announced she was pregnant, and she was keeping the baby, and not dropping out of school, then that's what everyone talked about.

"Wait for what?" Maddy asks.

I think of how I kept waiting for somebody in authority to question me about Leila, or inform me of what they knew, and how nobody did. I think of how the first anniversary of Leila being gone was at the same time as Xander's first baby was born and we sat in the church for the christening and I realized we would never mark Leila's departure from our lives because there was no official demarcation point for us to measure from.

"Paige? Are you going to say something?"

I think of how Faye called me out in the middle of the day because of our shared story — our lost sister — and how she wants me to write this important story about a woman who's gone missing, and I've always said I wanted to write a story about our sister going missing, and I think maybe this is the time, and if not now, when, and I clench my fists, and take a deep breath and tell myself I just have to say the first sentence, then it will be out there.

Maddy's phone rings and she reaches for it, and I say, "No! Please wait!" *Do it. Say it.* "There's a reason I should write this story. There's a reason I have these print-outs. My sister sent them to me because our sister disappeared fifteen years ago."

***

"Sit down." Maddy points to the faux fur chair on my side of her desk. She clatters away on her candy-floss pink keyboard, then turns her monitor to me. "Two-thousand words for the weekend supplement two weeks from tomorrow. Obviously we hope she's found by then, so your angle needs to allow for that. You can talk about speculation — 'What could have happened? What do people think?' and so on, but also 'How has it affected the community?' and how does it affect you to be covering this story as somebody who has lived a version of it?"

While Maddy's jumped straight to business, I'm still sorting through my feelings around facing my inner demons in an effort to rescue my career. She's gone quiet now and is looking at me with her hands folded and her entire body still.

I clear my throat. "So, um, I'm writing it?"

"That's what you want, right?"

"I ... yes ... I want to write it." Or, at least, Faye wants me to write it. I very much want to be able to write it. It's just that now Maddy's willing to assign it to me, there's only one person to blame if I fail. And it's not Maddy. "Will June OK it, though?"

June is our publisher. People who put a positive spin on her personality and work style call her "no-nonsense." Everybody else calls her "scary."

"June left for her niece's wedding in Australia this morning. She'll be gone for twelve days. I want the piece from you in ten days so we can edit it and design it so she won't be able to say no."

"Right." I swallow. The pressure's mounting. I have to complete my first feature-length story in ten days. It has to be good enough to ensure my terrifying publisher can't say no. And, oh yeah, it's about a deeply painful and, until now, hidden aspect of my family life. "So, a week from Monday?"

"Before 5:00." Maddy nods. "Now, I have an important question for you."

"Yeah. OK. Shoot." It's an apt expression. I feel like I've put myself on a firing line.

"What the hell, Paige? I've known you for nine years. We're supposed to be best friends. How have you never told me this?"

She's right. I can see how it's a shock for her, too. "Are you angry?"

She sighs. "I'm troubled. I feel like you should have wanted to tell me. I don't know why you didn't."

"I didn't want to tell anyone. And I *did* tell you. Other than people who knew because of living there when it happened, you're the first other person I've told."

"I understand," Maddy says. "Of course I do. But, at the same time, I don't know how you walked around holding this thing inside and never showing it. I'm finding out all those things I thought were just personality flaws — the reticence, the reserve, the inability to commit, the emotional brick wall — are actually by-products of an unhealed childhood wound?"

I lift my eyebrows. "Sort of like your tendencies to over-please, over-share, and over-commit?"

She grins. "Aw Paige, I wish you could have told me before."

"Aw, Mads, I'm glad I have now." I pull her desk calendar toward me. "So, I guess I'd better get a move on."

"Yup. I'll lighten your workload as much as I can, but like I said earlier, we're short-handed. I'm still going to have to assign you a few stories."

"I thought I was off the hook thanks to my lack of curiosity."

"You brought me this story. You pulled yourself back from the brink."

"So, I've proven myself worthy of covering library board meetings and traffic light replacements?"

Maddy gives a wide smile, showing all her bright white teeth. "More than worthy, Paigey."

I suppose I should be happy not to be fired. Dave may charge me substantially less than market rent, but I still have to pay it.

"I suppose that means I'd better get a move on." I gather my things. "My niece is riding at Oak Copse this afternoon — the stable where Wren went missing — so I guess I know where I'm going."

I'm in the doorway when Maddy says, "One more thing."

I adjust the strap of my messenger bag. "Uh-huh?"

"You know how we've won the regional award for long feature writing for the last two years in a row?"

"Yeah." I have a guilty twinge as I remember telling Maddy I didn't think much of the writing style of the woman who won last year. Sour grapes.

"I don't have an entry for this year. Or, at least, I didn't."

I stop fiddling. Am once again filled with the discomfort of being handed the very opportunity I wanted, with the only limiting factor being me. "Really?"

"I don't see any reason not if you write it the way it could be written." She gives me a long look. "So, write your heart out, Paigey."

Four

My route out of the city is first lined by sound barriers with high-rise build-ings poking over them, then big-box stores, then suburban clusters, with the final site comprising razed-flat, bulldozer-adorned fields and a sign promising Your future home! Single-family, semi-detached, and townhomes!

A half-hour drive from downtown, with the city creeping ever-nearer, most people wouldn't consider Oak Junction remote. Yet, despite how quickly I can drive there today, it wasn't easy to leave.

Growing up, everyone said, "I'm outta here, first chance I get," "Once I grad-uate, I'm never coming back," "You won't see me at the high school reunion."

For people learning a high-demand trade, or those with parents who had built a big university fund, that was easy to say.

Ten years ago, I had neither parents, nor a university fund.

I slow for the sharp chicane that means nobody can drive into the Oak Junction valley by mistake. People don't arrive here by taking a casual wrong turn.

Nor do they leave casually.

When I finally and fully committed to going, it meant attending school part-time while I bussed tables, cleared trays, and scrubbed dishes and counters in the university cafeteria. It meant living in a basement apartment so inadequately heated that my shampoo froze in the bottle. It meant, sometimes, being hungry.

It seemed worth it because I had assignments to land, Journalism to do (capital "J" intentional), success to seek, none of which I could do in Oak Junction.

Of course, even as Dave made my life easier by removing the prospect of imminent starvation, realizing my journalistic goals seemed harder and harder.

Until now. They're right in front of me. I just have to make them happen.

"Shit!" I slam on the brakes. Directly ahead of me, standing in the middle of the long, straight road that leads to the junction at the heart of the valley, is an animal I very nearly missed seeing. He's a mix of light and dark — his thick grey coat highlighted with hits of yellow and bright white — just like the patchwork sun and shade of the tree-lined road. I stare at him as heat flushes through me, rushing a split second behind the surge of adrenaline that hammers my heart and steals my breath.

He stares back at me with golden eyes, which are probably what saved both of us — glinting in a shaft of mid-afternoon sun. One minute you're driving along a public road in the middle of a sunny afternoon — the next you could be hitting a coyote. Or, if you're Wren, one minute you're sitting in the peaceful countryside in the middle of a sunny afternoon, and the next you're ... what?

Good question.

The coyote shakes his head and pads off the road, slipping between two tree trunks. I shake my head and ease my foot onto the gas.

Enough daydreaming. Pay attention. See what's in front of you.

Go and get that story.

***

The Oak Copse parking area is equal parts dry dust and gravel. The ashy cloud hanging in the air tells me Faye arrived just seconds before me. I park next to her and open my car door to hear Charlotte and her friend Pen chattering as they grab items from the cargo hatch of Faye's car. "I hope I'm riding Dream," "Ugh, Dream is *so* slow!" "Well, he's better than Freya who refuses *everything*," "Why did you have to remind me? Last week Rose told me I was jumping ahead of my horse — I bet anything she puts me on Freya to test me."

Charlotte *whumps* the hatch closed, the girls' boots crunch away across the gravel, and I walk around to Faye's door. She looks up from her phone and the corners of her eyes crinkle with genuine warmth. "Paige! You came!"

The sight of my diligent sister tossing her phone, email still open, into the passenger seat makes me laugh. "Of course I did. There's a story you have to help me with."

She gasps and jumps out of the car. "Are you serious? You're writing it?"

"I pitched it to Maddy, and she said I have ten days to submit."

"Well then. There's no time to waste. Follow me!"

Faye leads the way down a corridor between two fences with content-looking horses grazing on either side. We emerge into a field with a worn path around the edge. It's narrow, and I'm happy to keep following my big sister for now.

The humid air, the sun-crisped vegetation, and the feeling of the hard earth under my feet spin me back to my last summer with Leila when we spent long days on the property our brother Rowan ran as a campground.

Leila and I mowed the areas around the campsites. We bundled the wood Rowan chopped to sell to campers. We weeded the gardens and picked up the garbage. He pitched it as a summer job but, looking back, I realize it was his way of keeping an eye on us at a time when our mother was finding it harder and harder to stay sober.

It couldn't have been easy for my older siblings. They were all trying to get their own lives kick-started and Leila and I shouldn't have been their responsibility — still, they did what they could.

The good memories flood back now. Rowan taking us into the grocery store for popsicles. Outfitting us with work gloves and cheap summer sneakers from the rack in front of the hardware store. They were so thin I wore through the soles by Labour Day, but I loved the way they felt on my feet. It was like going barefoot without all the scrapes and dirt.

"You OK?" We've entered a wide-mowed path winding through a mostly evergreen woodland and Faye has fallen into step beside me.

"Fine," I nod. "Just remembering what it was like to work for Rowan."

"That summer was really bittersweet for me," she says. "I was glad when you told me you were moving to the city to go to school, but the selfish part of me found it hard that you were just gone — I thought you were moving out for the summer, not forever."

She's remembering the more recent time I worked for Rowan — the summer I decided to go to journalism school. "I'm sorry," I say. "I didn't know. Or didn't think — speaking of selfish."

"Don't be silly," she says. "You were doing exactly what a twenty-year-old should be doing. It was just hard for me to know how to treat you. You weren't my kid, but you were my kid sister."

We walk for a few seconds, our feet quiet in the thick grass. I shoot her a sideways glance. "You did fine."

She sighs. "I don't know. I always wonder. Maybe that's why I've brought you here — so this time I can be more sure I've done the right thing."

We've emerged into a clearing. There's a massive log to one side. When I look more closely, I see it's actually a tree trunk lying on its side with a splay of roots facing the trees.

I turn to Faye. "When you say 'here ...?'"

She nods. "Yup. Right here. This is the last place anybody saw or heard from Wren."

Five

"Where exactly are we?" I cup my ear toward the sound of engine brakes reverberating through the summer air. "Are we that close to the highway?"

"We're not far as the crow flies," Faye says. "But what's even closer is the Trans-National trail."

Thanks to a grade seven geography exercise which involved local map-making, I can picture the trail as a seam connecting the community. Starting by the ferry landing, running parallel to Rowan's land, skirting the outdoor centre behind the high school, and continuing to cut through properties and cross roads until it eventually intersects with the engine-brake highway.

"The trail's about five-hundred metres that way." Faye points along the mowed track which, presumably, continues onto the next jump on the course.

Five hundred metres. Half a kilometre. In the city, I can walk that in less than three minutes.

"Does this track go all the way there?"

"Not this one," Faye says. "The cross-country course winds around the property — this is about as far as it gets from the stables. There are lots of smaller, twisty paths that weave through the woods around here, though. I'm sure quite a few of them hit the trail."

With the engine brakes gone, the only sounds in the clearing are the singing of birds, buzzing of insects, and somewhere in a nearby tree the chatter of a squirrel who, presumably, wishes we weren't here.

Although the track we followed in is well-established, it's still only about half as wide as a country road, and in the direction Faye pointed it's even narrower, with tree branches arching over it.

I turn in a complete circle, my eyes skimming the treetops that surround us. "I know we walked here in just a few minutes, and I know where the trail and the highway are …"

"… but it feels like we're in the middle of nowhere, right?" Faye says.

"It really does."

"Which is why, even though there were hundreds of people on the property that day, whatever happened to Wren, nobody saw it."

Something about my sister's words sends a shiver fizzing up my spine. I'm suddenly very glad I'm not here alone. If I was, I'd be skedaddling right this minute, but because Faye's here, I give in to the pull of that huge tree trunk. I walk over and touch the sun-warmed bark. I place one hand on top of it and, with the other, press the place on my breastbone at the same height, and marvel at its height.

"I know," Faye says. "It's incredible that they jump that."

I shake my head. "You're sure they do?"

She points to the flags nailed to either end. "Red on the right, white on the left. So, yes, they jump it."

"Amazing." I use the word in its truest form. I'm completely amazed. "I can't decide if I want to see that or not."

Faye laughs. "For now, how about we go see Charlotte jump? I promise you, her jumps are much smaller than this one."

***

Back at the sand ring, Charlotte points Freya — or is it Dream? — at a jump, while Faye strides around the perimeter of the fence, capturing photos and video.

I settle on the low ringside bleachers and enjoy the country breeze, which makes the warmth of the long-fingered rays of the sun welcome on my skin.

A man drives a tractor along a lane between the farmhouse and the barn. A cat low-belly stalks something in the grass by the edge of the ring. A woman and a small girl get out of a parked car and sit on my left side at the far end of the bleachers.

A peaceful scene. Safe and happy people. Yet a woman who lived and worked here isn't safe. A cloud obscures the sun and, in its shade, I shiver.

Meanwhile, to my right, a tall, slim girl has led a tall, slim horse out of the barn and across the graveled area.

She's moving around, adjusting buckles and straps. An older woman standing near her is taking photos on her phone.

"Here, let me see those." The woman obediently puts the phone into the girl's outstretched hand. She flicks through the photos. She squints and sighs. "That one's OK ... whoa, hard no ... Mom, I told you, you can't take photos from that angle."

The mother leans in. "But that one shows your nice teal saddle pad."

"And her withers that make her look like a giraffe."

"I think she's beautiful, and I'm sure anyone who wants her wouldn't care that her withers are a bit bony."

"Right. Which is why I'm training and selling her and you just take photos." The girl swipes again and hands the phone back. "That one's nice. You can post it, and use 'scopey' 'fancy' and 'bestkeptsecret' for your hashtags."

"Paige!" I was so busy eavesdropping and wondering what "scopey" means and what "withers" are that I didn't notice Faye climbing up beside me.

#bestkeptsecret heads into the ring, calling over her shoulder. "Try to get her in the frame this time. The last videos you took were useless. They were all close-ups of my face, which, I'm sorry, won't sell the horse. And don't shake so much. Queasy-cam might work for low-budget horror movies, but we don't actually want prospective buyers to throw up."

"My goodness, if Charlotte ever spoke to me that way I'd lock her in her room for a week."

I nudge Faye in the ribs. "You would not. You didn't even have the heart to make Coco stay in her crate when you were out so she wouldn't eat your houseplants."

"Aw ... Coco ..." Faye sighs. "She was such a good dog."

"See? You're such a softie. She was a terrible dog. Remember when she ate the prime rib you were marinating for your fifth anniversary?"

"Well, Coco didn't know any better. She was just following her nature. Addison, on the other hand ..."

I look across at the girl in question. "I don't know much about horses or riders, but the two of them look like they should be in a magazine."

"Oh gosh, that's her project horse — she bought her untrained and wants to sell her for twice what she paid for her — and she imported her other horse from New Zealand."

"New Zealand?!? How do you even transport a horse from New Zealand?"

Faye rubs her fingers against her thumb. "By spending five figures." She shakes her head. "I'm sure I deserve to be struck by lightning for gossiping like this. The fact is, sometimes I think Addison's spoiled, but she's also very ambitious — she's aiming for the next Olympics."

"When you say 'aiming' ... I don't know how these things work in riding. How serious is that?"

"She has it in all her social media bios — 'Canadian Olympic prospect.'"

"Ah," I say. "Then it must be true."

"Well, it's serious enough that her mother mortgaged her house to fund it, and I know that's true because I registered the mortgage on title for her, and you never heard that from me, because of client confidentiality."

I run my fingers along my lips. "It's a secret."

Faye continues, "I really shouldn't say bad things about Addison because she lets Charlotte ride her horse. In all honesty, I think she's hoping we'll want to buy the horse for Charlotte — which we won't — but you're right that she's very pretty, and Charlotte loves riding her."

Paige bites her lip to keep from smiling too broadly. This chatty, light-hearted side of Faye is one she hasn't seen before. Another benefit of reconnecting with her sister as a grown-up. "Keep gossiping — it's entertaining and maybe I'll learn something to help me write this story since I have no idea where to start."

Faye snorts. "Well, don't say I didn't warn you — because they make my gossip look like tea party small talk — but there's this online horse forum where riders talk about other riders, horses, coaches, farriers ... you name it, it's fair game. They're meant to be helpful — share advice — and some threads do. Others, though ..." She shakes her head.

"They spread rumours that are sometimes quite vicious — Charlotte came to us in tears once because she used her allowance to buy a plush rainbow belt bag to hold her phone while she was riding, and someone on the forum said only sad wannabes would use something like that. We ended up blocklisting the forum site on her phone. However, as in most gossip, there are sometimes kernels of truth, so you might want to check them out. I'll send you the URL."

"Do they talk about eventing? Because I haven't the first clue."

"Don't worry," Faye says. "I have a way to fix that. In fact ... Rose!" Faye scrambles down from the bleachers and snaps her fingers at me to follow. We meet Rose at the fence.

Faye introduces us, then tells Rose, "Paige is a journalist. She's writing a feature story on Wren's disappearance and I was hoping you could help with her research."

"Of course," Rose says. "Anything to find her. What can I do?"

"Well, to start, I thought you could give her a jump judging assignment at the horse trials tomorrow."

Wait ... tomorrow? My first instinct is to object, then I remember two things. One, it's not like I have any competing social demands and, two, I have a story to submit in ten days. Faye's right — I should take advantage of an immersion course in eventing.

Rose nods. "Sure. Definitely. As it is, we never have quite enough jump judges, so if you come, I can give my mother-in-law the day off."

"Maybe your mother-in-law should supervise me? I don't have a clue what I'm doing."

Rose laughs. "Don't worry — it's easy as anything. I have a training deck I can email you if you want to look it over tonight, but you'll get the hang of it in no time."

"Right. If you say so."

"She does," Faye says. "You'll be fine."

I turn to my sister. "Have *you* ever done it?"

"Faye's helped us out many times," Rose says. "We appreciate her help, and yours tomorrow, and — most importantly — I appreciate you following Wren's story."

"Speaking of which," Faye speaks up. "There is one particular thing about Paige volunteering tomorrow."

"Which is?" Rose and I say it at the same time.

"You need to put her at Wren's station."

There it is again — that shiver that seized me when I was out in the clearing with Faye. The one that made me think how glad I was not to be there alone.

"Thanks for that," I tell my sister.

"My pleasure. I can't think of a better way for you to understand what happened on that day."

As long as I don't understand it too *well.* I bite the words back, because I can see Faye is genuinely pleased to have set this up for me and it hasn't occurred to her I'd be uncomfortable about it.

So I won't be. I'll just come back out here tomorrow, and I'll learn.

It'll be fine. Lightning doesn't strike twice ... right?

"... Paige?"

"Sorry, I missed that."

"I was asking if you want to come back and have dinner with us."

"Oh, yes!" Charlotte has slid off her horse in time to hear Faye's invitation. "Come for dinner, Auntie Paige!"

"It's a lovely invitation, honey ..."

"... *but* ..." Faye's raised eyebrows fill me with guilt. It's been twenty-four hours since she called me out to her office and in that short time I feel closer to her than I have at any other time in our relationship. It's tempting to just say, *Yes, of course, I'll come.* She's right, though, there is a "but."

"But," I say. "I was thinking I should try to meet up with Xander."

Faye snaps her fingers. "Yes. Fantastic idea. You absolutely should."

"Aww ..." Charlotte may be fourteen. She may look sixteen, or even older. But she can still whine like a seven-year-old.

"Ah-ah!" Faye shakes her head. "You know this is a no-whining zone. Auntie Paige is going to jump judge tomorrow, so she'll come pick you up at 7:45 and you'll have lots of time together."

I catch Faye's eyes and mouth, *Seven-forty-five?*

She nods. "That's late. You should try traveling to off-site horse trials. Sometimes the horses load when it's still dark out."

"That's just the thing — I *wouldn't* try that." Her eyebrows lift again, and I add, "But, of course tomorrow will be very informative and it will be great to spend time with Charlotte, so 7:45 is no problem at all."

"Now you get your horse groomed," Faye instructs. "Because all this talk about dinner is making me hungry."

"See you tomorrow, Auntie Paige!" Charlotte waves as she leads her horse away. "Don't forget sunscreen!"

"Or bug spray!" Pen adds.

"Or a hat!" Charlotte calls.

"Or your water bottle!"

The girls head to the barn, giggling and calling out items as they go. I'm trying to ignore them on the grounds that it's not an Everest expedition and I can't truly need trekking poles or bear bells.

"I don't need bear bells, do I?"

Faye grabs me in a hug. "They're messing with you. What did it take us — eight minutes to walk out there? I went in my work clothes."

Of course, she doesn't mention that the easy walk to the not-Everest location is one that the last jump judge didn't return from. She does, however, give me an extra fierce squeeze.

I return it.

I could get used to this.

"Great idea to meet with Xander," Faye tells me. "Say hi to him for me."

"Will do. I'll see you tomorrow morning."

She winks. "Bright and early."

Six

Twenty minutes later, I'm sitting at a corner table in the Oak Junction café. When Leila and I were kids, my mom would bring us here on her payday. Even though she made us split a basket of fries, and never let us order dessert, just eating somewhere other than the scuffed table in our small bungalow made it an enormous treat.

Plus, there was one really nice waitress who used to bring us sheets of paper and a juice glass full of crayons, and on really special days, an ice cream sundae with two spoons.

It feels weird to come in and know I can order what I want. It reminds me that even though I don't always feel like it, I'm a grown-up and, also, that even though I often feel poor next to people my age who went to law school, or med school, or who took up a lucrative trade instead of going to journalism school, I'm still very lucky. I'm certainly well-off compared to my mother, who was always scrambling for hours at the garden centre where she worked for minimum wage.

My brother said he'd meet me here for his dinner break, and while I wait I sip a lemonade, and watch a steady stream of people pick up takeout. I use the guest Wi-Fi to follow Faye's link to the horse forum she told me about.

Specifically to a thread called "Barn Talk," which opened the day Wren went missing with the following exchange:

RedRibbons: Were any of you at Oak Copse today? Is it true that one of the jump judges is missing?

AlwaysEventing: I was grooming there. I didn't know about it, but my friend was also jump judging and she said one of the cross-country jump judges stopped answering her radio in the middle of the afternoon and nobody saw her after that.

ChestnutMare: Does anybody know what happened?

AlwaysEventing: My friend said the volunteers searched at the end of the day, and the police came out after.

RedRibbons: The police? So they think somebody did something to her? Who is she, anyway?

AlwaysEventing: On Facebook, they say her name is Wren Sheedy.

ChestnutMare: Oh, I know who she is. I went to an equine first aid course at Oak Copse. They used Wren's gelding for bandaging. He was a cute palomino. She seemed nice. She tied a mean spider bandage. Even though I don't know her well, it's terrible to think somebody would hurt her.

VersMarais: I wouldn't assume that's what happened.

AlwaysEventing: What do you mean?

VersMarais: I'm just saying there's often an explanation for situations like this. If you know her, there might be a simpler reason she's dropped off the radar.

RedRibbons: Do you know her?

VersMarais: I heard a couple of things.

AlwaysEventing: Like what?

VersMarais: Well, it's not a secret, so I guess it's OK for me to say. I know someone who rode at the last barn Wren worked at. She had to leave because she was sleeping with the owner's husband. If she's done it once ... Also, I think there was something else.

RedRibbons: What kind of "something else?"

VersMarais: I'm not sure enough to write anything here, but I heard it was a "leave and we won't get the police involved" situation.

AlwaysEventing: Wow. Makes you look at it in a different light.

I tap my fingers on the café table. It definitely does.

Before I can think too much more about that, the door swings open again, and this time my brother fills the space. The siblings in my family come in three sizes. Slight, like my slender mother. Leila and Rowan both fit that bill. In-between, like both me and Faye, who have a bit more height and are slim, but not tiny. Then there are Macy and Xander. Above-average height with broad shoulders — even if he wasn't wearing his uniform, Xander would look the part of a police officer.

"Sis." Xander opens his arms and I step into them. The polyester of his short-sleeved uniform shirt isn't particularly soft against my cheek, and he has the smell of a big man who's been wearing body armour on a hot day.

As he squeezes me, I wonder, *Do we do this? Are we huggers?* Then I think of the hug Faye gave me as I left Oak Copse. I guess I'm redefining my relationship with my siblings, so the answer is, yes, we must be huggers, since that's what we're doing now.

Xander's voice rumbles through his chest into my ear. "Have you been around horses?"

So, maybe I have the smell of my day on me as well.

Still, neither of us rushes out of the hug, and when we do step back, Xander keeps a hand on each of my shoulders and says, "It's good to see you."

The strangest feeling swamps me. *I have a brother*, I think. Which, of course, I always have, and have always known — I have two, in fact — but in this moment I truly *feel* it. I wonder if maybe all along I could have — *should* have — talked to Xander about Leila. I feel a surge of bravery — maybe I *will* talk to him about Leila.

The waitress lifts her hand in our direction and points to a table. *I'll be right over*, she mouths.

We pull out our chairs, settle into our spots, and turn our faces to the friendly waitress who brings us each a glass of water and scribbles down our orders. As my brother tells her what he wants, I note the smile lines around his eyes, and the grey hair at his temples — they make me think of Leila — of how by simply standing still in time it's as though she gets younger as the rest of us age.

Xander turns back to me. "To what do I owe the pleasure?"

Of course he'd be wondering. Although I see him several times a year at our big group gatherings, I've never sought him out just because. Never to have a chat, grab a coffee, or catch up.

My guilt makes me want to lie — "*Just to see you*," "*To find out how the kids are doing*," "*To say hi*."

But I have a story to write, so I choose to be straight-up with him. "I've been out at Oak Copse."

His eyebrows lift. "What were you doing there?"

"Charlotte rides there. Faye called me. They're both upset about Wren Sheedy's disappearance."

"And you have questions."

I think about that for a second. "Yes, of course, I do. Faye does. And Charlotte. But I'm also ..." I search for the best word to describe the sensation I got out in the clearing where Wren was last seen. The feeling that's settled over me that I can't shake. "Uneasy. And, full disclosure, I'm writing a feature story about Wren."

"Right," Xander says. "So you're asking as a journalist? And you're asking me as a police officer?"

I think about that for a second. Take a deep breath. "Sort of."

Xander gives another eyebrow lift.

"This isn't an official interview. I won't quote it in my story. But, since nobody's written about her disappearance at all, I need background. I need to figure out what the story is."

"So ... it's dinner between siblings, but one happens to be a journalist, and one happens to be a police officer."

"My *favourite* police officer," I say.

"It's not my case."

"But you must know *something* about it? Even just as a community member who happens to also be on the police force?"

"I'll tell you what" — Xander points to the waitress carrying two big plates toward us — "we'll eat our food, and catch up on family stuff, then I'll tell you what I know."

***

Xander leans back, pops his final fry into his mouth, and says, "So ... facts."

I lean forward. "Facts are my favourite thing."

"Off the record. Off the top of my head. Not telling you any secrets — because it's not my case, so I wouldn't know any."

I nod. "Understood."

"Let's start with you telling me what you know."

"I know she was jump judging at the Oak Copse horse trials a few weeks ago. I know she stopped answering radio calls partway through the afternoon. As far as I know, nobody has heard from or seen her since."

Xander nods. "Those are facts."

"I know her employer, Rose — the owner at Oak Copse — organized a search of the property and they didn't find anything. I know Rose called the police. As far as I know, the police didn't do their own search."

"I'm reiterating here that it's not my case."

"I heard you the first two times you mentioned that."

"Paige ... don't shoot the messenger."

"Yes, sorry, Mr. Messenger. Please message away."

The waitress fills Xander's coffee cup, and he takes his time adding milk and sugar, then lifts his eyebrows at me. I get the message. *Let him talk. Don't interrupt.*

"Not all investigation takes place on site. There are things you can learn by looking at maps of the area — how close it is to the Trans-National trail. How that leads to the river, and crosses roads that lead to the highway."

"Meaning?"

"Meaning, for a rural location, there are a surprising number of ways in and out of Oak Copse."

"For someone to take her."

"Or for her to go on her own."

I want to ask more about that, but I also want him to keep talking, and he's already warned me once, so I just bite my lip and nod.

Xander's eyes land on my teeth-trapped lip and he smiles. "There are details about a person's past to look into — their family, former relationships, prior work situations."

My mind flits to that accusation on the forum, that Wren had a problematic affair at her last job. "Do you know anything about those?" I ask.

"Since we're talking about facts, I can tell you her grandparents raised her on a reserve on the Quebec side. It's about a two-hour drive from the ferry."

"Nothing else?" I ask.

"No other *facts*," he says.

Before I can push, he adds, "Another avenue of investigation is to look at other things that are going on in the area, which is where I could be more helpful."

"Meaning?"

"Like I said, I don't know much about Wren or her disappearance, but there is something I know a lot more about. Or, I should say, some*one*."

"I'm listening."

"There's this guy. He showed up about six months ago with a trailer load of horses."

I wait. Wait some more. Finally ask, "OK, and ... what?"

"He moved onto Ed Cormier's property."

Ed Cormier. The name is there, in my brain. My memory's grabbing at it but I can't quite catch it. *Ed Cormier. Cormier.* I snap my fingers. "Julie Cormier!"

Julie was in my class. Where my family got by with little extra to spare, the Cormiers were dirt poor. Literally dirty. Julie sat in front of me in grade four. I used to stare at the back of her hair, which was always tangled and frequently had small twigs and leaves stuck in it. "Julie Cormier smells funny," I told my mother once at dinnertime.

"Don't you ever say that to anybody else," she told me and pulled away the bowl of ice cream she'd just given me for dessert. "And no dessert for you."

Later, as I was falling asleep, she came into my room and sat on my bed. "I'm sorry for getting angry before. It's just that I went to school with Julie's mother. Her family's had bad luck and I don't want you making it worse."

"I didn't know," I told her.

"I know you didn't, and from now on I'll sometimes send two desserts to school in your lunch and you can give one to Julie, OK?"

I said OK, but I didn't mean it. I didn't always get dessert myself, so if I ever had two, I wanted to keep them both. Plus, I really didn't like the way Julie smelled and didn't want to get too close to her.

As it turned out, I didn't have to worry about it for long. "She died," I tell Xander.

"Yes," he says. "In a snowmobiling accident. Ed was driving. I try to give him the benefit of the doubt — that nothing could mess you up worse than being responsible for your little sister's death — but no matter how you look at it, he's a menace."

"In what way?"

"You name it. Cigarette smuggling — really any kind of smuggling. Breaking into cottages. Car theft. Domestic assault. I'm positive he burned down a barn for the insurance money — it was full of chickens, which all died — but we can't prove it."

"So, this guy you're talking about moved in with him?"

"He moved onto his property. Ed's in prison right now."

"And ... I'm not sure I'm following."

"Well, a background check on this guy shows everything and nothing."

"Meaning?"

"Other than the garden variety stuff — impaired driving, and theft under five thousand — he doesn't have any convictions, and nothing violent."

I think of how I feel guilty when I jaywalk, then think of my brother's life where people with impaired driving and theft offenses are no big deal. "But?" I ask.

"Charges are a whole different story. He came here from up north — past Sudbury — and before that, he was in Manitoba. I called my colleagues in both places and got the same story — he was dealing horses and people complained he misrepresented the value and/or the health of the horses, that he tacked unauthorized charges onto horses they bought from him, that he reneged on negotiated prices, and when they showed up with their trailer, he asked for double the agreed-upon amount. There was more, but that was the gist of it." He grimaces. "Unfortunately, most of that stuff's hard to prove. Guys like that don't put things in writing. And, when enough people complain, they move on."

"Why did you check up on him? Is that a normal Oak Junction thing? Will I need a police check if I move back?" I mean it as a joke, but something in me stills for a moment. *Move back.* Where did that come from?

I'm relieved when Xander doesn't pursue it. "I've been doing this for long enough — sometimes you just get a feeling about someone."

"So, what *is* your feeling about this guy?"

"Two things."

"Which are?"

"One is that people tend to keep doing what they know and what they've learned how to do. If I moved somewhere else, I'd try to transfer to a new police service. Or, if that failed, I'd look for security work. If Rowan moved —"

I finish his sentence, "He'd open an ultimate field wherever he lived — but what he has is more of an obsession."

Xander laughs. "Sure, but it's true, right? Some people make complete changes but, realistically, not that many."

"So, if this guy has always been crooked, and it's usually had to do with horses ..."

My brother nods. "I see no reason that would be different here."

"What's the second thing?"

"He'll need contacts. He won't be able to operate in a vacuum. He's brought horses here ..."

"... so, he'll be seeking out horse people who are already here?"

"Anyway, I've been watching this dodgy horse guy and somebody's disappeared from a horse farm." Xander shrugs. "It could be a coincidence."

I remember my investigative journalism prof standing at the front of a classroom writing, *That's too coincidental to be a coincidence* written on the board. He pointed at the sentence. "When you hit a coincidence, ask more questions."

"So," I say, "There's a shady horse guy who lives at Ed Cormier's place, named ..."

"Jeb. Jeb Dixon."

"OK." I pull my notebook out of my bag, open it to a clean page, and print Jeb's name.

"What are you doing?"

"Making a note." I say it automatically, but as Xander takes a sip of his coffee, I realize that's not quite right. The note is just the physical manifestation of what I'm actually doing, which is starting a new project.

In other words, committing.

The nice waitress slides two chocolate and butterscotch sundaes onto the table. They're scooped into thick tulip-shaped sundae glasses and topped with whipped cream and multi-coloured sprinkles.

I reach reflexively for the one closest to me, expecting it to be snatched away at any second. Back when Leila and I had two spoons for one sundae, she was just that much quicker than me; grabbing the base and sliding it in front of her with a wink and a laugh. "Gotta work on those reflexes, Paigey."

I hesitate. "I didn't order this."

The waitress winks. "You didn't have to, hun. That's your brother's favourite." Then she gives me a wink with her other eye and my memory starts spinning again ... until it's cut off by Xander speaking.

"Paige, I know this strikes close to home."

There it is. The opening to take a leap and talk about the sister we never discuss. "For both of us," I say.

"It's natural for you to take an interest. It's good for you to take an interest ..."

"But?" His tone tells me there's clearly a *but* coming.

"But the circumstances might not be the same."

"What do you mean?" I ask.

"Just sometimes you have to trust the people investigating might know more than you do. Like I said, they definitely know more than I do."

"You're going to need to explain."

"It's nothing specific."

"Specific or not, there's something else. You're looking at the menu, but we've already eaten." I may have never lived with Xander — or, at least not while I can remember, but we share DNA. It's not just the eye contact evasion. He's answered my question the way I answer other people's questions when I'm holding something back:

Maddy: "Do you like them?" when she gave me a pair of sparkly, dangly earrings I'd never wear in a million years.

Me: "They're just like the ones you have that look so good on you."

Dave: "What do you think of the new paint colour for the pub bathroom?"

Me: "It's very green."

Every single blind date Maddy's set me up on over the years: "I had a lot of fun. I'd like to see you again."

Me: "I'll be out of town next week. Let's circle back after that."

Xander shifts in his chair, fiddles with his napkin, looks me in the eye, then away, then back again. "There's no good way to say it."

"As in, you're worried about how it will sound?"

"Pretty much."

"I'll give you a pass. Whatever it is, saying it so I can understand is better than not saying it."

Xander sighs. "The thing is, Paige, from what I've heard, there's a question about whether she's actually missing."

I blink, give my head a quick sideways shake. My voice lifts in tone and volume. "Well, she's clearly *missing*."

Xander tilts his head, gives me a direct look.

"Fine, yes, I said you had a pass. I'm taking a deep breath. Please explain."

"Apparently there are rumours."

"What kind of rumours?"

"Something about trouble at a previous employer ... and that's really all I know, but I can imagine that would lead investigators to wonder if that trouble followed her here, or like I said about our friend Jeb, whether she could have gotten into the same kind of trouble in a new place."

I narrow my eyes. "Your colleagues think she's a floozy and they think she's been a floozy here, too, is that right? Which, even if it's true, doesn't mean it's OK for her to drop off the face of the earth and for nobody to find out why."

"Come on, Paige ... the police have to consider factors that would make it more likely that somebody left of their own accord — that they might be in a situation that makes them not want to be found."

I shake my head. Mutter. "*It's Leila all over again.*"

"Excuse me?"

I lift my gaze and lock my eyes on his. "Our sister. Nobody looked for her because they decided she was probably a party girl. She was probably out living it up. She probably didn't want to be found."

"That's not true."

"That's one-hundred percent true." He's shifting in his chair. Clearly uncomfortable.

I think of Dave — of how he handles customers who've had too much to drink. Who are teetering on the edge of going home and sleeping it off, or picking a fight. He's kind to them. He calls them "buddy." He calls them a friend, or a cab. Nine times out of ten, he keeps them from getting into trouble, keeps himself from getting punched, and keeps his bar from being damaged. When I comment on it, he always shrugs, and says, "More bees with honey."

What would Dave do? I straighten my back and swallow my rising anger. "What do you think happened to Leila?"

"I don't know." It's not Xander's words that capture my attention — it's the catch in his voice. "I don't know, Paige. I was a new recruit. I was away at police college. I knew Mom wasn't in a great place to look after the two of you. I hardly knew either of you two girls ... I thought Leila would show up. When I got back from training, that's what everyone said, 'She'll show up. They always do. Just give it time — you'll see.' They were the ones who had been here while I was away." He looks at me. "I thought they knew something I didn't. I didn't want to rock the boat. I'm sorry."

I reach out and touch his arm. "It's not your fault. It's the fault of whoever took her, or hurt her — because, I'm telling you, Xander, somebody did. I *did* know her and she would never have left me. I also know the things they said about her weren't true."

"What things? I never heard anything."

I sigh. "I can see that none of your colleagues would pass the rumours onto you, but they swirled around the high school. Leila was beautiful and guys liked her. She laughed at them while still liking the attention, which is totally normal for a sixteen-year-old girl. It's also pretty normal for teenagers to say vicious things about someone who turns them down. I heard words like cock-tease, and slut every single day ... and, remember, Leila and I went to high school with Chief O'Ryan's daughter, so you can bet he was hearing the same gossip. And it wasn't just at school." I dig into a zippered pocket of my bag, pull out a print-out of the OJJ story about Leila that I keep there, and pass it across to Xander.

I watch his eyes flick left to right across the lines. I watch the tensing and release of muscles in his forehead and around his eyes.

When he's done, I tell him. "It's not true. She didn't 'frequent' The Mule. She and I got a ride there one time — *once* — and Rowan spotted us within five minutes and drove us home, with all kinds of warnings about what he'd do if he ever saw us there again. And the 'older male' thing — what is that? Considering we didn't have a dad around, the only 'older males' Leila had contact with were you, Rowan, and any of our male teachers."

Xander opens his mouth, but I cut him off before he can say anything. "If you're going to say maybe she was with an older guy I didn't know about, that would be all the more reason to be worried about her, and look for her — not to assume she left on her own and was just fine."

He tilts his head. "Yes, Paige. Thank you. That's exactly what I was going to say."

I feel the heat creep into my cheeks. "Sorry. It just makes me mad."

"Understandably. It's a lot for you to deal with."

"For both of us. She's your sister, too."

"Yes, she is," Xander says.

"And Wren is just as important to lots of people as Leila is to us."

"Message received."

"As long as we're both on the page that rumours aren't facts."

"We are, indeed, both on that same page. I'll keep my eyes and ears open and if there's anything I can tell you, I will. Is that good?"

I smile and reach both hands across the table to squeeze his. "It's great."

His phone vibrates, but he doesn't break eye contact with me. "It's amazing to see you, Paige. To talk like this. I know your upbringing was ... disjointed, I guess? We all loved you, but we were wrapped up in our lives. I often think if we'd had it more together — made you feel more at home here — maybe you wouldn't have wanted to leave so badly." Then he does glance at the phone. "I should probably ..."

"Yeah." I stand alongside my brother, and hug him — because that's what we do — and mumble, "For the record, I didn't leave because of anything any of you did, or didn't do, and ..." I'm about to tell him I always knew he loved me when I get slammed from behind so hard the breath whistles out of my lungs.

"What the ...?" Xander's strong hands push me to the side and he steps forward to confront the guy who just barreled into me full-force.

"My bad, my bad, my bad ..." The guy puts his hands in the air and sways gently. "Sorry, officer. Sorry, lady. I just tripped."

"You didn't 'trip,'" Xander says. "You're loaded."

He's not wrong. The guy is the picture of inebriation. Bloodshot eyes. Sallow skin. And the smell coming off him ... he's sweating alcohol.

"Nah-nah-nah ... Just need some food." He lurches to the counter and tells the girl at the cash, "I'll have a burger and a Bud."

"I can give you the burger, but I can't serve you beer."

"'Course you can, darlin' — you just take it out of the fridge and give it to me."

The girl can't be much older than Charlotte. She folds her arms in front of herself. "You know I'm not your darlin' and you know you're not getting anything to drink in here."

"Goddamn think-you're-better-than-me, uptight goody-two-shoes," the drunk guy growls. "Give me a drink if you know what's good for you."

Despite the July afternoon warmth, the menace in his voice makes all the hairs stand up on my arms. I have a sudden flashback to my childhood house — to voices yelling in my mother's bedroom and to Leila grabbing my hand and pulling me to the side door. "Come on! I found a robin's nest. I'll show you."

It's not a memory I'm consciously aware of, or one I've revisited before, but as I stand here it's so stark, and clear, and feels so real, I shiver.

The teenage girl just lifts her eyebrows. "Ah, the drunken threat. Strong tactic. What are you going to do? Throw up on my shoes until I give you a drink? Keep slurring your words until I just have to serve you?" I love her spunk.

The drunk guy doesn't appreciate it, though. He roars, "You always were a brat, Maisy Jane. Your good-for-nothing father should have spanked you more!"

The girl looks like she's having trouble holding in her giggles, but both the older waitress and Xander have stepped to the counter. "Go to the kitchen, Maisy," the waitress tells the girl, before turning to the drunk. "Ryan, I'll be happy to give you a coffee, on the house, but we've been over this before — we can't serve you alcohol when you've already had as much as you have."

Ryan lifts his hand, wags his finger in the air. "You old hag. Just because you don't know how to have fun, don't you dare ..."

"Right. That's enough." Xander puts a hand on each of the man's shoulders. "You've outstayed your welcome."

He turns him to face the entrance and shuffle steps him to the door and out onto the porch. The waitress and I follow.

It's interesting that all the wasted guy's bravado and offensive backchat has stopped now that Xander's piloting him out of the café. Not only is he a drunk — he's a drunk who's only aggressive to women. I like him less and less.

"Did you drive here?" Xander asks. "You'd better not have."

"Nah, man. Stupid doctor took my license away, then the damn bank took my car away."

"He hitchhikes," the waitress tells Xander. "George Finch won't pick him up anymore." She turns to me. "George is our local Uber driver." As she speaks, I notice her nametag. **Marge**.

We watch Xander manoeuvre the unsteady Ryan down the stairs and across the parking lot into his car labeled **Oak Junction Police**. Ryan gets the front seat, which is more than I think he deserves.

***

I collect my things, pay Maisy, and head out to my car. There's daylight left, but the faint crescent of the moon is already visible and the night calls of crickets and other insects fill my ears.

The air smells distantly of fresh-cut hay, and close up of sun-warmed surfaces giving up their heat. They're familiar scents I associate with the summer — small-town sleepiness. Sleepy, if you don't count missing women, and aggressive alcoholics.

Nothing's ever quite as it seems on the surface.

"Paige!" I turn to face Marge, hurrying down the stairs. *Did I not pay the right amount? Did I leave something inside?*

I wait for her to call out, but she comes all the way across the parking lot and in a low voice asks, "Did I hear you asking your brother about Wren? And saying you're writing a story about her?"

I wonder if I'm about to be told to mind my own business, or whether I'm going to hear more of the "she's not really missing" category of gossip. "Um, yes ... I was. I am."

"Well, you should probably know. Since she's gone."

The breeze that lifts my hair away from my face is warm, yet her words — and the way she says them — make me suppress a shiver.

"That Ryan" — She juts her chin in the direction Xander's car took — "he was always a bit of a mess, but the business with Wren made it much worse." I didn't expect Wren's name to come up in conjunction with the sloppy drunk I just met. I want to hear more, so I bite my lip and let Marge continue. "His marriage was tricky ever since their child was born with her condition, but they were hanging on. Then Wren showed up ..."

Here it comes. I steel myself to hear more of the gossip Xander mentioned. *Wren was a home wrecker. Wren was a tease who unfairly tempted Ryan.*

I've done Marge a disservice, though.

"... she was a charmer, that girl. She'd come in here, full of life, cheer the whole place up. Someone like Ryan Martin — always looking for something better, easier, more fun — well, he was attracted to her right away, and she had a way of making people feel special. He got it in his head there was something between them."

"Are you saying he ...?"

"I'm saying it was a messy situation. Hard on everybody. Wren hated it — he didn't hide that he was after her, and when she pushed back and told him he'd got it wrong, he didn't hide that he was angry. She stopped coming in here — I think she stopped going a lot of places — to avoid him. And his wife, of course, everybody was talking ..." She shakes her head. "And since then, his drinking's gotten even worse."

I know what that's like. During the period when my own mom's drinking got worse — before she started spending most of her time at her boyfriend's place in the city — it was painful to go anywhere in Oak Junction with her. Even if the attention wasn't unkind, it was unmistakable. Eyes on us. Whispers behind our backs. My mom might have been the only person who didn't notice it — both Leila and I were keenly aware of it.

I imagine Wren peering through the café windows before coming in. Looking over her shoulder while at the cash. This time I'm not able to stop the shiver that grips me.

"You said she's 'gone' ..." I notice, unlike everyone else I've talked to, Marge refers to Wren in the past tense. "What did you mean by that?"

Marge takes a hold of my arm, just above my elbow. "You know, hun. I saw you shiver. Might be nobody wants to say it, but there it is. You can look at it using statistical probability, or you can go by the shiver in your bones, but either way, that girl's not alive anymore."

Seven

If I hadn't shivered before, that statement would make me.

Marge turns to face the building across the road, its facade lit by one of Oak Junction's eight streetlights. "It's times like this I wish the old Journal was still publishing." She turns back to me. "No offense, but you shouldn't be the first person writing about that missing girl."

Maybe I don't take offense, but I do go on the defense. My shoulders tense, as does my jaw, and I have to bite back my first retorts:

— *Somebody* has *been writing about her*... in the Barn Talk forum. Of course, that helps make Marge's point. In the absence of fact-checked journalism, rumour-driven social media posts and forums are flourishing.

— *The OJJ didn't write about my sister back when they could have — or at least nothing useful.* But that's personal. My family may be finally coming around to talking about our sister, but I'm not ready to discuss her in a public parking lot.

"I'm here now." Just three words, but they come out stronger than I expect. More like a promise than a statement.

Marge nods. "So you are ... and so you should be."

It's an oddly pointed statement. "What do you mean?"

Marge says, "Hun, you of all people can write this story. I used to bring you and your feisty sister crayons, and she'd draw hearts — write my name in them — give them to me to take home. I'll never forget her, and you won't either, but there's plenty who find it easier to forget her, and Wren, and others like them."

How can something as intangible as an emotion give such a strong physical sensation? If I didn't know better, I'd swear there's a band squeezing my heart. "That was you?" The words come out as a whisper.

Marge laughs. "I guess I've aged more than I thought. To be fair, it was easier for me to recognize you because I saw you with your brother."

Her wink from earlier. *Of course.* My memory clicks everything into place. Two sundae spoons, two small girls, and a kind waitress whose face I never really noticed because it was her apron that was at my little-girl eye level.

All of a sudden, Marge pulls me close and tightens her arms around me in a way that feels like the band I imagined around my heart just moments ago. "I'm glad you came back."

It's been such a long time since I've had a real, full-on, no-strings-attached hug, and these last couple of days I've had so many. I hug Marge back. The woman pats my back. "Now you drive home safely."

I turn right onto the road heading back to the city. But only for a hundred feet. The exchange with Marge — my reflection on the Barn Talk forum — reminded me I didn't finish reading the post.

I turn left, into the driveway of the old Journal building, dig out my laptop and find the window still open just the way I left it when Xander showed up.

The timeline running down the side of the page tells me the next part of the discussion took place a couple of days after the thread opened:

RedRibbons: I saw on Facebook that woman from Oak Copse, Wren, is still missing. Does anyone know more about that?

AlwaysEventing: My friend rides there. She normally gets taught by Wren, but the owner, Rose, gave them their lesson yesterday.

ChestnutMare: Something must have happened to her. I read she left everything behind. Who would do that?

VersMarais: Did you also read that the police don't agree?

RedRibbons: What do you mean?

VersMarais: They aren't looking for her. Don't you think that says something? The police can tell when someone leaves on their own.

ChestnutMare: But what about the things she left behind? And her horse?

VersMarais: The apartment wasn't hers — right? It's a staff apartment. So she probably didn't own much of the stuff in it? Her car might not be worth much. And her horse — it's expensive to keep horses, and Oak Copse is nice — maybe it seemed like a chance to leave him at a good home. Also, what are the most important things you take every time you go out?

RedRibbons: My phone.

AlwaysEventing: Money and ID.

VersMarais: Right. Has anyone said she left those behind? Just asking ...

RedRibbons: The other day you said there was something else she might have been in trouble for where she worked before — what was that?

VersMarais: I still don't have all the details — but maybe the police do. Maybe that's why they're not looking so hard for her. Maybe they know why she left.

"Who are you?!?" This VersMarais person has my blood boiling. The way they just "suggest" things that are so destructive. I remember when I was first living with Faye, I was halfway up the basement stairs when I heard her chatting with a neighbour in the kitchen. "It may not seem like it now, but this is probably for the best for Paige," the woman said. "She can be surrounded by the good influence of your family now."

Polite poison. Benign barbs. The kind of thing that's hard to call someone on, because they hide behind false innocence — *I didn't say Leila was a bad influence — you're too sensitive.*

To give Faye credit, she never invited that woman into the house again, which was a relief, but the lingering nastiness of her words stuck with me, and VersMarais rekindles it with everything they write.

I step out of the car, and try to focus on the beauty of the wisping clouds, tinged pink and orange by the setting sun, flecked with the tiny dark silhouettes of a passing flock of birds.

On impulse, I climb the front steps of the building up onto the porch. The boards need paint, but are solid underfoot — I have no worry they're going to give way.

I try the door simply because it's in front of me. I don't expect it to be unlocked, and it's not.

I move over to the big front picture window. Lean my forehead against the cool glass and cup my hands around my eyes. The sun is low in the sky now, and with the trees growing close around the building, it's too gloomy to see much. One desk is visible, and my brain fills in a couple more, deeper in the room. That could be a memory from childhood, or it could be my imagination.

The only other thing I can make out is newspaper. News*papers*. Everywhere. In stacks on the floor. Drifted across the desk.

Are Faye and Marge right? Would it be different if the paper was still running? Would there be a local reporter out at Oak Copse, down at the police station, asking questions, demanding answers?

It doesn't really matter, because the paper isn't running and there are no local reporters here. I pull my face back an inch or two from the glass. Just enough to shift my focal point — so my own shadow reflects back to me.

My phone buzzes and I jump back from the window. I suddenly feel very exposed, up here, on the porch, nobody else in sight. The forest grows up tight to the back of the building, and my car looks small and lonely down on the weed-laced gravel.

I hurry back to the car, slide into the driver's seat, lock the doors, and turn the key in the ignition as fast as I can.

It's that feeling again — the same one I had in the clearing with Faye. Mounting panic, short breath, quickened heart rate.

Illogical, I tell myself.

Then I wonder if Wren had this feeling. If she told herself it was illogical.

As I drive home — as I make that sharp turn from the Oak Junction main road onto the highway — I wonder about Leila as well. About whether she took this same turn one day of her own volition, or was taken, or if she ever left at all.

Eight

A HEAT WAVE'S BEEN sneaking up the way they do in this city. It starts with the nighttime temperatures creeping a couple of degrees higher every night. Then the humidity layers in, and before you know it, the overnight "low" is twenty, feeling like a muggy twenty-five, and that's before the sun even rises.

I spend the night sprawled, coverless, directly under the ceiling fan in my stuffy bedroom — kept from a proper sleep by heat-driven dreams and sweat-sticky skin.

The dreams have me failing at jump judging because I have absolutely no idea how to do it, failing at writing Wren's story because it turns out robot line painters were actually what I was cut out to cover, and failing at finding Wren because I don't even know what happened to my own sister.

There's also the little matter of Dave. A spear of light slices into the apartment when he opens the door. The post-last-call sounds of him getting ready for bed are so familiar to me. His bare feet quiet on the wooden floorboards. The kitchen faucet running as he gets a drink, then the bathroom faucet as he brushes his teeth.

It's one reason I sleep with my bedroom door open — so I can listen to this routine. Knowing he's home is reassuring and should help lull me to sleep.

However, knowing he's sleeping in nothing but his boxer shorts on the other side of a thin wall makes me want anything but sleep.

Especially when the creaky floorboard just in front of my bedroom door groans. My eyes fly open and I can see his silhouette in the glow of the security light that washes in through our back windows.

What if he said my name right now? What if I said his?

He doesn't, and I don't either. After a long second he moves off, into his own bedroom, where he also sleeps with the door open.

We aren't in a romantic relationship. We don't owe each other anything. But I've always liked the feeling of companionship I get when we both sleep with our doors open.

At the very least, it lets me know he hasn't brought a one-night stand up for a behind-closed-doors marathon.

Then I'd really get no sleep.

***

"I'm lost," I whisper to Charlotte.

I skimmed the volunteer information sheet before going to bed last night and from it I took two main things:

1) Lunch will be provided.

2) Bring a camp chair, sunscreen, bug repellent, and toilet paper.

With my eyes blurred by confusion at everything else, I missed the part about downloading a scoring app ahead of time.

Rose is standing on the farmhouse porch facing a loose semi-circle of about twenty people — nineteen women and one man — walking us through using the app. "... you just enter the competitor number and their information will come up on the screen, then you select the result ..."

"Not found," I mutter. "The only thing on my screen is 'not found.'"

Charlotte reaches over and taps me back to a previous screen. "You have to select the number of your jump first."

"Oh. Right."

"Auntie Paige, you're not *that* old. This shouldn't be so hard for you."

Pen nods. "I know, Wren is just the same. She always takes paper scoring sheets and she's about the same age as you."

"Wait," I say. "There are paper scoring sheets?"

Charlotte wrinkles her nose. "There *are*. But they're really only for backup. With the app, the results go up in real time."

"All the same, I'll take some of that paper, thank you very much."

Rose is still talking about the different options available to select for each competitor and, sure enough, my screen is now showing far too many buttons for my liking.

I whisper to Charlotte again, "I thought this was a yes or no kind of thing. Like they either go over the jump or they don't."

"Ninety-five percent of the time it is," she whispers back. "And ninety-nine percent of those will be 'clear.'" She points to the corresponding button on my screen.

"And the rest?"

"It probably won't happen."

There's no time to emphasize how unhelpful that is, because a woman asks, "If someone falls at my jump, how do I get the medic?" and I experience a whole new level of angst at the thought of falls, and injuries, and medics.

"Call the medic on the radio." Rose holds a radio up over her head. "The radio is your lifeline, so test yours when you pick it up and we'll do a radio check before we start. And I have clipboards with paper sheets for anyone who wants a backup for the app."

"Oh, yes please." I join the other volunteers in the press toward the table with the radios and the clipboards, but Rose holds up her hand. "First, let me introduce your support team. For anyone who doesn't know them, this is Nate." She nods at the man standing to her right. I recognize him as the tractor driver from yesterday. "He'll be on the course in a golf cart. He'll bring you anything you need, including water and lunch." Cheers go up for lunch and Nate. "He'll also work the gates for us."

"Over here" — Rose nods to her left — "is secretary extraordinaire, Kimberly. She'll be in the control hut with me all day and you probably won't need to contact her, but she's a trusted resource for any questions."

"We're all here to help, but it's going to be a busy day. We won't be monitoring you or your jobs — if you need help, you need to ask, otherwise we might not notice. OK?"

A ripple of nods moves through the assembled volunteers.

"Now," she says. "Feel free to approach the table."

***

We stride along the same path I took with Faye yesterday, only this time I have a camp chair banging against my leg and the smell of bug repellent cloying at my nostrils. One pocket bulges with my app-laden phone, the other with my radio lifeline, and I'm clutching a clipboard jammed with scoring sheets. Across the top they read, **Thank you for volunteering to be a jump judge. Your decisions are of critical importance in determining the final standing of each competitor.**

Not much pressure then.

"We're stationed at the jump after yours," Charlotte said as we left the volunteer meeting. "We'll drop you off on our way there."

Thank goodness, because the trees and grass are beautiful — and they all look the same. We reach a fork and I would have stayed left if Charlotte hadn't said "It's this way," and led me right. I shift my chair in an effort to evenly distribute the bruises it's giving me.

Pen waits for me. "Good for you for bringing a chair. The first time I jump judged I forgot and turns out there was an ant's nest where I sat. My butt was covered with little red bites for a week!"

"Chairgate — I remember!" Charlotte calls over her shoulder.

"More like 'nochairgate,'" Pen laughs.

I love listening to their chatter: "I hope Nate comes to us early so we get first choice of subs," "My dad loaned me his good camera so I can get action shots,"

"I hear Izzy Yeates is bringing that new mare of hers from Ireland," "I can hardly wait for the nine-one-one division."

"What's the nine-one-one division?" I'm thinking of my jump judging duties and wondering if I should have brushed up on my first aid basics.

"Ha!" Pen says. "It's the pre-entry division. You'd think all the problems would be with the prelim riders over the big jumps, but wait and see all the run-outs, and wobbles, and falls in pre-entry. It's not the horses that cause the problems ... it's the riders!"

She waggles her eyebrows and Charlotte shoves her. "She's saying that because I'm riding Addison's mare — Paris, the one you saw — in pre-entry this afternoon."

"I didn't know you were riding," I say.

"Neither did I. Rose's daughter, Em, told us Auckland was sore the other day, so I assumed Addison would scratch him from Ironwood —"

I lift my eyebrows and Pen explains, "It's a big competition in Quebec. Addison's finish at the last horse trials here qualified her to move up to the two-star level with Auckland, and there are only a few of those held in Canada every year — one of which is at Ironwood this weekend."

"Right. Thank you." I turn to Charlotte. "So, you thought Addison would scratch ..."

She nods. "And stay here and ride Paris. But she asked me to ride Paris, and she's gone with Auckland, so I guess Em made a mistake, or Auckland recovered quickly."

Charlotte crosses her arms. "You just wait and see, Pen, we'll fly this course." She turns to me, "And don't worry about the nine-one-one thing. If someone falls, you just have to radio for the medic and stay out of the way."

"You could try to catch the horse," Pen says.

Before my stomach can lurch at that thought, Charlotte shakes her head. "No, you really don't have to. And you're actually not supposed to touch the rider. At that level, the falls are pretty small, but if they fall the wrong way, you never know. So just wait for the medic!"

"Don't worry, I'm going to have him on speed dial, or speed radio, or whatever."

I don't recognize the final approach to the clearing I'm stationed at, but I do recognize the hulking log. *Hello, old friend.* As before, it draws me over, and I spread my palm across its rough surface.

Charlotte points to a shallow inlet along the forest's edge. "I'd put your chair there. Nate will come by in the golf cart and tell you if it's OK, but it should be fine. It's where Wren put hers."

She pauses for a minute, then sighs. "It's so hard to think about Wren not being here. I don't know how you did it when it was your own sister."

"I didn't know you knew about her."

Charlotte nods. "A few years ago, I saw a picture of her in one of Mom's old photo albums. I got her to tell me about her. Now I think about Auntie Leila most days."

Auntie Leila. I've never heard her called that. She's probably never heard herself called that ... unless she's miraculously leading the perfect parallel life I sometimes imagine for her. In Australia, in a house next to a beach, with a partner who loves her, raising adorable kids.

Charlotte's still talking. "Mom says you knew her best, though. Maybe you can tell me some things about her?"

I swallow hard and nod. "Of course."

"Cool." With the resilience of a teenager, she breaks into a wide smile, then turns ninety degrees and points past the tree trunk. "Pen and I will be down there at jump seven. You can radio us if you need anything."

I set my chair where Charlotte pointed, watch the girls walk out of sight around another bend, and under the white-cloud-dotted blue sky, with sunshine pouring into the clearing, I shiver.

I'm here because a woman nearly the same age as me — doing the same thing I'm doing now, right down to sitting in the same spot — went missing from here a few weeks ago.

I walk back to the jump. Although it's undeniably huge, it's more the sheer density of it that amazes me. It's solid all the way through.

What would happen if you hit this thing?

Nothing good.

I know it happens. I made the mistake of searching "horse cross-country" and "horse trials." I saw falls so spectacular that I can't blame people for wanting to post them on the Internet, even though they're truly of the gasp-inducing-turn-away-only-look-back-from-between-fingers-covering-eyes nature. This sport is dangerous, which means that in these still and pretty woods, injury, and even death, are a distinct possibility.

Which, of course, is why I'm here. To mitigate the expected risks.

But what about the unexpected risk? The one that's so unlikely, and almost unbelievable, that everybody's back — dozens of young girls and women fanned out throughout the forest even though the very last time they all gathered, one of them went missing and has never come back. How can anybody mitigate against that?

***

By noon, I've learned quite a lot.

Like if I don't push the correct button on my radio, nobody can hear me. It only takes a couple of embarrassing moments when I'm saying, "Jump six in place," and control is asking, "Jump six, are you there?" for me to get it. As I'm frantically trying to get them to hear me, I feel a jolt of panic imagining the time at the last horse trials when control was asking, "Jump six, are you there?" and the answer was no.

I've also learned how fast, and loud, and powerful a sport this is. How the horse and rider carry their own whirlwind with them, sweeping into the quiet clearing with pounding hooves and breathing so heavy it's as loud as the hoofbeats, and the rider's voice crying, "Whoa!" or "Go!" and almost always finishing with "Good boy!" (or girl) as they exit right and power on to Charlotte and Pen at jump seven.

I love it.

On the one hand, I wish I could do it — on the other hand, I'm glad I don't. Both morning divisions have required competitors to jump the hulking tree trunk, and while Charlotte was right — they've all flown over like it was a skinny branch lying on the ground, landing feet from the base — my heart has been in my throat every time.

There's also a stark dichotomy between the isolation of sitting in this clearing with a thick swathe of forest behind me and no other people in sight, yet being a necessary strand of the web created by the radio. Not only do we radio check before each division — confirming one-by-one we're all in place where we should be — there's also a constant roll call as we report in on each competitor over each jump. Every three minutes a new horse-and-rider combo starts and I can track their progression around the course by listening to the sometimes-crackly, sometimes-clear reports from my fellow jump judges.

I already know jump judge three is Scottish, judge nine must be experienced, because she covers three jumps — 9A, B, and C — and judge twelve is often confused. Judge fifteen is frequently late or misses reporting in at all. "Nate, can you please take her a radio with a fresh battery?" Rose, who is control, asks.

Because we're all so connected by our radios, I startle and look all around me when, halfway through the morning, an angry voice roars into the quiet of my clearing. "That refusal was your fault! What a stupid place to put your chair!"

I recognize judge nine's calm voice replying, "Sir, you're going to have to take that up with control."

"You can guarantee I will. I'll be filing an official complaint."

"Yes, sir. That's the correct course of action. I need to ask you to step back — there's a rider approaching."

"Oh, now you care about obstructing riders on course ..." There's a sneer in the man's voice that makes the hairs stand up on my arms.

"Nate?" Rose's voice comes through the radio.

Nate's talking before she can say anything else. "Already on my way."

After that, there are no more aberrant transmissions. Immediately after the finish judge radios through the last rider for the division, Rose's voice comes through. "Jump nine — did everything get sorted out?"

She replies. "Nate moved him along. He'll be heading your way soon."

Rose laughs. "Oh, he's here. We'll take care of him. Just wanted to make sure everyone was good out there. Enjoy your lunch breaks."

I hear a hum. Nate and his golf cart appear bearing a cooler full of neatly arranged brown bags labeled, **Turkey**, **Roast Beef**, **Veggie**. As I'm choosing, he asks, "How's it going?"

"Good, I think. Nobody's yelled at me, at least."

He shakes his head. "Perspective ..."

I choose a veggie sub and he opens a second cooler filled with ice and drinks. "I was going to ask," I say. "Is it really that important?"

"It depends what you consider important. Believe me, it's not like that guy was on track to win the division today, and even if he did, the prize money wouldn't cover his expenses to get here. However, if he was trying to get an MER, a refusal sets him back."

I set the sub and drink in my chair. "MER?"

"Minimum eligibility requirement. If you want to move to a higher division at a federation-recognized event, you and your horse need to complete a certain number of events at your current division, and part of that is having no cross-country faults."

I remember Pen explaining that Addison's results at the last horse trials here qualified her to move up. "Ah, so if he was trying for that, today's outing doesn't count."

"Correct. But I doubt it was that." Nate grins. "He was just being ornery."

"I assume I'm using the scoring app correctly. I just keep hitting 'clear' and 'send.'" I hold up my clipboard. "I'm also writing everything down."

"If there was a problem, they'd tell you."

I laugh. "Or send you out to tell me."

"True enough. Em — that's jump judge fifteen — didn't need a fresh battery. She was talking to her boyfriend on Discord. Fortunately, she's our daughter so we can ground her if she doesn't pay attention. Do you know what's up for this afternoon's divisions?"

"Something different, I'm guessing?"

"Yes, we can't have the entry and pre-entry riders jumping that tree trunk."

"The nine-one-one division."

Nate lifts an eyebrow. "I see you're getting a hang of the lingo ... that we never repeat in front of the pre-entry riders ..."

I mime zipping my lips shut.

"The tree trunk's done for the day. The next division will jump this large single log, and the one after that, this small log pile."

"Right. I was going to ask about those. They weren't here when I came out in the middle of the week."

Nate shakes his head. "We set quite a lot of the cross-country course. I build new jumps and swap them out for the old ones which I repair or repaint. We cut new trails and hold new divisions — this is the first year we have star-certified levels. I spend a lot of time moving jumps around with the tractor."

I look at the tree trunk and raise my eyebrows.

Nate laughs. "Right. No, not that one. That was a gigantic oak that died near here and it took six people, a tractor, and an ATV to get it to that spot. It's one of the few jumps we never, ever move."

"Charlotte said my chair was good here for judging the trunk jump. Should I move it for this afternoon?"

He gets out of the golf cart, strides over to the chair, then pauses.

It hits me that when judge six — Wren — stopped responding, Nate was sent out here to check on her.

I should ask him about that. In fact, to do a good job writing this story, I *have* to ask him about that.

There's something in his stance, though, that makes me hesitate. Something that brings it all back to me — the feeling of being the closest spectator to somebody who's disappeared. I feel it often myself as the last person anyone can be sure Leila saw.

That proximity makes you think. It makes you play with time. *What if I'd stuck around a few minutes longer ...* I wonder if Nate thinks, *What if I'd gotten here a few minutes earlier ...?*

My hesitation costs me. He straightens his shoulders, moves the chair a couple of feet, slightly adjusts the angle, and says, "You should be good here, and there's still room for you to shift over if you want to stay in the shade." Then he points at the cart. "I have to deliver the rest of the lunches — call me if you need anything!"

I look at my brown bag sandwich and, instead of settling into the camp chair, wander over to the big jump. With a little heaving and grunting I get myself up on it and eat my lunch with the sun-bathed wood warm under my skin and a slight breeze ruffling my hair and for a moment — just a tiny moment — I feel a tug to just stay here forever and never leave.

And, even though that's the opposite of what happened to Wren, somehow the sensation makes me feel closer to the woman who was here, then was gone.

***

It's amazing the difference a day can make — or even half a day. Where this morning I was apprehensive, head swimming with instructions, and terms I didn't understand, now with the nine-one-one — *whoops*, pre-entry — division well underway, I'm enjoying the process.

The radio lets me simultaneously chart the approach of the next horse coming my way, and the progress of whichever horse has most recently passed me by.

When I hear, "Clear over jump five," I know there's a horse coming my way. I lean forward and turn my head to the left. Sure enough, soon the tattoo of hoofbeats builds, and within seconds I see the next horse and rider combination. Nine-one-one, or not, most of them still sweep over the jump with no difficulty, at which point I tap the big, red Clear button, then Send and press the button to speak into the radio, "Clear over jump six."

Finally, I make a check in the "clear" column on the paper scoring sheet on my clipboard.

I've had my first non-clears this afternoon. There have been several refusals — a couple with full-on sliding stops in front of the jump and one that was no surprise at all, even to a non horse person like me, with the horse slowing down the minute the pair entered the clearing, and the rider begging, "Come on," and "Let's go" in a tone that didn't even convince me.

In all cases the riders made a big circle, sweeping past only a few feet in front of my camp chair, and re-approached the jump with a lot of kicking and yelling, including one girl who yelled, "Hyah!" in a way I thought only happened in cowboy movies.

Despite Pen and Charlotte scoffing at my use of paper, I'm glad I brought the sheets. I scribble little notes explaining what happened. If anyone asked why I marked a refusal, I could explain why.

It's a funny thing to be sitting in this clearing as the competitors flow through. On the one hand, I'm sure they all know I'm here. Usually the rider's eyes fly to me, only to flick back to the course. Very occasionally they address me, "Hello!" or "Beautiful day!" or "Thanks for volunteering!"

Mostly, though, they ignore me and I try to be ignorable. Sitting statue-still, holding my breath, hardly blinking.

"Rider seventy-two on course!" The announcement crackles the peace of the clearing and I enter 7-2 into the app. **Charlotte Edmonds** it tells me. **One Night in Paris.**

Now I have a dilemma. Do I acknowledge Charlotte? Should I encourage her? I've learned nobody's allowed to coach riders on course (and it's not like I have any wisdom worth imparting anyway) but should I wave? Or will that be distracting?

It's not the biggest problem I've ever faced, but I'm having fun out here. I feel like I've become a decent jump judge. I want to do the right thing.

Be quiet, I decide, which is why it's so lovely when Paris canters, ears forward, eyes bright, into the clearing, and Charlotte sings out, "Hi, Paige!" as they stride toward the jump and clear it with a foot to spare.

My voice is as sing-songy as Charlotte's as I declare, "Rider seventy-two, clear over jump six!" and as I check off the clear column on my sheet, I think, *I'm glad I came to do this.*

***

An hour — and dozens of riders — later, it's over. Rose's voice comes across the radio, thanking everybody for our time and inviting us back to the volunteer hut where we'll find food, drinks, and freezies.

As soon as I stand up, I realize I have to pee. It's a long way back through the cross-country course and across the fields to the port-a-potty.

I turn to the woods — this, after all, is why the volunteer sheet said to bring toilet paper. Directly behind my chair, the scrub is dense, but there's a narrow deer trail about twenty feet further on. As soon as I step into it, the temperature drops a couple of degrees. And even though I'm just a couple of feet in, everything sounds different from in the clearing. There's a muffling effect from the trees which sharpens my awareness of my own breathing, and the cracking of twigs under my feet.

I hear a snap off to my left. I turn, but there's nothing to see. My hand flies to my back pocket, to the radio. Would it be of any use, though? Is control still monitoring this channel?

I shake my head. It's full daylight in the middle of the summer, and despite the abundance of trees, this isn't a wilderness area.

Still, whether it's the physical vulnerability of the actual act of peeing in the woods, or just the first unfocused moment I've had after hours and hours of scoring and radio checks, but it hits me full-force that *Wren could have been right here.*

Right where I am. On a day much like this. Just minding her own business — or taking care of her business.

I hold my breath. Don't want to move. From this lower, squatting vantage point, I scan the space around me. Lots of green. The occasional shaft of sunlight penetrating the leaves. Nothing man-made that I can see. No unnatural colours — like the bright red of the volunteer t-shirt I'm wearing.

Don't be stupid, I tell myself. If Wren was this close to the course, someone would have found her long ago.

Except, *would they*? Leila could have been anywhere back when she went missing. Even if you assume she went missing between the school and our house, that stretch contains kilometres and kilometres of shallowly treed areas. Hundreds, or thousands, of people drive along those treed roads every day. But if you don't look — up close, on foot — you won't see, and if you wait any time at all, foliage will grow, and seasons will change. Leaves will fall, then snow, and by the time the season comes back to what it was when someone went missing, bright colours have faded … that's as far as I want to go in my imagination. I don't want to think what a whole year would do to Leila, or Wren, in the Ontario outdoors.

Or to myself. I scramble upright, hastily reorganizing my clothes, and experience that frenzy so many people know, but remains so hard to explain, of feeling both far too alone, and simultaneously watched: panic in the woods.

I have to get out. I rush back the way I came, stumbling on a root, pushing past a sharp branch. It's ridiculously, pathetically close — the sunlight, the openness, my camp chair, the jumps.

I breathe hard for a couple of seconds, swab away a line of blood from where the rough branch broke the skin on my forearm.

"Auntie Paige?" I whirl around to see the willowy forms of Charlotte and Pen walking toward me from the direction of their jump. "Are you OK?"

"Uh-huh." I nod, focus on taking a deep breath in, and letting a deep breath out. "Fine." Of course I'm fine. I was barely the length of a tape measure into the woods. The two girls were always just a little way along the path.

"You're bleeding," Charlotte says.

"Just a scratch."

"I'd be freaked out," Pen says.

"Pen!"

Pen turns to Charlotte. "Why not say it?" She looks at me. "I was telling Charlotte I wouldn't want to sit here alone. It's kind of creepy. Especially since nobody knows what happened."

"Auntie Paige is going to find out what happened," Charlotte says.

"Is she?"

"My mom says she is. She's writing a story about Wren going missing." Before I can respond, she turns her focus to me. "We should be your first interviews. After all, we were here on the day, and we were some of the closest people to where she was sitting."

"Just like you, today," Pen adds. "See? Creepy."

Charlotte ignores her. She looks at her phone. "We're here now. We might as well do a reenactment."

"A what?" Pen asks.

"We'll walk back to our jump to show Paige where we were, and describe exactly what happened, and that will help her get started on the story."

Pen sighs. "But we carried all our stuff this far."

"We'll leave it here and pick it up on our way back through."

"In that case, I'm in!" Pen says. "Come on, Paige!"

Nobody asked me if I was in. But the girls are already halfway to the bend on the way back to their jump.

I lean my folded camp chair against theirs and head off after them.

I've had enough of being alone in this clearing for today.

Nine

Charlotte and Pen's station is much more enclosed. Right before we reach it, the trail branches — "If you go left here, there's a jump out of the woods into the hayfield," Pen tells me. We stay right, though, stepping into an area wedged with a couple of jumps and trees growing tight overhead. There's only one spot where the sun shines clear through to the ground.

"We sat here." Charlotte stands in the sunny patch.

Pen nods. "It rained most of the week before the last trials and the bugs were terrible. This spot — because of the sun and a bit of breeze — was the only place we didn't get eaten alive."

My phone vibrates in my pocket. The message isn't important, but it reminds me to open the voice recording app and press the big red button. Lines skitter up and down the scrolling timeline as the app captures Charlotte's voice. "It was the second-last division. Entry. I know because I was waiting for Annabelle Ling to come through on her new gelding."

"That's right." Pen snaps her fingers. "The one she got from that roping barn, then tried him eventing."

"One rider came through and everyone reported in except Wren. We noticed, but it's easy to miss one report if you just don't press the button all the way down …"

"… or maybe have to go to the bathroom," Pen says.

"Right," Charlotte nods. "Or sometimes you get distracted listening to so many radio calls all day that you're not even sure if one happened or not. Like, I remember in the morning I thought Addison had a refusal, but I was obviously wrong because she went clear and got her MER." She taps her ear. "It all gets mixed up sometimes."

"Anyway," she continues. "We didn't worry about it the first time, but Wren didn't radio in for the next rider, either. And, of course, we didn't know it, but later we found out she didn't enter her scores in the app. Rose — control — asked Wren — jump six — to radio in. She didn't. I started to walk along the trail —" Charlotte starts along the path back toward my jump, and says, "Come on, we might as well head back while we talk."

Pen and I jog to catch up to her. Charlotte continues, "I heard the next horse coming, so I went back to where Pen was. Wren didn't radio that one in, either, and that's when Rose asked the starter to put a hold on the course."

Pen speaks up. "We asked Rose if she wanted one of us to go check on Wren, but Nate radioed in and said he was nearby with the cart so he'd go."

The three of us are re-entering the tree trunk clearing. "So, he must have come in from that direction?" I ask, pointing to the path which leads on to jump five. "Since he didn't come by you?"

"Probably," Charlotte shrugs. "But there's also a junction closer to the hay-field where a bunch of trails meet. There's a spur that comes off that and joins this trail between jumps five and six. He could have come that way."

"Honestly," Pen adds, "There are so many offshoots and little trails we don't know all of them."

I'm used to looking at the clearing from the other side — arriving from jump five. I take it in from this angle … and nothing jumps out at me. Other than the hulk of the tree trunk jump, that is — the shadow from the sun falls on this side of it, making it look even more ominous. The clearing's still sunny and quiet, ringed with trees. The only sign of disorder is the pile of our belongings dumped where we left them.

"What happened next?" I ask.

"Nate radioed Wren wasn't here. He said he'd look for her. We heard him calling for her."

"Over the radio?"

"No — we could hear his voice at our jump. Calling 'Wren! Wren! Are you around here?' ... something like that," Charlotte says.

"Uh-huh. Maybe 'Are you OK?'" Pen adds.

I look back toward Charlotte and Pen's station. Despite the visual blockage of the trees, it's not that far. I think of the sound of the truck air brakes traveling all the way from the highway. It seems reasonable that the girls would hear Nate if he yelled loudly enough.

Charlotte continues, "They were trying to figure out how to start the course again, without Wren, because there was a horse waiting by the start box and a bunch more in the warm-up. Rose told Nate he might have to stay here, and he said he was supposed to go to the trailer parking area to help somebody whose truck wouldn't start. I didn't want to come over here because Pen and I promised our friend Amanda we'd video her when she came through our jump, but I was just about to radio in and say I'd do it when Rose said Addison was at the hut and she could come out."

"And?" I prompt.

"And it restarted," Pen says. "For the rest of that division they left three minutes between riders instead of three-and-a-half and we caught up some time."

"And you walked back with Addison?"

"Um, no ... she was already gone when we got here, but Wren's chair was still here, so we picked it up to bring back. Right, Char?" Pen turns in a complete circle. "Charlotte?"

She was here a second ago, but Pen's right — Charlotte is nowhere in sight. I wonder if Pen's heart is whacking against her chest the way mine is. *Oh god, Leila, Wren, now Charlotte.*

"Charlotte!" There's a shrill edge to Pen's voice that tells me she's thinking the same thing.

I try to yell, but it comes out as a croak. *Swallow hard and take a deep breath* ... and Charlotte trots into view. "Hey!"

"What on earth? Where did you go?" Pen asks.

"To get the rake from the junction — I remembered about it when I told you Nate could have come that way. I noticed the footing was pretty churned up here." She's carrying a hefty metal rake and, as Pen and I watch, she vigorously rakes the area in front of the tree trunk, uses the back of the rake to smooth all the loose debris, then stomps it down with her boots. "Here, help me. If we compact this down the weeds and grass will grow in by the next trials."

As I obediently stomp next to her, I want to tell her, *You scared us*, and *Don't do that*, but I also don't want to make her think twice about doing perfectly acceptable and normal things. Just because I've carried around a hyperawareness of the dangers of the world since I was fourteen, doesn't mean I want Charlotte to.

Instead, I work next to her, pressing the earth flat with the soles of my boots and I bask in the relief of watching her next to me. She's fine. It was a false alarm. It was much ado about nothing.

I have dreams sometimes that Leila's with me. That we're getting ice cream at the café together, or sitting side-by-side on the school bus, and I think, *See? She was never missing — it was all a bad dream.*

The relief in those dreams is flooding. The dismay when I wake up is crushing. It's nice, right now, to hold on to the relief and know that's the real feeling.

***

We shoulder our camp chairs and head back, with a brief detour to let Charlotte slot the rake back into a PVC pipe strapped to a tree trunk. There's a shovel in another pipe next to it.

"That's an interesting setup," I say.

"Nate keeps a few of them at spots along the course to make it easy to — well, to do what we just did." She points to a bag hanging from a hook next to them. "There's a saw and a hammer in here — all the tools you might need for an emergency repair."

We continue on, following the mowed path past jump five, then jump four.

"When did you realize something was wrong?" I prompt to get them talking again.

"Not for a while, to be honest," Pen says. "There's always a lot going on at the end of the day — you'll see when we get back. The jumps in the show-jumping ring and the warm-up area have to be taken down, or moved. There's garbage to collect. The barns here are busy — people taking care of the horses they rode, or exercising horses they didn't ride. Plus, just the usual stuff of cleaning stalls, feeding, turning horses out."

"Yup," Charlotte says. "When we got back Pen helped one of our friends braid for an off-property show she was going to the next day. Addison texted to ask me to take Auckland's braids out, so I did that."

"Is that normal?" I mean Charlotte taking Auckland's braids out, but Pen answers.

"Sure. We all help each other out. It works out because Charlotte and I help people who have their own horses, then they sometimes let us ride them."

Charlotte nods. "The barn was clean and quiet, and most of the trailers were gone, and people were heading over the to barbecue area when Rose stood up on the porch ..."

"Like this morning?" I ask.

"Right. She asked if anyone had seen Wren since the show ended. Nobody had, and Rose said she knew we were all tired and hungry, but she'd appreciate it if a few people would volunteer to go out and walk the property to look for Wren before the sun went down."

"And?"

"And everyone did. Just about everyone. She organized us into groups of four. She sent a couple of groups to walk through the hayfield, and to walk the fields on either side of the driveway, then she sent a few groups back through the course but gave each of us a different route to take so we'd cover all the spurs."

"Very organized."

"Rose is super-organized. She also asked each group to look into the edge of the woods wherever we looked. So, for example, our group stretched out like this —" Charlotte moves a few feet away and walks parallel to me, while Pen goes right to the edge of the trail and skirts the trees, looking in as she goes. "There was another one of our friends who looked in the woods on the other side."

This time I don't even need to ask. Charlotte volunteers. "Nothing. Not even garbage." She sighs. "When we got back in, everyone was hungry, but also worried. It wasn't fun like the barbecues normally are. Rose called the police."

"What did they do?"

"I'm not really sure. They showed up just as Pen's mom came to get us. It was pretty dark then. There were only two of them in one car. They didn't bring a dog or anything. I don't think they went out looking that night, but I'm not sure."

I wave my hand at her. "Don't worry. You've told me a lot. It's fine."

They've told me so much, in fact, that I'm overwhelmed.

We've reached the main stable yard again which, as Pen said it would be, is a hive of activity. Nate's driving a tractor with a trailer hitched to it and people lifting poles onto the trailer. The grounds are busy with horses wearing loose, light blankets, being walked or grazed, usually by groups of girls, many with ribbons clipped into pockets or waistbands. Jack Russell terriers scamper between people and horses.

"What's with the Jack Russells?" I ask.

Charlotte shrugs, "It's a horse thing."

We stop by the jumping ring and Charlotte says, "I have to go in and groom Paris and deal with her tack, which is ..." She wrinkles her nose. "... fully *yuck*."

"I'll help," Pen says.

I hold my hands out toward them. "I can hand your radio in if you like — I'm going to take mine back anyway."

The girls head toward the barn and I turn the opposite direction, toward the secretary's hut, with Charlotte calling, "See you in front of the house for the barbecue!"

***

As I walk along the driveway, I recognize the vice-principal from my high school. Earlier today, I saw my brother Rowan's boss from his first job at the nearby outdoor education centre, and the woman running the concession stand used to work at the convenience store at the junction.

I grew up here, but after Leila disappeared, I disengaged. From activities I used to do, from school, from my community.

Then I went to journalism school in the city and the only reason I didn't also disengage from my family is that they kept inviting me — well, in all honesty, Faye kept inviting me — to holidays, birthdays, and anniversaries.

It means I've been in Oak Junction for every Easter, Thanksgiving, and Christmas for the last ten years, as well as a few milestone birthdays, and the births of nephews and nieces — driving in from the city, eating and chatting, and driving back again. I never sleep here.

Some quick mental math tells me today is the longest time I've spent in Oak Junction for a decade. It's strange that it took a woman's disappearance to lure me back.

The secretary's hut accomplishes a lot for a small building. Results sheets tacked along one long side, flutter whenever there's a breeze. Riders run their fingers along the close-printed lines. A large photo backdrop stretches across the hut's other long side, stating **Oak Copse Horse Trials** on repeat. There's a line-up to stand in front of it, and the riders currently in place are giggling and bumping one-another while a couple of mothers implore, "Smile" "All at the same time" "Stand closer together."

A folding table stands on the covered front porch, and in the relative darkness beyond the open door I get the impression of a hive of activity, with laptops open on tabletops and Rose's voice directing someone I assume must be Nate — "Let me know when you're ready to start the barbecue."

Behind her, the back door's open and a gust of the afternoon breeze whistles through the building, making a gentle rustling sound as it lifts and resettles papers.

There are wipes in a cylindrical dispenser with a sign taped to it: **Please wipe down your radio.** I'm doing just that when a woman I recognize from the organized chaos from when I first arrived this morning — Kimberly — appears in the doorway. "All good? Anything I can help you with?"

"Just returning a couple of radios — do they go in this basket?"

"Yes, that's great. Thanks."

I freeze. "Shoot! I just realized I left my score sheets in the pocket of my camp chair." The camp chair that was over Charlotte's shoulder last time I saw it. "I can go get them ..."

She shakes her head. "Don't worry. As far as I know, the app worked perfectly — no glitches — although I can double-check with Rose. Which jump were you at?"

"Jump six."

It's not that the woman loses her smile — it's that she holds it a shade too long and stills her whole face around it, like she's containing a reaction. She lifts one finger, sticks her head back into the hut, then reappears with a natural smile back in place. "You're good. They have all your data."

"Thanks. Good to know."

"Of course. Thanks for volunteering!"

"It was fun. Do you work here?"

She laughs. "No, just a veteran volunteer ..."

"Mom, mom, mom!" A little girl with a big smile reaches up to the porch railing. "Can I have my money now? To get an ice cream?"

"Here you go." She hands her daughter a five-dollar bill and we both watch as she joins up with two other girls and all three head toward the food truck parked at the end of the parking area. The girl wears a brace that comes out of the top of each shoe and reaches about midway to the back of each calf.

Kimberly catches my eye. "She has cerebral palsy. It's why I volunteer here. Rose got certified so she could teach my daughter. She was amazing about it. Have you noticed Rose has a slight limp? She said it's one of the reasons she loves riding — because she doesn't limp on horseback — and she wanted to share that with Avery. Now there are four local kids who all ride in her therapeutic riding class."

I'm embarrassed that Kimberly caught me staring at her daughter. "Her braces are so bright." *What a stupid thing to say.*

Maybe it wasn't the worst thing, though. Kimberly smiles. "Oh, the agony of choosing them. She wanted ponies so badly, but unfortunately that's not a pattern they come in. She went back and forth between flowers, and moons and stars."

"I like the moons and stars."

"Excuse me." A woman bustles up beside me, nudging me sideways. "You've overcharged us for our temporary stabling ..."

Kimberly winks at me so quickly I wonder if I've imagined it, then turns to the red-faced new-arrival. "Hello, Peggy, let's look over your account ..."

Don't you know she's a volunteer? I want to ask the woman. Dave and his servers get their fair share of complaining customers at Page Turners, but at least they're paid to deal with them. It's the second time today I've witnessed somebody laying into a volunteer and it feels so wrong. Then again, it's clear Kimberly knows how to handle this woman, so I give her a quick salute and turn back to the house with its promise of dinner.

***

As I approach my car, I notice my camp chair slid between the back wheels. Charlotte must have realized she was carrying it as soon as I headed off to the secretary's hut. I open the hatch and slide the chair in, pulling the unneeded score sheets out of the pocket and shoving them in my bag, then turn to the barn to see if the girls are done their chores.

"Auntie Paige! Thank goodness you're here!" Charlotte's standing behind a horse I don't recognize. As I get closer, I can see she's holding onto the horse's leg.

"What's up?"

"Pen's helping turn the horses out, and I just finished the most perfect standing wrap, but the velcro is knackered, and I can't let go to get the masking tape or the whole thing will unravel."

"Tell me how to help."

Charlotte jerks her chin toward a side entrance a little further up the aisle. "There's a roll of tape in Addison's locker. The lockers are on either side of that door. Addison's is the last one before the door on the right side. It has her name on it."

"I'm on it."

Addison's locker looks expensive. All the lockers are the same — because they're all built into the barn — but where everybody else's names are Sharpied onto cards slipped into holders, Addison's has three engraved nameplates on it: Addison Keating, It Happened in Auckland, and One Night in Paris. Classy.

There's a lock hanging open on the latch. When I pull the door open, I'm hit with the rich, tannin-based smell of leather and the clean smell of peppermints.

The locker is jam-packed. To my inexperienced eyes, it looks like Addison has two of everything — including saddles.

"It might be on the floor," Charlotte's voice drifts around the corner. "I think I knocked it down earlier."

Sure enough, when I crouch down, there's a roll of tape lying on the bottom of the locker. I pick it up and wish I hadn't. It's covered in something sticky. Now my fingers are tacky. Yuck.

Charlotte must have knocked something else to the bottom of the locker. I think it's one of those wipes they give you in restaurants to wipe your fingers when you eat wings. Perfect.

Once I'm holding it, though, I realize my mistake. It's the same size, and the printing on it is the same colour as a wet wipe, but it's actually a sachet of powder. **PBZ** it says. Something horse-related, I assume. I can't see an obvious place that it fell from, so I prop it up on the inside trim at the bottom of the locker where it won't marinate in the molasses any more — because I'm pretty sure that's what's currently coating my fingers.

I pull a length of tape out for Charlotte to smooth into place and leave her to tidy the locker while I search out the barn dog, who cheerfully licks my sticky fingers clean.

Ten

THE FARMHOUSE IS NOW fronted by folding tables adorned with bottles of ketchup, mustard, and relish. Muffled swearing lures me to the side of the porch where Nate's struggling with a propane canister.

"You OK?"

"This stupid thing. I was sure it would run out at the last barbecue, and I planned to change it then, but ..." He hesitates. "... the barbecue got cut short, and I forgot about it, and — of course — here I am with a property full of hungry volunteers and an empty propane tank."

"Yikes. Do you need me to go somewhere and get a full one?"

"Oh no. I have a replacement tank. It's just a pain to change, and I haven't put out the cutlery or the napkins or plates."

"Well, I can do that. No problem. Where are they?"

Five minutes later, I'm installed in a camp chair and I have a rhythm going — roll a knife and fork in a napkin, perch them on a plate, push to the side, and start the next one. Much like dishwashing, I find the repetitive chore soothing. While my hands are busy, my mind can wander over the things I've learned today and how they might fit into this story I'm supposed to write.

I've listened to enough true crime podcasts to know Wren's disappearance could fall into one of three broad categories: she left herself, an outsider took her, or someone she knows took her.

Of course, there's always the possibility she somehow had an accident, or got lost, but my time in her chair makes that seem unlikely. It's true I ventured into the woods for a pee, and Wren might have done the same, but I still don't see how she could lose her bearings — I didn't, and she knows the property much better than me.

The main argument against the lost-or-hurt argument, though, is the timing. First, why would she get up in the middle of a division — in the three minutes between horses? There are plenty of longer breaks between divisions — logical times to get up, move around, stretch, pee in the woods. And, if she did get up mid-division, and something went bizarrely wrong, she couldn't have gotten far. Nate was there within minutes. He called her, with his voice carrying at least as far as Pen and Charlotte's jump. If she was conscious, she would have heard him and could have replied herself. If she was already unconscious at that point, she would have been so close to the track somebody would have seen her when Rose sent the search party back out.

I'm not saying it's *impossible*, but to me that theory is ninety-nine percent *improbable*.

Which leaves the others.

Did she leave by herself? Well, she could have. She's fit and strong and knows the area. She could have sent her last radio transmission, jumped up from her chair and started walking, fast. By the time Nate was calling her name, she could have been well on her way to the Trans-National trail.

As a theory, it's one-hundred percent possible, but is it probable? My gut says no, for a few reasons:

- Partly because, again, why do it in the middle of a division, when people would notice right away? Why not wait for one of the longer breaks, or until after the last competitor of the day, or go in the middle of the night, or any other time at all?

- Also, I've only heard about Wren from people who care about her and, naturally, they don't think she'd just walk away.

- Finally, because the chat on the forum suggesting she took off because she was in trouble, rubbed me the wrong way. It seemed sly and cowardly.

Those, however, are feelings, and I should probably look for something closer to fact, so I put that in the back of my mind and move on to the other possibility: somebody else made her disappear.

Xander's candidate, Jeb Dixon, pops into my head. Well, he would, wouldn't he? He's got all the right ingredients to make a perfect villain: criminal history, suspected by a police officer and, most importantly, not any of the lovely people I'm currently surrounded by.

Like the group of chattering girls pressing around the table right now. Charlotte, and Pen, and Addison, along with three or four others with the same long hair pulled back through the opening of "Oak Copse" baseball hats, wearing the same brightly belted breeches and knee-high socks, and all talking about wildly different things at the same time.

"I'm starving!"

"Look — Freya slobbered all down the front of my shirt."

"Ooh, do you think there's going to be cake?"

"I still can't believe we knocked that one jump down."

"Auntie Paige, this is Justine ... Auntie Paige?"

I take a second to isolate Charlotte's voice from the others, and to realize she's talking to me.

"Oh, hi Justine, it's nice to meet you." I recognize the girl's two long braids tied with bubblegum-pink ribbon — she came through my clearing sporting that same bright pink on her helmet cover, her horse's leg wraps, and more. "I loved your pink-polka-dotted shirt today!"

Charlotte introduces me to another girl who asks, "Is it OK for me to take one of these plates?"

"Of course," I say. "That's what they're here for."

They all leave as quickly as they arrived, clutching their plate-napkin-cutlery combos and still chit-chatting, with one of them saying, "Your aunt is *so* nice, Charlotte ..."

Obviously, I don't want any of them to have had anything to do with Wren going missing.

Next up to the table is a group of volunteers. I recognize some of their faces from this morning's information session, and some of their voices from their radio check-ins. While they may look different physically, they all wear red shirts like the one I'm wearing. Their skin is flushed from sun and fresh air. "Jump six!" one of them laughs when I say hi. "I recognize your voice."

Of course, I don't want any of them to have hurt Wren either, which is why it's reassuring that they likely couldn't have. Their voices forming a running commentary on the radio also create an alibi, in the same way Wren's silence pinpointed her absence. Still, I should ask if anybody else missed a radio check-in around the time of Wren's disappearance.

It's getting hard to remember all the questions I need to answer. I fish in my bag for my notebook, but with everything I needed to pack for today, I left it at home. The score sheets are there, though, with their clean, white backs. I pull out a pen and write:

> *1. Check where Jeb Dixon was on the day of the last horse trials.*
> *2. Check if other jump judges missed radio calls.*

While I'm writing, one more comes to mind:

> *3. Find out more about the outside competitors — is anybody who competed at the last horse trials a viable suspect?*

Not surprisingly, I don't want anyone I've met today to have been responsible for whatever happened to Wren. But, assuming something happened to her, somebody *is* responsible. Somebody who knew her well enough to have a reason to make her go away. Somebody who knew where everybody — Wren included — was stationed. Somebody who could move around the property freely with nobody wondering about it.

"Excuse me? Hello! I hope you're all hungry!" Rose's megaphone-enhanced voice snaps me to attention. "I won't keep you long, other than to say, on behalf of the organizing committee" — She sweeps her arms wide to indicate Nate and Kimberly standing next to her, just like they did this morning — "you've all worked very hard, and done a great job, and Nate tells me the food is ready, so please enjoy!"

I wait out the initial rush to the barbecue. I watch Rose turn to say something to Kimberly. I watch Nate jump down over the stairs to get back to his station at the barbecue.

I think that I already like them all.

I think they all knew Wren well, knew where everybody was stationed, and can go anywhere they like without explanation.

I still think Wren deserves my best effort in writing about what happened to her, but I also think it might be harder than I expected.

***

"Are you literally just eating pickles?" Faye asks.

I crunch the last one from my plate. "They're good. And Dave's burgers have spoiled me for anything else ... not to diss Nate, but I really can't go for store-bought patties anymore. And I'm also eating carrots." I lift one to show her.

"Right," Faye lifts her eyebrows. "*Dave ...*"

"Yes. Dave. My roommate-slash-landlord. Who owns a pub. Who cooks burgers." Even as I work to keep my voice even and casual, I feel heat in my cheeks.

"Paige! You live with him — you've lived with him for years — and we've never met him."

"I don't live with him the way you mean."

"Mm-hmm. Your cheeks are as red as chili peppers."

They burn just as much, too, but I'm not about to admit that to her.

"Aw, Paige. The whole time you lived with us, I never had to shoo anybody out of your bedroom. You've never brought a plus-one to any of our holiday, or birthday, or anniversary dinners. You've never talked about a partner. You're smart, and funny, and pretty," she winks, "— good looks run in the family — so I can only conclude you must have some kind of love life and you're avoiding talking to me about it."

I buy myself time by crunching a carrot. I think of how nice it's been to finally talk about Leila. I think of how hard it is feeling the way I do about Dave and having nobody to share it with. I take a deep breath, summon all my nerves — this feels even harder than talking about our missing sister — and blurt out, "OK, I like him. Liked him. Way back, not that long after I moved in, I hit on him."

My gut twists remembering it, and my cheeks get even redder admitting it, but kind of like when you finally get the nerve to rip off the band-aid and your skin burns with the pain, I have that lovely after feeling of knowing at least it's over. It's out there.

Well, almost.

Faye shakes her head. "I'm sorry. I'm going to need more details than that."

"Oh Lord, I'm going to need more pickles if I'm going to tell you this story."

"Easily done." Faye takes my plate. "I won't be a minute. Hold that thought."

I smile. It feels good to let my sister take care of me. Again. I watch her lift the pickle jar up from the table, then hold it to the light. Empty. *Not to worry*, she mouths. She looks around, spots Nate, points at him, then holds up her finger. *Just a minute.*

It's one of those moments where everybody else is occupied and I'm left alone without even my plate of food to keep me occupied. I turn in a slow circle, sliding my eyes from the house where Faye's following Nate in through the door, to a couple of garage-type buildings where I suspect the golf cart and other assorted means of transportation live. Next to them is a small barn. From its size, and construction of square logs and white chinking, I suspect it must be the property's original barn. Beside it, and directly across from Nate and Rose's house, are the show-jumping and warm-up rings, now looking very quiet with the jumps tidied away.

The cars of the people milling around me are angle-parked along the side of the warm-up ring, then there are several metres of gravel, then the bulk of the barn. It's new — sided in metal — it's huge, it's solid, it has multiple entrance doors, and at the near end, there's a set of stairs leading up to a single residential-type door.

Wren's apartment, I'm guessing.

With no sign of Faye, I decide to take a stroll over to Wren's stairs. It's a very short stroll. About fifty metres, I'd say. I look back at the farmhouse Nate just led my sister inside. I don't want to think about those rumours on the forum, but … if there's any truth to what they said — if Wren does have a history of sleeping with her bosses' husbands — the distance of an Olympic-sized swimming pool is all that separates Wren and Nate's homes.

Proximity. Affairs have started because of less. And this situation is full of all kinds of proximity — work and living arrangements. Nate, and Wren, and Rose. It's not impossible. I need to at least consider it.

The big double barn doors are propped open. Beside them, and under the stairs, is parked a small car. The car is like mine, the stairs are like the ones I use to get up to my apartment over the pub, and my parking spot is under the stairs, like Wren's.

I wander over to look into the car windows. The inside of the car is clean, but not empty. There's a box of kleenex in the console. A crate slotted full of CDs sits on the transmission hump in the back seat — they seem to be arranged by spine colour. The CD player holds a spring-loaded phone holder.

I get the strong feeling of a life interrupted. Not a life in chaos. Not a life being tidied up for somebody to leave, or worse. Just a life being lived and, for some reason, the person living it isn't here to keep going.

Maybe because, again, the inside of Wren's car looks very much like the inside of my own. This is what someone would see if I just walked away and left my car here.

I'm saved from getting too deep into that unsettling thought by girls' voices drifting out of the barn. "Did you read the post on the forum saying Wren owed people money where she lived before?"

What the …?

"Really? No. I mean I read the other post — about the …" The girl drops her voice to a whisper. "… *affair*. But I didn't know about the money. Do you think it's true?"

"I don't know. My grandma always says, 'No smoke without fire.'"

My cheeks are warming again, and this time it's because of a very different emotion than when I was talking about Dave.

Two girls who I recognize from Charlotte and Pen's gaggle step out of the barn. The one closest to me flashes me a big smile. "Thanks for volunteering today!"

Butter wouldn't melt. It's almost scary how teenage girls can say something so destructive one moment, then seem so sweet and polite the next.

After Leila disappeared, I stopped using the bathrooms at school. It wasn't worth it to overhear sly remarks like, "Oh, god. I can't listen to one more person talk about 'poor Leila Turner.' She probably got knocked up by some deadbeat and left town."

But then, when the guidance counselor paid a visit to our homeroom — "I'm available to talk to anybody who is struggling, or has information, about Leila Turner," — the same girls threw their hands up to say, "She's so sweet," "I just hope she's OK."

"Paige! I have your pickles!" If anything could snap me out of my downspiraling reminiscing, it's my sister yelling at me about pickles.

I stride back to Rose and Nate's lawn, where Faye's waiting. "I also got the last grape popsicle — I know they're your favourite."

I lift my eyebrows. "Pickles and popsicles?"

Faye laughs. "Yeah. It is quite the combination. Something I would have eaten when I was pregnant."

I snort. "Well, no danger of that for me."

"Ooh — nice segue." Faye sinks into a Muskoka chair at the edge of the lawn and pats the one next to her. "I got you pickles. Now you spill the beans."

I sigh. *Where to start?* I do the thing I did in Maddy's office — tell myself *Just say the first sentence*, and I take a deep breath and tell her about that night. The sangria. The exhaustion. The working with Dave. The failed pass.

I rub my forehead. "God, Faye, it was so mortifying. And terrifying. I scuttled off to bed and tossed and turned all night, convinced he'd ask me to move out in the morning."

"And?" she asks.

"Well, obviously he didn't. So I dodged that bullet."

"I wasn't really asking about that."

"Mostly it's great. We're good roommates and good friends. We have fun. But there's this awkwardness whenever anything comes up around dating, or sex. Like we're both right back in that cringey, embarrassing moment which we desperately don't want to talk, or think about."

"The not talking about it — how does that work for you?"

"I don't want to talk about it. See what I did there?"

"Seriously, Paige."

"Seriously, Faye. Obviously, in retrospect, I can see it doesn't work, but at the time it was the easy way out, and now I have no idea how to change it. Plus ..."

"Plus what?"

"Plus, what am I going to say? I made a pass at him and he rejected me. If I bring it up again, it's like I didn't listen to him the first time and he'll have to reject me again and I'll have fresh, new pain layered on top of my old pain scar-tissue."

"Or not."

"What do you mean?"

"Did he really reject you?"

"Sorry, was I just talking into the wind?"

"He said — do I have this right? — 'This isn't why I offered you a place to live.' I don't hear a 'no' anywhere in there."

"Come on, Faye. It wasn't a yes."

"Paige, you heard no — which I understand — but I hear a guy saying, 'Hey, I'm not a creep who lured you into living here for sexual reasons.' Maybe all he wanted to hear was, 'Don't worry about it. I want this.'"

"No." I shake my head.

"Is that, 'no' you don't believe me, or 'no, shoot me because I could have been having sex with a great guy all along?'"

"Faye?"

"Yeah?"

"This is too much for me to think about right now."

She lays her hand on my arm. "OK. I'll leave it alone after I ask one more question — all those years when none of us talked about Leila, how did you think I felt about her?"

"I ..." I shake my head. I don't want to say I thought she had forgotten about her — moved on — it feels like a stupid thing to think.

"Let's put it this way — now that we've started to talk about her, has your impression changed?"

I nod. "Completely. The same with Xander."

"And guess what? It'll be the same with Rowan and with Macy." She sighs. "My point is, Paige, it's easy to assume things. To think you know how someone feels, or what they mean. A lot of times, after you talk to them, you find out you have it all wrong."

The popsicle is melting into the bowl Faye propped it in. I pick it up and bite the end off, enjoying the sharp hit of the synthetic grape flavour.

"Do you know why you've never met Dave?" I ask.

"Why?"

"Because he doesn't know."

"He doesn't know ... about Leila? You've lived with him for four years and he doesn't know you have a missing sister?"

I shake my head. "Why would he? Until a couple of days ago, I hadn't even talked about her with you."

"Oh my goodness, Paige. You've got to talk to him."

She's not joking. The minute I got the deadline for this story, I also got a deadline to tell Dave something I should have told him years ago.

"You already knew that, though, right?" Faye says.

"I did."

"I know. Sorry. It's the mother in me. I'm compelled to give advice even when the person already knows full well what I'm telling them. Just ask Charlotte — she's banned me from talking to her before she competes because I tell her to smile, and to keep her back straight, as though she doesn't already know those things."

I smile. "It's sweet. Maybe because I missed out on that when I was a kid, I don't really mind."

"Yeah." Faye sighs. "Mom wasn't at her best in those last few years. She was different when she was raising us older kids. Not perfect, but more stable, and more focused on us ... maybe we could talk about it some day. If you're interested."

"We can talk about lots of things now," I say. "However, one thing I should talk about is information for this story — or else I'll never get it written. Specifically, how can I find out who was volunteering and competing at the last horse trials?"

"Easy — ask me. Kimberly had a conflict that day, so I stepped in as secretary. I kept backups of the lists on my laptop and I still have them."

"Right ..." If Kimberly wasn't here that day, maybe I need to rethink my top three suspect list. "I thought Kimberly was always the secretary? Was she out of town or something?"

"No. Nothing like that. Avery was riding in the grasshopper division, so she came in the late afternoon to watch her, but for most of the day, she had a family obligation she couldn't get out of. Of course I said I'd help. To be honest, she'd already done most of the work anyway. I just used her lists. And Addison was there."

"Sorry, I don't follow."

"Not only is Addison good with digital photos and social media. She's a technology whiz in general. When Rose and Nate started using the scoring app, she figured out a lot of the glitches. Kimberly's an amazing secretary, but Addison also pops into the hut a few times during each show to make sure everything's running smoothly. So having her as a back-up was really helpful."

"Right ... so ... I'm asking."

"Excuse me?"

"You said to ask you for the lists — I'm asking."

"Not a problem. I can email them to you when I get home ... hang on ..." Her brows furrow. "What's he doing here?"

I follow her gaze to a man walking across the parking area to the lawn.

A man I last saw being removed from the Oak Junction café in my brother's police car.

Before I can ask Faye anything about him, a little girl screams, "Daddy!" and runs across the lawn toward him. She has a distinctive gait, and even more distinctive leg braces sporting a moon-and-stars motif.

Kimberly's daughter.

Marge's words jump into my head: "His marriage was tricky ever since their child was born with her condition ... then Wren showed up ..."

Oh my god. Wren's stalker, Ryan, is Kimberly's husband.

With Wren gone, it seems Kimberly's life might be a lot easier — that definitely holds her spot on my suspect list.

Eleven

Faye's finally coaxed Charlotte and Pen into her car, but not before inviting me over for dinner tomorrow night. "I'm not sure how useful the lists will be if you just stare at them on your own. I can help you with context."

My first instinct is to say, *no, thank you* — in the last couple of days I've already spent far more time in Oak Junction than I can remember since I lived here. Then I think, *why not? What else am I doing?* And Faye's right — there's nothing more certain to freeze me in my tracks than a spreadsheet full of names and numbers that I didn't put there.

As I wave them down the driveway, Rose comes up beside me. "How did the day go? Was it helpful being stationed at Wren's station?"

"I learned a lot — about how everything runs, and about how much work you put into it."

"It's what we do. It's our job." She winks. "But it's a fun one."

I like her. I'd like to be sure she isn't involved in Wren's disappearance. "Now that I have a general idea of what happened on the day, is there any chance I could talk to you one-on-one?"

"The day after an event is always quiet," she says. "All the horses who competed today will rest tomorrow, so most of my regular lessons are canceled — can you come by?"

"I'm having dinner at Faye's, so could I come in the afternoon?"

"See you then!"

***

I've driven along these roads so many times in this suspended time between day and night. When no part of the sun is visible, but its glow lines the horizon, suffusing the air with an orange haze.

It's probably the most dangerous time to be out driving. The deer are active, the woods they hide in near-dark, car headlights not-yet-effective, and human eyes the least able to adjust and pick out anything on the pavement that shouldn't be there.

It's part of the reason I take it slow. The other reason is because the events of the day are churning through my head. I've felt almost every emotion today. Of course, there was joy — all those horses and riders thundering through my clearing, wearing broad smiles. All the riders walking around the grounds with ribbons hooked to their belts. All the children coming away from the canteen with lemonade and ice cream.

There was sadness, too. The girl who led her limping horse back past my jump not five minutes after I'd marked them clear. She was blinking back tears as she explained to me — "An old injury. I thought he was better." And, of course, the pervasive knowledge I was sitting in a missing girl's place.

Fear, I felt that. Anger — even coming through the radio it affected me. And triumph, both reflected from other people's accomplishments and for myself when I didn't mess up my jump judging. Doubt, too, though. What have I taken on? I've learned so much today, but I feel further behind than I did before.

Because now I have to figure out what to do next.

Think about that later. My mind won't, though, even as I try to make it focus on the waning light, the bend in the road ahead, the famous Oak Junction monster pothole that never quite goes away, and can eat the suspension of small cars like mine.

Do what you know.

"I write news stories."

Exactly.

"I don't solve crimes."

To write a news story you research and interview people, then you double-check the facts and the answers …

"It's not the same."

It is, though. Filter out the gossip. Find the facts. Look for the lies.

"What do you mean?"

If somebody took her, there are things they can't tell the truth about. Check the facts. Find the lies. Then you'll know.

"You're crazy." I shake my head. "I'm crazy. Arguing with myself. I'm not even good at writing news stories."

So do better.

How?

Start now.

***

Two things are niggling at me. One, a nagging thirst which has me longing for a pint — or two — of cold lemonade, and two, the forum post the girls were talking about in the barn. The one about Wren owing money. I didn't see a post about money.

As soon as Rachel slides my lemonade in front of me, I open my laptop on the bar and go back to the forum main page to search for VersMarais — because they've got to be behind it — and a new thread shows up, this time under "Off Course" — "for topics that don't fit anywhere else."

I guess slagging off a missing rider wasn't deemed to be proper "Barn Talk?"

I click and find all my old friends have migrated over:

AlwaysEventing: Did you guys join the Find Wren Sheedy group on Facebook?

RedRibbons: Yeah, people are talking about organizing a search. Do you think that would help?

VersMarais: Not if they're searching around here. That's the last place she'd be.

ChestnutMare: What do you mean?

VersMarais: If she owed money to the wrong people, there's no way she'd stick around here. The whole point of leaving is to get somewhere they can't follow her.

AlwaysEventing: Wait, what? Did she owe money to people?

VersMarais: Remember before I said there was something else I heard about her? She had bad debts. If she's done it once ...

AlwaysEventing: How do you know? What do you mean by "bad debts?"

Good questions, I think. Girl should be a fact-checker. If she *is* a girl ... *don't jump to conclusions*, I remind myself.

VersMarais: I can't give any details because the people involved agreed not to say anything if she left, but maybe this time Wren couldn't make a deal and she had to go, fast.

ChestnutMare: I don't know what to think. I didn't know her and it's confusing between what's on here, and the Facebook group, and the things people are saying.

VersMarais: Whatever. I don't find anything confusing about somebody sleeping with the wrong people and owing money, then leaving town, but if you're confused, maybe you should take some time to think it over.

Wow. What a charmer. I can't figure out how sometimes the most abrasive people are the ones other people listen to.

"Did you want any lemonade with your ice?" Dave points at my ice-filled pint glass.

"I was thirsty. I drank the lemonade pretty quickly."

He takes the glass, refills it, then slides onto the stool next to me. "So."

I take another long sip of the lemonade, savouring the bite — Dave uses the bare minimum of sugar, and I appreciate it. "So, I'm a little dehydrated."

"From ...?"

I know what he's asking. Where have I been? What have I been doing? What's made me dehydrated? It's not that we owe each other these answers, or that we live in each other's back pockets, but out of common courtesy and friendship we have an established level of mutual sharing … which I've broken over the last few days.

I'm so tired, though. Partly from the early start, and the fresh air. Partly from the emotions of rekindling feelings about my siblings — here and absent. And, ironically, partly because of the conversation with Faye which drove home that I owe Dave an explanation.

Thinking about what I need to tell him makes me too tired to tell him.

"Charlotte — my niece — was riding at a competition in Oak Junction today. I volunteered at the event."

"I thought you didn't like spending much time in Oak Junction."

"I never said that." I know I'm being unreasonable, because even if I didn't say those precise words, he's right, and I've never hidden it, which makes the edginess in my voice uncalled for.

"That's true. But you don't go very often, and when you do, you tell me, 'I'm not staying long.'"

"It's complicated."

"I can understand complicated things."

I hear more than that. I hear, *I can understand you*. It makes my chest hurt and my throat ache. I want to accept his invitation to talk, but it's not Dave that I doubt — it's me. I don't know where or how to start to tell him something I should have mentioned years ago.

"Hey, babes!" Maddy leans her head between us, putting an arm around each of our shoulders. "How are my two favourite people at Page Turners Pub?"

Dave transitions to his host face. A smile that displays his one, deep, cheek dimple, but doesn't extend to his eyes. He hops off his barstool and gestures for Maddy to take it. "I was just about to get Paige another lemonade refill — what can I get you?"

***

Maddy sips at the virgin daiquiri Dave brings her. "So, tell me how the day went."

Before I left Oak Copse, I sat in my car and scribbled down a few more thoughts — specifically the names *Rose*, *Nate*, and *Kimberly*. I slide the sheets in front of Maddy and talk her through them. "So you see, the next step is to talk to each of them. I'm meeting Rose tomorrow, then I'm going to Faye's, which should help me get some more information … what?"

Maddy's rubbing her temples. "Listen, Paige, of course you can try to find out what happened to Wren. If you manage that — or even get information that will help — that's a good thing."

"But?" Because there's definitely a but in her voice.

"But you might not, and especially not during the deadline we have. You sold me this piece on the fact that your own sister went missing. The personal angle means it's a good story whether or not you find out what happened to Wren. The fact that she's missing at all is the story. It affects people. It affects the community. You know that better than anyone." She pauses and looks me straight in the eyes. "The question, Paige, is are you able to write it? I know it's hard, but can you do it, and do you want to? Or are all these notes a way of distracting yourself from the personal stuff?"

I think about the people I've already talked about Leila with — Xander, Faye, Marge, and Maddy herself — and how it went OK. "I want to. I think I can." My eyes slide to Dave, serving someone at the other end of the bar.

"You haven't told him?" Maddy asks.

"Not yet." I sigh. "I know I have to. I've already talked about it with Faye. I just can't figure out how to start."

"Has Dave ever not been there for you?"

"You know the answer to that."

"And did I freak out when you finally told me?"

"It's different."

Maddy nods. "It definitely is. You owe him more. He'll be hurt if he finds out any other way. Don't hurt him."

"I don't want to," I say. "I never want to hurt anybody, but sometimes I seem to do it anyway."

"Well, this time it's very easy not to. You know what you have to do." She stretches, yawns, and says, "Speaking of things you have to do ..."

"What now?"

"I said you'd still have to write some regular stories — how do you feel about covering the rubber duck race on the canal tomorrow morning?"

Twelve

WHEN THE FIRST RAYS of the sun hit my face, I groan and pull my hair across my eyes. It smells like dirt and horses. Like Oak Copse. Like home and missing girls.

I want to roll over and go back to sleep. But I have an assignment to do. More than one. Yes, the duck race, which is the main reason I left my curtains open so the sun could wake me. But I have a deeper driver now. It's a new feeling for me, but a good one.

So, before I can give in to the softness of my sheets and the comfort of my pillow, I swing my sleep-heavy legs over the side of the bed and head for the shower.

***

The ducks launch from a set of the navigation locks our city is famous for, which explains why this has to happen early. On a sunny summer Sunday, there will be reams of boat traffic wanting to travel from the river into the canal.

Under the still-fresh rays of the early morning sun, several people stand atop the lock gate, holding up the ends of a bigger tarp than I've ever seen. At the lockmaster's signal, they let go, sending thousands of cheery yellow rubber ducks bobbing free in the river.

Excited children bob, and jump, and run, and whirl after them, yelling, "Which one's ours?" and "Are we gonna win?"

I stop feeling tired and start smiling.

I follow the slow procession of duck chasers along the bank, asking people what prompted them to participate. The funds raised go to the hospital and on this bright day, surrounded by dogs, and children, and volunteers handing out balloons, and offering free face-painting and washable tattoos, I hear story after story about loved ones who were sick and recovered because of their treatment, or who died, but with dignity.

Tears run down one woman's face when she tells me about losing her son, and I apologize for asking. She places her hand on my arm. "No, it's a gift to talk about him. As long as I can share my memories of him, he's still part of me."

I manage a quick "thank you" before stepping aside and taking several deep breaths. I put my sunglasses on so nobody will see my pink-rimmed eyes and send a silent apology to Leila. *I'm sorry. I didn't know any better. I didn't forget you. I'm going to talk about you more from now on.*

I have enough quotes for my story, so I let the crowd carry me along.

Beside me, one man tells another, "The only way your duck could beat mine is if you cheated and got away with it."

A little boy tells his sister, "If I win, I'll share the prize with you."

Fun, happy, heartwarming. I'm already thinking how to weave happiness and sadness into my story as I wander to the finish line, where I'll try to get a few words from the winner.

***

Then, I drive straight to Oak Junction. Do not return to the pub. Do not risk running into Dave.

I'm a coward. Last night, under the pretence of walking Maddy to her car, I left the pub with her, then went up to the apartment by the back stairs. I heard Dave come in at 2:00, but I pretended I didn't. If he heard me leave before 7:00 this morning, he pretended he didn't.

I could do the right thing, be a strong person, tell Dave the whole story, and do it while enjoying his famous avocado-mustard-brie melts.

Instead, I order lunch from Marge at the café.

I work on the rubber-duck-race story between spoonfuls of very-good tomato soup and when I finish the cheese biscuit I ordered, Marge brings me another one. "It's the last one, and it's a funny shape, so you might as well have it."

"Does anyone really care what shape the biscuits are when they taste this good?" I ask.

She smiles. "Honestly, brunch is the busiest part of our Sunday. There won't be that many people in between now and late afternoon when we'll get our Sunday dinner takeout orders."

I look around at the room filled with bright light and empty tables. "It's nice for me that it's quiet like this — I got my entire story written. But maybe you wish it was busier?"

"Ah no. For me, this is what it's all about. I'm a baker, so I've always liked getting up early, serving breakfasts. I always wanted the café to close after lunch — being open 6:00 to 2:00 would be perfect for me. I'd like nothing better than to just clean up now and go home."

"Why don't you? Not today, I mean — but why don't you change your hours?"

Marge sighs. "There's no other restaurant in the valley. Without trying to, we've become a community hub. Here …" She ducks behind the counter and comes back with a binder, which she places on my table. When I open it, there are pages of clippings with headlines about times when people gathered in the café — during the big ice storm over twenty years ago, and through the floods that hit this area fairly regularly. Most recently, after the big tornadoes that decimated the original strip mall across the street. My fingers rest on the familiar

Oak Junction Journal masthead at the top of each page, and I gaze across the street at the empty newspaper office.

Marge's voice brings me back to attention. "We didn't even close during the pandemic. That's when we pivoted to takeout, and it's still about half our business." She sighs. "I'm proud of the role we've played, but I'm also tired."

Marge does look tired, and seeing the dark circles under her eyes gives me a pang of guilt about Dave working tirelessly at the business that subsidizes my rent.

I owe him so much. I owe him the truth.

***

I owe Dave, I owe Leila, I owe Wren.

The thoughts set up a rhythm in my head as I drive to Oak Copse.

I owe Maddy, I owe Faye, I owe Charlotte.

Which, of course, is why I'm driving to Oak Copse. Because I can serve them all by doing my best on this story, right now.

Well, except maybe Dave. But nobody ever said Dave wasn't exceptional.

I owe Dave …

Thirteen

"Do you ride?" Rose asks as I stand blinking in the cool dim of the barn, waiting for my eyes to adjust from the bright warmth of outside.

Ride bikes? Before I can ask what would be a very dumb question, considering I'm standing in a *horseback riding* barn, I give a final, quick double blink and say, "No."

"Do you want to?"

Before I can say, *Also, no,* she continues. "I saddled Pudding for you. She wasn't ridden yesterday — she's my retired eventer from back when I competed. I thought it would be nice if we rode and talked."

"Of course it would be nice to ride and talk." I say it, because it's true. In general. For a lot of people, it would be nice to ride and talk even if I'm not at all sure I want to do it. I also say it because I like Rose — best be careful about that. After all, she's one of my top-three suspects. In fact, maybe this is her way of bumping me off. Put me on Pudding, take me out to the field, and let the horse kill me.

"Why is she named Pudding?"

"Because she's old and sweet."

I squint my eyes. The horse doesn't have a swayed back, or a grey-speckled face. Then again, she's standing with one leg cocked and her lip drooping. There's also a nameplate on the stall next to her that confirms she's named **Pudding**. Maybe if she was called Tempest, or Rogue, I'd think twice, but I decide to take a gamble that Pudding's as docile as Ruth says.

"Let's go," I say.

We follow the route I've already walked so many times in the last few days. By the end of the day yesterday the soles of my feet were achy, and it's nice to be up on Pudding's back, letting her four feet and strong back carry me ... even if my backside will probably feel worse tomorrow than my feet do today.

Rose is surprisingly trusting. She supplied me with a helmet, and rubber boots with a small heel on them — "So your feet don't slip through the stirrups," which, *yikes*! — then gave me only three instructions: "Keep your heels lower than your toes," "Use your core strength to sit nice and tall," and "She knows what she's doing so don't mess with her."

Thinking about it, I guess the trust she's displaying is in the horse, more than in me.

Which is fine. So far, the horse does seem trustworthy. She walks at a lovely clip, which has a distinct rhythm to it. Her ears are forward and she's clearly interested in the walk, but not to the point of deviating from the line we're taking behind Rose and her horse.

As we walk over lush green grass, under a searing blue sky, between white-fenced paddocks full of grazing horses, I take a moment to acknowledge I'm not objective about Rose Not at all. This is a special experience, she's given it to me, and I want to like her.

It's fine, I tell myself. *Nobody's impartial. Recognizing your bias is most of the battle.*

Sure, I should just keep telling myself that.

Rose's horse halts and so does the obedient Pudding. I scratch her neck. I'm starting to like this horse.

"Do you recognize that pony?" Rose points across the nearest paddock at a cute black pony with a big white splash on his belly — adorable and memorable from yesterday's competition, even to a complete horse ignoramus like me.

I nod. "Now that's a pair who really rocked the matching turnout — I loved how her fuchsia helmet cover matched his saddle pad."

"The family who owns him switched to our barn late last season. I told them I didn't have any training spots open, but Wren could coach their daughter. Everything went well — in fact, they won their division at the first event where Wren coached them. They earned enough points to qualify for the Eastern Canadian Eventing Championships, which was the final event of our season." Her voice trails off.

"OK ... but?"

Rose sighs. "Yes. There's so often a but with horses. As always on the morning of an event, we were up at a godawful hour. Wren came to me and said the pony wasn't right."

"What does 'not right' mean?"

"Good question. It's fairly easy when a horse has a huge gash, or a fever, or nasal discharge, but 'not right' is a tough one. When you know horses — when you're around them all the time — you just kind of know sometimes, and that's what Wren was telling me. Something was wrong with the pony. She couldn't tell me what, but she knew."

"What did you do?"

"Wren called the family to explain, and the mother told her to load the pony on the trailer anyway. Wren said no."

"What did they say?"

"They were ... not happy. They drove out here. The daughter was crying. The mother charged into the barn and said the pony looked perfectly fine to her. She found me loading the trailer and said, 'Are you going to let some incompetent employee ruin my daughter's season? Fire her, or lose us as clients.' When I said I was standing by Wren's call, she told her husband to phone the old barn and see if they had room in their trailer to come and get the pony and take him to the event."

I can't imagine how the pony is still here after all that. How do you walk back from calling somebody incompetent? From threatening their job to their face.

"What happened?" I ask. Pudding reaches her nose around and bumps my toe with her nose, and my heart gives a little flutter that puts me firmly in Wren's protect-the-horse-at-all-costs shoes.

"The daughter came running out and grabbed her mother's arm and screamed 'Cupid is lying in his stall, biting his sides!' That's a classic sign of colic, which can — and does — kill a lot of horses."

I state the obvious. "He's not dead."

"Getting the vet out early always helps. Because Wren noticed there was something wrong, and didn't send him off on the trailer, we could get him treated, and he's totally fine." Rose pauses, then continues. "No, that's not quite right. It wasn't just that she noticed — which was impressive enough — it was that she stood up for what she believed was right, even when it would have been easier to give in. It's the true definition of being a horse person — putting a horse's needs before your own. She would always do that."

"What about the family?"

"Oh, they backtracked instantly. The woman wasn't the type to apologize, but she told both Wren and me she was under a lot of stress, and the thought of disappointing her daughter was just too much ..."

Rose nudges her horse forward and Pudding follows again, only this time we're out in the open field and able to walk side-by-side.

"So, are you telling me Wren has enemies?" I ask.

Rose wrinkles her nose. "No, that wasn't exactly what I meant to tell you. More that she's principled. If you didn't like her, you might say stubborn ..." Before I can say anything, she continues, "... but most people like her."

"So, what do you think happened to her?" I ask.

She shoots me a sideways glance. "I know what I *don't* think happened."

"Which is?"

Rose holds up a hand and starts ticking off fingers, one by one. "I don't think she got bored and decided to leave. I don't think she was in trouble and decided to leave. I don't think she had a mental breakdown and decided to leave."

There's definitely a theme. Rose continues, "I don't think she was suicidal, and I don't think she got lost in the woods."

"Also …" She puts her reins in one hand and uses her free hand to rub her forehead. "… I don't think she's just going to show up any day now." When she looks at me again, her eyes glisten with gathering tears. "I understand the police go by statistics, and what they know, but I know Wren, and I know she's not OK, or she'd be here."

She exhales. "Sorry. It's just hard. All of it. It's hard to believe she's actually missing, and since I don't fully believe it, I wonder if maybe I haven't done everything I should, but when I reach out to the police, they say 'just give it time.'"

"It's normal to be upset," I say. "Also, for what it's worth, I put a fair amount of weight in your instinct that Wren probably didn't leave on her own." I could add that growing up with my mom gave me pretty outstanding skedaddle radar. Leila and I both knew when she was about to get out of Dodge for an extended period. There was an unmistakable energy in the house, which was so clear that Leila would raid our mom's purse for money and car keys and drive to the big Walmart on the road into the city to stock up on enough food and toilet paper to last for a while.

We've entered the course now. I recognize it — of course I do. I was here just yesterday — but it looks so different. Maybe it's because of the lack of people. No jump judges with camp chairs and umbrellas. No approaching or retreating competitor hoofbeats. Maybe it's because I'm on horseback, which gives me a much higher vantage point than I expected and lets me see further into the woods on either side of us.

"Have there been a lot of searches?"

"I organized a foot search late on the afternoon she disappeared. All the volunteers joined in, and there were lots of dogs around, too. Nobody saw anything and none of the dogs sniffed anything — other than the occasional squirrel. Since then I've set up a system for when riders go out on hacks —" Rose responds to my lifted eyebrows. "Trail rides, like we're doing now. I've been asking them to ride on different parts of the property on different days, and even to take public trails that go off our land. Every trail in the area has been covered at least twice and nobody's ever found anything."

There's no doubt the property is vast, and there are a lot of trees out here, but being on horseback shows me how much more ground riders can cover. It does seem like if there was anything to find, at least one person out of all those riders would have seen something.

Rose's phone rings. "Sorry, this is a call I've been waiting for all day. It'll just be a minute or two." She rides a few steps away and Pudding shifts. Just that tiny movement is enough for me to glimpse something red in the trees.

It's not far in. I look back toward Rose, who has her back to us. As soon as I turn around again, there's the red flash — clear as anything now that I've seen it once.

I give Pudding's sides a tentative squeeze and she obligingly moves forward, right to the edge of the trees.

Whatever it is can't be more than twenty feet away. Thirty at the most.

Rose's voice drifts to me. "… in that case, you should start the insurance coverage from the morning he gets on the truck …"

I decide if Pudding's willing to go into the trees, I'll check out whatever it is. Otherwise, we'll wait for Rose.

I look right at the red thing, squeeze the horse again, and whisper, "Come on, let's go."

She goes.

She goes much more quickly than I expect. She lowers her head and weaves between trees, and I realize the thing might be more like forty feet in, and I'm so busy keeping my eyes on it that I almost don't notice the branch at the exact height of my head until it's right in front of me.

I duck, but the wood scrapes the top of my helmet (I guess helmets aren't just for falls). Since I've stopped looking, Pudding stops walking. She just waits for me to tell her what to do next.

I straighten, take in the deflated red balloon stuck in a notch of a tree that most likely once had helium in it, and with my heart rate and breathing still quite a bit above normal levels, I ask Pudding to turn around.

She does it easily as though to say, *Yeah, I wondered why you wanted to come in here.*

The way back out is all about self-preservation. I lie along the horse's neck to minimize my chances of decapitation and I let Pudding carry me back to the clearing, feeling incredibly vulnerable.

"Goodness!" Rose says. "Where did you go?"

"Sorry." I feel quite sheepish at this point. "I saw something in the woods, but I nearly took my head off on a branch."

"Ah ..." Rose nods. "Yes, that's a rookie mistake. But I see you learned quickly. The neck grip is always a safe bet."

I'm relieved she hasn't told me off — or told me to get off her horse — she'd be perfectly within her rights to do either, but I also can't shake the feeling that danger might always be closer than I think.

We walk in silence for a couple of minutes until we reach my old familiar clearing. *Wren's* clearing.

"This jump ..." I say.

Rose smiles. "Pudding's jumped that in her day."

"Has she?"

"Sure. Ride her up to it."

I do the same thing as I did to reach the red herring in the trees — look, squeeze, and ask — and Pudding walks calmly right up to the jump.

"You did it. Very good — you're a natural."

I laugh. "Was this all a recruitment effort to get me hooked on riding?"

"Is it working?"

"I can definitely see the attraction. Although not in jumping something this big." Riding up to the jump on Pudding just confirms how truly huge it is. "I thought it would look smaller from her back."

"Horses are fine with that jump, but it definitely freaks the riders out. To horses it's wide and solid, easy to see, and they know exactly what to do. The riders ... they talk to each other — 'Have you seen the size of the tree trunk jump?' 'Would you jump it?' — this jump has an unfair reputation."

"Speaking of which ..." This is something I don't want to mention, but I have to. "Have you read the Barn Talk forum?"

"Come on." Rose rides us out of the clearing and along the path. She's silent for a few seconds. I wonder if she's going to ignore the question, until she sighs and asks, "What poison are they spreading now? Oh, wait, I bet I know. They say Wren was sleeping with Nate."

"So, you read it?"

"I don't have to read their rehashed slander. About a week after I hired Wren, I ran into our neighbour from up the road at the feed store. She said, 'I'm surprised you'd want to bring that girl onto your property — didn't you hear she broke up the owners' marriage at the last place she worked?'"

"Wow, that's quite the neighbourly chit-chat."

"I know. I was so tempted to set her straight. When I interviewed her, Wren told me what happened. It's sad that she felt she had to, but the horse world is small, and gossip spreads lightning-fast, so I can see why she thought it was better to bring it up herself."

"What *did* happen?" I check myself. "I'm not asking for the story — I promise — and of course you don't have to tell me. I'm just curious."

Rose waves her hand. "It's probably better for more people to know the truth — it's the best way to kill the rumours. Wren was in a relationship with the barn owner's ex-husband before she even worked at the stable. He was the one who recommended her for the job. So all that talk is a bunch of lies, but with one tiny kernel that's nearly true — just enough to keep the gossip going."

"What did you end up saying to your neighbour?"

Rose snorts. "I told her I appreciated her concern, but I didn't think Wren was my type, so I probably wouldn't start sleeping with her."

The laughter hits me in the gut first, bubbling up and taking my breath as it spreads. I clutch at my stomach and for Pudding's sake try to hold in my whoops. It isn't the funniest thing I've ever heard, but it's the right humour at the right time.

I wave my hand feebly in Rose's direction. "I'm ... so ... sorry ... it's ... just ..." I shake my head. When have I laughed like this? I can't remember. Although I remember Leila used to laugh like this. It was fun to watch her — like she'd gone somewhere else, but I knew it was a good place. I'd give so much to know she's in a good place now.

The thought gives me the pause I need to take a deep breath and rally. "Whoa, I don't know why that made me laugh so hard."

Rose grins. "Because I'm funny."

"You are," I agree, and we ride on in companionable silence. Now and then, Rose points something out to me — a jump with a story, a fox sliding through the trees. I slap at flies on Pudding's neck, and Pudding looks after me with her careful, even walk.

"How is it?" Rose asks. "The riding? A lot of adults are scared to try."

"I like it. It's much more tiring than it seems. Sitting up straight and quiet doesn't sound like hard work, but I can feel it catching up with me now. I'll be sore tomorrow."

"You're right that sitting straight and quiet is harder than it seems, and not everybody can manage it. You've done great, and I'm not just saying that."

"This might sound weird, but I'm not sure if I could have done it even a couple of weeks ago. I have a lot on my plate right now, and some of it's heavy, but I just realized I'm happier than I've been in a while."

Rose shakes her head. "It doesn't sound weird at all. Riding — and horses — show us things about ourselves we didn't know."

"Thanks," I say. "Normally I wouldn't share like that, but I feel like I'm sharing all over the place these days." I think of Dave. Well, *almost* all over the place. "At any rate, I don't think I could be scared on this horse. Thanks for letting me ride her. I can tell she's special."

I have the impression Rose is going to say something, then a fly lands on her horse's neck and she flicks it away. When she looks up, we're approaching a gate which opens into a leafy tunnel. At the end I can see the wall of the barn, and Wren's car parked under the apartment staircase. There's a paddock beside us with a pretty golden horse grazing in the middle of it.

"That's Wren's horse, Shine," Rose tells me. She talks me through dismounting — "take both your feet out of the stirrups, swing your right leg over her back, bend your knees" — It's not graceful, but I get down in one piece. As we walk through the gate, my legs have that strange feeling, like when you just get off a boat. Wobbly, and like I need to double-check to make sure they're there.

Outside the barn, Rose pauses. "Back to Wren and why she'd never just walk away. Look at this."

She fumbles with her phone, then hands it to me with a video playing. I recognize the Oak Copse sand ring. There's a girl, her slight stature emphasized by her tight jeans and a fitted tank top. The pink streaks in her long hair swinging out of the back of her baseball cap tell me it's Wren running through the deep footing.

A horse trots behind her, neck arched. He has a long mane that swishes and moves much like the girl's hair.

Rose doesn't have to tell me that's Shine.

On the screen, Wren runs through a set of poles and Shine follows, lifting each knee high in a floating prance.

She turns and hops over one jump, then another. He does, too. At the end of the line of jumps, she giggles in that high, pure way most people lose after childhood. The horse snorts and tosses his head.

Rose takes the phone back. "So?"

"Some people in the forum said she might have left her horse here, so he'd be in a good home, but ..."

"But, you see now, right?"

I swallow hard. Nod. "I see there's no way she'd leave him."

Fourteen

Twenty minutes later, Rose and I are back at the paddock gate, letting our two horses out with Shine.

They both drop to their knees, roll, then stand, shake, and trot out to meet Shine.

"Paige?" Rose asks.

"Yes?"

"There's something — I'm not sure if I should say it — it's hard to know."

"I'm happy to hear anything you have to say." I ready myself for a revelation about Wren. Something less complimentary than the picture Rose has painted so far — someone Wren was sleeping with that she shouldn't have been. Or a time when she crossed the line when confronting a client — from being direct to being offensive. "I can protect you as a source."

I'm not prepared for what Rose actually says. "Wren reminds me of your sister."

My first thought is Faye. Because Charlotte rides here, so of course Rose knows Faye. But free-spirited, pink-haired Wren could never remind anyone of chino-wearing, president-of-the-school-council Faye. Also, Rose wouldn't hesitate to mention Faye.

She has to mean Leila. "You knew her?" I whisper.

"She used to ride her bike out here. Normally we can't have random people hanging around the barn … but I liked her. She learned how to muck out stalls and clean tack. I gave her a few riding lessons in return." There's a catch in Rose's voice. "Not enough. I wish I'd done more."

As Rose is talking, I think of how I woke up the morning after the horse trials — how I smelled horses and thought of Leila.

I thought it was just because I'd been back in Oak Junction, but was there more? Did I smell horses on my sister before she went missing? Did my subconscious make the connection?

Whenever I think of Leila, I think of all the things I don't know, but maybe there are things I do know … if only I knew how to access them.

"I'm sorry if I've upset you," Rose says. "Maybe I shouldn't have said anything."

"No. I'm glad to know she used to come here."

"She used to ride Pudding."

"Right." I look out at the horse I just told Rose is special. Who took care of me, so I never felt nervous. "I'm glad I got to ride her, too. Thanks for that, and for telling me, and for being kind to my sister."

"Did you ever find out …" Rose starts, then stops. "Sorry. It's none of my business."

"Of course it is. You opened up to me about Wren. I think it's something we have to do — talk about them so they don't get forgotten." I shake my head. "I don't know anything about what happened to Leila, but that's my main motivation for writing this story."

"I can see that. I guess it's a big part of my motivation to help you."

As we head back through the tree-lined path, I ask Rose, "Is there anything missing from Wren's apartment?"

"I don't know."

I stop in my tracks. "Don't you own it, though? I would have expected you to go in."

"At first I thought the police would want to look through it, and I shouldn't go in — you know, like a crime scene. They never did, but now it feels like I'd be violating her privacy if I do."

It's hard to believe nobody's gone into the apartment of a missing woman. No wonder rumours flourish — somebody says, "they haven't found her phone, or wallet" and in the absence of facts the statement goes unchecked. For the sake of the story, and for Wren's sake, the apartment needs to be searched.

This is where it gets hard. I don't want to violate Wren's privacy, and I don't want Rose to think I'm pushy. I never want anyone to think I'm pushy — it's why I haven't been doing my best work — it's so much easier to let things go, than to probe for more details or facts.

Considering my motivation to go to journalism school was to right the wrong that nobody followed up, pushed, or hunted out the story when my own sister went missing, it's inexcusable that I haven't been doing it myself.

I just got on a horse and rode it through a cross-country course (even if it was at a walk). I just walked that horse to the gate and set it free. These are things I've never done before. If I can do them, I can do my job.

"We should go in."

Rose's nose wrinkles. She blinks.

She's going to say no.

I haven't done enough.

I take a deep breath, roll my shoulders back, and prepare to dredge up something of my personal story that will convince her. *You can do it*, I tell myself. *You have to.*

But before I need to say anything else, Rose nods. "You're probably right. I should go in. I think if you come, I'll feel better about it. It won't feel like I'm snooping."

"Let's go, then." I sound far more confident than I feel.

***

I stand behind Rose at the top of the staircase, waiting while she unlocks the door. The stairs are high enough to give a view out across the property. The horses we just turned out graze peacefully beside Shine — two with gleaming dark coats, and Shine a bright golden highlight. Straight ahead in the woodlot, a breeze stirs the leaves, which make a soothing rustling sound. To the east is Nate and Rose's snug farmhouse with the wide porch Rose spoke from when she sent us all out on our search.

There's a chair tucked in the corner of the landing and I can imagine Wren sitting in this peaceful spot with a coffee in the morning, maybe a glass of wine in the evening. With her much-loved horse grazing nearby. One more strike against the notion that she chose to leave.

A slight creak draws my attention back to the door, and I follow Rose inside.

I take a deep breath and order myself, *Be observant, take pictures, take notes.* On that very first inhale, I'm hit by the overpowering smell of bananas. Straight ahead, on a breakfast bar that separates the kitchen from the living area, is a bowl of fruit containing bananas past even the banana-bread stage.

Rose goes around the breakfast bar to the sink. "A coffee cup and a cereal bowl left in the sink. Other than that, spotless."

She's right. The bananas might have a strong smell, but nothing in here suggests neglect. There's a blanket folded neatly over the arm of the couch. The counter is bare of both dishes and crumbs.

"How does someone leave their room if they're going to walk away and never come back?" Rose asks.

I'm hit by a strange disorientation. It's a feeling I remember from when I was a kid running a high fever, or from back when I'd go on the occasional bender only to lie down on my bed and experience a sensation as though the whole world rotated around me before settling back down, but not necessarily in the same place.

How did Leila leave her room?

I don't even know. I can't remember. The time after Leila went was a blur. My mom, as she almost always was by that point, was away the day Leila didn't come home from school. I knew there was something wrong, but it wasn't until

Faye ran into me at the grocery store, spending the last of my money on bread and milk, that the truth became cemented. "Leila's missing," I told Faye.

After that, Faye drove me home just long enough to get my toothbrush, school clothes, and our hamster, Benny. I didn't even go into Leila's room. It's why I have nothing of my sister — why I didn't even have a photo until I printed out the old OJJ story.

Another family was living in our bungalow before Christmas — I found out later my mom was already months behind on the rent — so how Leila left her room is just one more gap in a long string of them.

"Paige? You OK?" Rose leans across the breakfast bar to lay her hand on my arm. "Is it too stuffy in here?"

"No, sorry. I'm fine." I yank my attention back to the here-and-now. To this apartment and this story. To the bananas darkening in front of me. "Just thinking. I read somewhere that nobody found her phone."

Rose nods. "That's another reason they figure she left of her own accord. She didn't leave a phone or a wallet behind. The police say it suggests she's gone somewhere and taken them with her."

I nod. "Same buzz on the forum. I wonder who had the idea first …"

The good thing that's come out of my brief trip down memory lane is a new resolve. I didn't even look in Leila's room. I'm going to have a careful look through Wren's.

There's nothing in Wren's cupboards, or her fridge, or her freezer that I wouldn't expect to see in just about anybody's kitchen. It's notable that her kitchen is much cleaner than mine. Dave and I are both big believers in clean kitchens, but there are two of us, so we just naturally have more stuff.

"Was she single?" I ask Rose.

"She lived alone. I'm pretty sure she had some kind of love life, or sex life, or whatever you want to call it — sometimes she'd go out after night check and drive in just as we were starting morning chores — but it was nothing we talked about, and she never brought anybody back here."

The rest of the living space backs up that assertion. The end of the sofa with the blanket over it also has an ottoman in front of it, and an end table beside it. Very much a setup for one person who doesn't have to share their couch comforts.

"Bedroom," I say.

Rose follows me. The bed's made — I'd be surprised if it wasn't. There's very little hanging in Wren's closet, but what's there is arranged by length. Her drawers are full of clothes made of denim and athletic fabric. All folded neatly, all smelling fresh. "Do you have a clothesline here?" I ask Rose.

"Wren used to put up one of those folding umbrella ones." Rose also sniffs over the open drawer. "She always smelled like the outdoors." She lifts her own shirt to her nose. "And like horses."

One drawer contains lacy, satiny items — mostly black. It backs up Rose's belief that Wren wasn't celibate even if she didn't bring her partners here.

There's nothing in any of the drawers I wouldn't expect to see there — no papers tucked away under the socks, or boxes shoved alongside t-shirts.

The most interesting things in the bedroom are the photos propped on top of the chest of drawers. Wren looks much younger in all the pictures. Her face is rounder and her hair isn't pink.

There's a shot of her in cowboy boots, standing next to Shine, who's wearing a big saddle with a horn. "That saddle …" I point to it.

"That's a Western saddle. From when Wren used to use him for roping."

There's a picture of Wren in a pretty dress standing on the steps of what might be a school, with two people who look too old to be her parents. Then one of a long table, jammed with food and people, all of whom are looking at the camera grinning. My favourite is of her standing, spreadeagled, on a covered bridge. It looks as though she's trying to hold up the roof. It looks as though she loves whoever is taking the photo.

"Do you know who any of these people are?" I ask.

Rose shakes her head. "All I know is she has family in Maniwaki. That was the true reason she came here to work — as opposed to that lie about her being fired. She was north of Toronto before, but from here she could do day trips to see her family."

Suddenly Wren seems more like me. A girl from a small place, not still living there, but not completely letting go, either. I snap photos of her photos and it feels more invasive than looking at her lingerie.

The bathroom is small, but contains everything one person needs. OK, it's more like tiny. Much too cramped for both Rose and me to squeeze in together. Rose peeks in and says, "I don't really see anything noteworthy."

I go in and open the medicine cabinet. This should feel more like prying than anything else, but I've gotten used to it. It has to be done.

Toothpaste. Toothbrush. Eyedrops. Band-aids. Cotton swabs.

No opioids, tranquilizers, or stimulants. No cannabis. Come to think of it, there wasn't any alcohol in the fridge, either. Erratic behaviour due to addiction is seeming less likely.

There's a pack of birth control pills, but I don't think much about those being left behind. I've known friends to be more or less religious about taking birth control, and I've also known people who have changed their minds and just stopped taking the pills for a variety of reasons.

The small bottle beside them is another story, though. It rattles when I lift it. It's probably a third full. "Do you know anything about these?"

"They don't look familiar."

"My mom took them. They're synthetic hormones for hypothyroidism. You have to take them every day."

"What I do recognize is this." Rose reaches past me and lifts a sachet from the top shelf. When she holds it up, I recognize it, too.

"I saw one of those sachets the other day — at the horse trials," I say. "I thought it was a wet wipe."

"It's Bute. It's a common pain reliever for horses."

"Like ibuprofen for people?"

"Similar. It's also an anti-inflammatory."

"Does Wren have this for Shine?"

Rose frowns. "I wouldn't have thought so. Shine isn't on Bute right now, and I'd expect her to keep it in her tack locker. Also, this isn't the brand we use."

She pauses. "I'm guessing maybe she brought it from the last place she worked? Maybe it was in her stuff when she moved and she just stuck it here?"

"Do you know when the horses here are on Bute? I mean, I don't tell other people when I take an Advil."

"You would if you were an athlete, or in the hospital. I have to know what all the horses are taking to avoid possible bad interactions and because certain medications are banned for eventers — or can't be combined with other meds. Like you can't give a competition horse both Bute and Banamine."

"Right. Banamine. I'll take your word for it." I line up the sachet of Bute, the small bottle of pills, and the birth control for good measure, making sure the labels are showing, and snap a picture.

"Alright, then," Rose says. "I feel better that we checked this out. I'm going to water Wren's spider plants before we leave. She killed a bunch of them right after she moved in and she was determined not to let these die — the least I can do is give them some water."

"No rush," I say. As soon as Rose is out of sight, I bend down and take a close-up photo of something that's caught my eye in the small trash can slid between the toilet and the vanity.

A condom wrapper.

Fifteen

"Do you have a compost heap?" I point to the black bananas.

Rose wrinkles her nose. "Just toss them in the bushes across the way. The squirrels will appreciate them."

I scoop them up, and try to keep my voice casual as I ask, "So, you said Wren never brought dates back here?"

Rose tips water into the final spider plant. "No, it was a paranoia thing with her. At one place she worked, she shared an apartment with another girl. That roommate picked up someone at a bar and brought him home. He wasn't a horse person, and he smoked. Wren woke up to the smoke detector going off. The guy's cigarette butt had fallen into the crack of the sofa and started to burn. Wren put it out with the fire extinguisher, but she was furious. She said you can never trust non horse people around a stable — they just don't understand the danger — barns go up like torches."

"Scary," I say. "I can see why she felt that way." So, how did the wrapper get there? Did Wren break her rule? Or was the visitor a horse person? I stick those questions in the "figure out later" file in my brain as Rose holds the door open for me, then locks it behind us.

As we descend the stairs, Rose says, "I feel better that I've actually checked through the apartment, so thanks for prompting me. You know, I assumed as soon as I called the police they'd be all over this place — it never occurred to me they'd think Wren could have left on her own." She sighs. "I also would have expected it to be a big story — to be covered by the press."

"Yeah," I say. "Both my sister and Marge at the café think the Oak Junction Journal would have covered it."

Rose shrugs. "It's hard to say. Let's just say they weren't doing the best work by the end and also ..."

"What?"

"Well, they didn't exactly give your sister's disappearance good coverage, did they?"

I nod. "I can't argue with you there."

She smiles. "At least you're writing about it."

"Yes. Although my editor keeps reminding me I'm writing more about the effect on the community, and about Wren herself, as opposed to the actual details of her disappearance."

"You never know, though, right?" Rose asks. "Maybe you'll stumble across the truth while you're doing it."

Before I can reply, there's movement inside the barn. All I can tell is that it's one of the riders. The barn is dim, and the girls all look the same to me (honestly, I could be blinking away at my own niece and I probably wouldn't know). Rose, however, proving the students are more like children to her, says, "How is Auckland today?"

Addison comes to the door where the light hits her, and I'm once again stricken by how put-together she looks despite the heat, and the horses, and the many sources of dirt and dust around here. "I just hand-walked him and he was as feisty as ever. No soreness that I can see."

Rose turns to me. "Now that would be a story for the OJJ if they were still publishing. How Addison and Auckland are powering toward their goals."

I snap my fingers. "Right. Charlotte said something about you qualifying for a big competition at the last horse trials here — she said that's where you were yesterday?"

Addison nods. "We went Intermediate at Ironwood. We have things to work on, of course, but for his first outing at that level, he was amazing."

Intermediate doesn't sound that exciting to me, but Addison's tone and the way Rose is nodding tells me it's a big deal. "That's great," I say. "Congratulations."

"Thank you. There were a couple of potential buyers there, so it was definitely a worthwhile outing."

"You don't want to keep him?" I remember Faye saying Addison is aiming for the Olympics.

She shrugs. "He's great, of course, but since this is going to be my living, I need to be practical. There's a price where every horse is worth selling. And if I keep building my reputation, I can attract high-level horses to ride, even if I don't own them."

I also remember what Faye said about Addison's other horse, Paris — "She's hoping we'll want to buy the horse for Charlotte" — maybe Addison's not *exactly* like all the other riding girls.

Addison turns to Rose. "Do you have a few minutes to watch me lunge Auckland just to confirm you don't see any soreness, either?"

That's my cue. "I should get going. Faye will expect me soon."

Rose tells Addison, "Get him going, and I'll meet you in the ring in a few minutes. In the meantime, I'll walk you to your car," she tells me.

"I can see why you find your students so interesting," I say. "They might look the same at first glance, but Addison couldn't be more different from Charlotte."

"You're right. Charlotte's a fantastic little rider — she'd have to be or Addison would never let her ride Paris — but she doesn't have the competitive edge Addison does. And Addison ..." Rose wrinkles her nose. "Let's just say where most other girls get distracted by relationships and school as they get older, she's become more focused on riding."

When we reach my car, Rose asks, "I know you said you're not investigating Wren's disappearance per se, but should I give you my alibi anyway?"

"It seems like you have the perfect alibi. If the day she disappeared was anything like yesterday, every single person on the cross-country course knows you were on the radio when Wren stopped transmitting."

"Not that I want you to think I hurt her, but radios are portable ... although, come to think of it, your sister was in the hut with me at the time."

I grin. "If it makes you feel better, I'll check your alibi with Faye when I get there. Assuming it checks out, though, you're one of the few people who absolutely couldn't have been at Wren's station when she dropped off the radio."

Rose gives a grim smile. "That's good? I guess?"

"I think it's good."

Addison walks Auckland toward us. Rose's eyes slide to her.

"Thanks for today." I tell her. "For telling me what you know, and letting me ride, and for my sister, too, all those years ago. I can see why she loved it."

As I set off down the driveway obeying Nate's twenty-kilometre-an-hour signs, with a quick wave out the window for Rose, I think the radio alibi is good for her.

Not so good for Nate, though.

If Wren didn't bring any outside partners back here, yet she had sex in her apartment — well, there aren't that many people it could have been. Only horse people, Rose said.

Nate's also probably the person who moves most freely around the property — so much so that it would be nearly impossible to say exactly where he was at any point in the day. Except for the time of Wren's disappearance — since he was the person who discovered she was missing, it's clear he was at her station then.

Finally, as much as I want to believe Rose's version of Wren's story, if even a small part of the rumours are true, maybe Wren does have a pattern of behaviour that would have led to an affair with Nate. Maybe Rose even knows — or suspects it — and is downplaying the rumours to protect Nate.

Although, would she protect him if she suspected him of having an affair? I don't know her well enough to be sure. What I do know is if Nate had a reason to make Wren disappear, he definitely had the opportunity.

Sixteen

I DRIVE BACK UNDER the flashing light at the junction on my way to Faye's and it makes me think of this place — of Oak Junction — of Dave quizzing me about how much time I've been spending here. Of my own thoughts, when I left here for journalism school — that I'd achieve success in quick leaps. That I'd probably have to move to Toronto to find an outlet big enough for my writing abilities.

I had a whole narrative built up in my head, how I'd go reluctantly, and I'd complain about the big city just like everybody else does. That when I came back here for short holiday visits, I'd find it charming, and maybe I'd run into one or two of my high school classmates and we'd all comment on the soullessness of Toronto, and the quaintness of Oak Junction — then we'd all go back to the big city.

That obviously hasn't happened, and I don't think I want it to. So many things look different to me now, including this place.

I don't think it's either somewhere stifling to be escaped from, or some idyllic small town to come home to.

In just the last few days, I've encountered friendship and hostility. Safety and danger. Good and bad intentions.

This place is complicated, and on that linguistic cop-out, I turn onto Faye's street.

***

Faye, no surprise, has a beautiful kitchen. I'd almost say it could be in a magazine, except there's soul in her decor. It reflects how she likes to live — practical and clean, with money spent on the things that are important to her.

For her wedding, Faye registered for a stoneware set so expensive I could only afford to buy her a single salad plate. That set is now discontinued and becomes more valuable every year ... yet those are the plates she has out for us to use tonight, and those are the plates her children have eaten from throughout their upbringing.

Faye's never posh, or perfect, to be pretentious. She's just those things because that's how she is.

"This looks amazing." When I say it, I mean everything. The expanse of uncluttered counter. Her island which has drawers and a sink and, by itself, is the size of my apartment bathroom at home. Even Charlotte, who probably should be at some sort of awkward, scribbled make-up, and statement clothing stage, slamming through the room without talking to us, instead appears freshly showered, wearing clothes that suit her and maybe a hint of tasteful lip gloss. She gives each of us a kiss on the cheek and her mother calls, "Have fun at Pen's!"

I giggle as we sit at the island by a huge bowl of salad. I lift my plate. "I think this is the one I bought for you!"

She laughs. "That's my favourite plate."

"Is it really the one?"

She shrugs. "Well, yes, in that every time I take a salad plate out, I think 'This is the one Paige bought for our wedding.' It was so sweet of you — I know how little money you had then."

And here it comes again — that upwelling of emotion that's seemed so close to the surface lately. The discovery that all along I've had bonds with my siblings I didn't even know about.

"Are those the lists?" To keep myself from sniffing, I point to stacks of paper next to Faye's laptop.

"Sure are." She winks. "It's not that I'm glad Brian's away" — My brother-in-law travels frequently — "but he would never go for mixing work and food."

I nod. "I'm with you. A little food makes work a lot more bearable."

She settles onto the chair next to me. "So, let's get to it. I prepared some things."

Turns out she doesn't just mean the salad.

"Why don't I explain, and you can stop and ask any questions."

Since that means I can eat while she talks, I'm good with it. I already have a mouthful of her delicious salad, so I shoot her a thumbs up.

"There are hundreds of people at each horse trial. All the competitors, their coaches, grooms, friends, and families. That's one group. Then there are the volunteers. Another group. Then the 'extras' — the medics, the woman who runs the canteen, the vet, the farrier, and so on. Good so far?"

She pauses, I smile, she continues.

"That's three main groups — competitors, volunteers, and others. The Oak Copse people are a subgroup who fit into one or more of those categories. The riders are mostly competitors, and some volunteer. Then there's the core group — sort of the 'executive' — Rose, Nate, and their family members who mostly fit into the volunteer and other categories. OK?"

My mouth is empty this time, so I say, "Yes. Agreed."

"To narrow these hundreds of people down to those who might reasonably be involved with Wren's disappearance, I'm assuming a few things." She holds up her fingers one at a time. "One, they'd need a reason to interact with her. Two, since nobody's found her, they had a way to move her. Three, they had to be in the clearing with her at the time of her last radio transmission, which was 2:15. Clear?"

"So clear, I'm going to stop stuffing my face so I can write this down." The packet of old score sheets is still in my bag, so I pull it out and write her one, two, three points on the sheet I already started scribbling on the other day.

"Let's do easy first," Faye says.

"I like easy." I sneak a forkful of salad before she gets rolling.

"The external competitors. Most of them wouldn't have any reason to interact with Wren. As you know, they just gallop through the clearing. Their grooms, families, and friends watch them in the dressage and show-jumping rings, but they don't follow them around the cross-country course. If they watched any part of the cross-country, it would be from the top of the hayfield where you can see half-a-dozen jumps at once."

"You're right. I didn't see a single spectator at my station."

My inclination is to discount the external competitors — which also means we've narrowed the suspect pool down by a couple of hundred people — but just to be extra-thorough I double-checked which competitors were at the trials when Wren went missing and which ones were also there yesterday. Almost all of them were at both."

"O-kay ... why did you do that?"

"I figure if they kidnapped or hurt Wren last time, they're unlikely to come back."

"That makes sense."

"I also searched to see whether any of the competitors were from either of the last two stables where Wren worked — they weren't."

"Smart thinking." I tap my fork against my teeth. "Speaking of searching ... can you search by owner?"

"Absolutely — who are we looking for?"

"Jeb Dixon."

Faye's fingers fly over the keys. "Not with an 'x.' Not with 'cks.' Not with just 'J' as a first initial ... why? Who is he?"

I tell her about Xander's suspicion. "I'd give it more weight if Jeb had a horse competing — if he was on the property anyway. But since he didn't have any reason to be on the property that day, if he was responsible, he would have had to plan it — to mean to find Wren."

I flash back to the condom wrapper. Xander doesn't trust Jeb because of his history with horses, but could that exact history be enough to gain Wren's trust? Could horsey Jeb be someone she was willing to invite to her apartment?

Faye's already tapping away, doing something else with her spreadsheets, so I push that speculation to the side of my brain. "I'm marking Jeb down as not-likely-but-possible," I say.

"Sounds good — OK, as to the 'outsiders' there aren't many, they've all been attending the horse trials at Oak Copse for years, with no issues, and most of them would never have crossed paths with Wren. We could look into the vet and farrier, since Wren would know them from their regular visits to the barn, but I still consider them unlikely suspects."

"I'm marking them low priority," I say, then do just that.

"The volunteers were older ladies who used to ride, members of Rose and Nate's families — for example, both their mothers, or riders, like Charlotte and Pen. Having an outside face like you is unusual, and there weren't any that day," Faye says.

"I have one question about volunteers," I say. "Did any of them — anybody other than Wren — miss any radio check-ins that you remember?"

She wrinkles her nose. "I can't swear to it, because I don't monitor the radio, but I don't think so. I remember Rose joking that Em was more reliable than usual because her boyfriend was jump judging with her, and he was doing most of the radio check-ins."

"Hmm, OK, just wondered." I make a note.

Faye says, "Maybe I'm being naïve, but I don't see a tween, or teen horse-crazy girl, or an elderly horse-loving woman attacking Wren. And if they did, they'd have to own up to it because I don't know how they'd hide what happened."

"I think you're right." I hesitate before continuing, because I've been thinking it, of course, but saying it out loud feels worse. "I think if something happened to Wren — an injury or worse — it would take a strong person to inflict it, and also somebody strong and with access to some kind of vehicle to move her out of the area and transfer her to a car or a truck to take her off the premises."

"Which would mean they'd need to have a license and access to a car," Faye agrees. "I think we're talking about an adult, but not an elderly one. Whatever happened, it was quick. Wren reported a rider, then three minutes later she didn't report the next one. After she missed one more, Rose sent Nate to look for her. It took him maybe five minutes to get there and her chair was empty. So, somebody had to incapacitate her and get her to a point out of Nate's sight within ten minutes."

If Nate's telling the truth. I'm not quite ready to say that out loud yet, though. Instead, I ask, "What does that mean?"

Faye sighs. "I think it means something I don't like. Going back to my original points, I think there are only a few people who know the property well, can move around it with nobody thinking anything of it, have the means to move somebody against their will, knew where Wren was at 2:15, and know Wren well enough to have had an interaction with her that could go wrong."

I wait. When she doesn't add anything, I ask, "Can you give me names?"

Faye gives what sounds like a grunt of pain. "Rose. Nate. Possibly Nate's sister, who was helping organize the ribbons that day. I guess I should say me ... although I was in the hut when Wren stopped answering, and Rose was there also, and Nate's sister, too. Which should make me feel better, but I don't like who that leaves. There has to be somebody else ..."

I clear my throat. "What about Kimberly?"

"I told you I was replacing her — she wasn't there that day."

"But she fits every other bill. You say she wasn't there, but more accurately, she wasn't *scheduled* to be there. Think about it — if she came onto the property, nobody would think anything of it, right? And her husband was making a fool of himself over Wren, so she had a reason to confront her."

Faye shakes her head. "I don't like to think of it."

"I don't like to think of any of it," I say. "But it happened. And you and I both know the only thing worse than finding out who's at fault is not finding anything out at all."

Seventeen

I'M GATHERING MY THINGS when Faye's phone rings. "Are you sure? I know *you're* sure. I mean, is Pen's mom sure? You've already slept over there twice in the last week ... fine ... yes, have fun and be a good guest."

"House to yourself?" I ask.

She sighs. "You know, when they were little it was my dream — just one night of having the whole place to myself — but Lissy's away at camp all summer, and Alex is always at one friend's cottage or another, and now with Charlotte sleeping at Pen's, turns out I miss them."

"They're fun. You did a great job raising them. I can see why you'd miss them."

"You could stay."

"I ... no ..." *I don't sleep in Oak Junction.* I can't say that, though, because it's just a silly rule I've made for myself. A silly thing I say to people who ask about me coming home — *Oh, I visit, but I don't sleep there.* Come to think of it, I don't even know what it's supposed to prove. Which means there's no good reason to stick to it. "I've had a long day," I finally spit out.

"All the more reason to stay. It's late and I'll worry about you if you drive home." I don't know if she sees I'm weakening, or if she's afraid I'm not, but she adds, "This is your home."

It's not, I want to say. But, of course, it is. I always think of "home" as the bungalow where I lived with Leila. Which means when I lost my sister, I also lost home.

But Oak Junction is my home, and this is Oak Junction. And I lived here in Faye's house for four years, which isn't nothing. She never asked me to leave. It was my choice to move to the cabin on Rowan's property while I worked for him, then to move into the city.

Faye would have let me stay, or come back, as one of her "kids" she misses when we're not around.

"Thanks." I echo her words to Charlotte. "If you're sure, I will."

***

I came down to my old bedroom to find crisp sheets on the bed, as though Faye's had it waiting for me all this time.

It's a nice feeling, but I have to admit I also feel a bit lonely in this big house with Faye, the only other occupant, in the master suite two storeys up.

When I lived here I was used to rapid little footsteps running or dog claws skittering across the floor over my head and sometimes, in the middle of the night a quieter creaking as Faye walked the floor with one of the kids who was sick, or couldn't sleep.

The dog nudges the door open and even though this isn't the same dog from when I lived here, he's from the same breeder and I'm not the only one who still refers to him by the old dog's name. "Hey, Otto." He hops onto my bed and curls up with a sigh. "Ah, that's why you're with me. My sister would make you sleep in your basket, wouldn't she?"

He gives a faint tail wag and closes his eyes, and I still feel alone.

No, that's not true. I'm not lonely in general. I don't want Maddy to be here, or Charlotte. I don't even dream of some random no-strings-attached hot guy (although I can't promise I'd say no, either). I miss Dave.

It's only polite to call him, right? So he knows not to worry when I don't come home?

No answer. Just his economical voice mail recording — "Leave a message" — which isn't long enough for me to enjoy the gravel in his voice.

I text instead. Faye invited me to stay over, so I'm in Oak Junction. Home tomorrow. Don't worry.

As if he would. No, that's not fair — Dave would worry. He'd worry about a car accident or some other mishap. He's a kind person. The bigger question is whether he'll care. Whether he cares, period.

I do. I want him to. But, again, being fair, it's not like I've told him I care. Why should he have to tell me when I haven't told him?

Rather than get a headache from this speculation, I decide to check the forum and let it give me a headache.

And ... mission accomplished. There's a brand-new post, still in Off Course.

> VersMarais: Any of you notice anything about the Wren Sheedy
> story?

> ChestnutMare: I haven't heard anything lately.

> VersMarais: Right. My point exactly.

> AlwaysEventing: What do you mean?

VersMarais: Remember I said if she was really missing, the police would be looking for her? Well, don't you think the press would be as well? Have you noticed there haven't been any stories in *The Star* or on the radio? Don't you think those places would be all over this if it was a real disappearance?

AlwaysEventing: Maybe they're just being respectful.

VersMarais: The news media isn't respectful. Not when there's an actual story to be told.

ChestnutMare: What's your point?

VersMarais: My point is, with the mainstream media not interested, other reporters might push in who are just looking to make things up and get a good story. I hope people are smart enough to ask questions if that happens.

I'm speechless. How can the queen — because I'm assuming VersMarais is a woman — how can the queen of making things up turn it around so she looks like the keeper of the truth? And encourage people to doubt any stories that do come out ... like mine.

It's unreal. It's infuriating. It feels ... devious. And it also feels like a big coincidence that Rose and I were just talking about news coverage — or lack thereof — today.

So, is this an actual coincidence? Or should I ask more questions?

I sigh as I put my laptop to sleep. Maddy would tell me there's only one answer, and it's always "ask more questions."

***

I'm trudging along the side of the road. The pavement is hot under my thin-soled sneakers, and the long strands of hair loosened from my ponytail keep blowing into my mouth and my eyes.

Somebody's cutting hay — the air is sweet with the smell.

"How much farther?" I'm putting as much whine into my voice as I can. I want my sister to be clear I'm not happy about walking. Not as far as the junction, and definitely not all the way home.

"You know how far it is," Leila says.

"I don't want to walk that far."

"We missed the bus. How else are we going to get home?"

We missed the bus because of me. Because Mom came home late with her boyfriend, and woke me up by fighting in the hallway outside my room. Even after her bedroom door slammed, I lay awake just in case it started again. I caught up on my sleep in math class and had to stay behind to finish my work. Leila waited, and we both missed the bus, and she hasn't blamed me.

So, I should stop complaining. It's hard, though, because being tired makes me whiny. I open my mouth to say my feet hurt (even though they don't, really) when I notice Leila glancing behind us. For about the sixth time.

"What are you ...?"

She grabs my arm and pulls me into an opening in a stand of trees. "Come this way."

"Why are we ...?"

"It's a shortcut," she says.

Now I know what Leila was looking back at. Or *who*, because there are footsteps rustling fallen leaves and crackling twigs on the path.

Leila nudges my back and whispers, "Run."

When we run, our follower does, too. My sneakers have no grip, and the path is hard-packed and worn smooth. I'm slipping, and sweating, and tripping on roots and rocks.

"Run!" This time Leila yells it.

Don't look back. I remember my grade four teacher saying it to us at the cross-country meet. "If you look back, you'll get caught. Focus forward and keep running."

I keep running.

Leila screams and I finally look, opening my eyes into the lamp-lit basement bedroom, to see Otto standing at the end of the bed barking.

He's fixated on the high-up window, front legs stiff, and teeth bared.

I feel completely exposed. Anybody could be out there, looking in. I flick off the bedside lamp, removing the spotlight from the bed, then I crawl forward and take hold of the ruff of Otto's neck. "Let's go," I whisper.

He's a good dog. He leads me up two flights of stairs and through darkened rooms to where my sister's sitting propped up with pillows reading.

When I appear with the dog, she pulls off her glasses and asks, "What happened?"

I mean to say, *Nothing,* or *The dog was upset,* or anything other than what I actually do, which is burst into tears.

It may have been ages since I slept in Oak Junction, but it's been even longer since I cried here.

"Oh my gosh, Paige." Faye guides me to her side and puts her arm around me. "Tell me what's wrong."

I sob out the details of the dream. "It really felt like I was losing her."

"I understand." Faye rocks us both from side to side until the repetitive movement eases my tears away. "You're going to sleep up here now, right?"

I wipe my cheeks dry. "It's your bed."

"Which is the size of one of the small islands in the Thousand Islands — I think you'll fit."

I laugh. "Sure, OK then."

I wait for Faye to draw the line at the dog, who's cuddled himself in between us, but she just scratches his ear and says, "He always sleeps with me when Brian's away."

She turns out the light and now, lying on the island-sized bed with my sister and the dog, I feel cozy instead of scared. Faye whispers into the dark, "When you came to live here, you seemed so grown up compared to my kids, but you were only fourteen, and you'd been through so much ... I don't think I gave you what you needed."

I reach out, find her arm, and squeeze it. "You did your best. We were all just doing our best. Plus, I think I turned out pretty amazing, don't you?"

The last thing I remember is both of us laughing.

Eighteen

I FEEL LIKE I'M playing grown-up sitting in Faye's orderly kitchen, drinking home-brewed coffee from a mug with no chips out of it and no gaudy logo on the side.

The ceiling fan shushes conditioned air over my skin, which, for once during this humid month, is cool and dry. I love my over-the-pub apartment, but it's definitely closer to student housing than to adult living.

I sip a smoothie whirred to a perfect consistency and containing exotic fruits I usually can't afford, and read my rubber duck story which Maddy posted late yesterday.

It's short. It's silly.

It's not half bad.

The details make the difference. It's just a few hundred words, but I made the effort to add in small things people said and did. It's something I haven't bothered to do for quite some time.

In the brief flash when I have confidence in my writing, I open a new doc and type, "You might think Wren Sheedy walked away from her life, until you see everything she left behind."

Keep going. A solid opening paragraph can make all the difference. *Write it.*

"Most obvious are the practical things. A car in good running condition. A spacious apartment full of clothes, family photos, and daily medication. There's a golden horse in a field right across from that apartment. A horse Wren raised and trained herself, and who she's brought with her everywhere she's lived. And there are the people who care about her. The ones who encouraged me to write this story."

It's less than a hundred words, but I like it. Both Maddy and I will edit and rewrite it a dozen times, but it's a foundation. I save it, then send a quick message to Maddy:

Duck race story looks good. Here's a quick intro I dashed out for the Wren story. Tell me what you think.

For the first time in a long time I truly care what Maddy thinks. Then I make the mistake of dividing the total word count for the Wren story by what I've just submitted. Panic grips me.

I've got to write more. Write faster. But I can't do that until I figure out what I'm going to say next.

And, because I'm worried about what to say next, I can't for the life of me figure out what to do next.

Check the forum.

Ugh.

That forum makes me feel so icky — which is exactly the reason I should track it.

I decide to ease in by checking the Find Wren Facebook group first.

The top post is the video Rose showed me of Wren and Shine, with the caption, Wren would never have left her horse. If anyone has information, please share it. Rose's work, I assume.

There are the usual comments which are nice, while meaning little. Emojis abound: hearts of all colours, hands clasped in prayer. One suggests organizing a vigil. Another wonders about a community-led search. Even if those intentions probably won't be backed up with action, the Facebook group is at least well-intentioned.

The forum, though ... it gives me the same feeling as the scribblings I used to see scratched into the thick paint of the school bathroom cubicles after Leila went missing. Those scrawled messages were the forums in the days before forums. Today they'd be turned into nasty memes.

— *What do you think happened to Leila Turner? Ask the football team.*

— *Leila Turner doesn't say no.*

— *LT + your boyfriend if you're not careful.*

For the rest of my high school years, I used the single-user bathroom in the guidance office. No graffiti and free tampons.

I have to visit the forum, though, if I want to know what's going on behind the scenes. What rumours are growing and spreading. What's influencing Xander. Or, at least, his colleagues.

I navigate to the Off Course page and am initially relieved to find nothing new there. Except ... last time the topic had just moved.

Be thorough, Paige — why does my inner voice sound so much like Maddy's these days?

I enter an x-ray search using the forum URL and Wren's name in the search bar, hit enter, then close my eyes, pinch the bridge of my nose, and take a deep breath before opening my eyes.

Sure enough — VersMarais is talking about Wren again. This time it's on a thread dedicated to out-of-country news.

VersMarais: For anybody who's been wondering about Wren Sheedy, I heard she got a job at a show-jumping barn in the States.

RedRibbons: Seriously? Where?

VersMarais: Somewhere in Upstate New York.

ChestnutMare: Where even is Upstate New York?

I'm astonished to see a side-thread discussion about this. A girl is missing and a group of people want to discuss the official boundaries of Upstate New York? Eventually RedRibbons gets the conversation back on track by asking the question I'm wondering about.

RedRibbons: How did you even hear that?

VersMarais: My cousin said they have a new junior trainer at her barn who moved from Canada and everyone wants to have lessons with her because of Canada winning the last Nation's Cup. She said this trainer doesn't have a horse with her, but said she was working on figuring out how to get her horse across the border. Sounds like it could be her.

RedRibbons: Or not at all. Maybe post again when you have a photo.

VersMarais: Wow. Bitchy much? Sorry if I hope the girl's safe and has a good job.

RedRibbons: If you want the best for her and the people who love her, you won't spread rumours that might not be true. Come back when you have facts.

I'm silently cheering for RedRibbons when Charlotte walks into the kitchen, stretching her arms over her head and yawning — her hair matted into a bird's nest on one side of her head.

"I thought you slept at Pen's last night?"

"I was supposed to, but Pen's big sister broke her curfew and came home drunk. She was throwing up — loudly, ugh — in the bathroom. Pen's parents were telling her off. It was chaos, so Pen and I came back here to sleep. She's still upstairs ..." Charlotte closes her mouth, lowers her arms, and narrows her eyes. "What are you doing today?"

I hope this kid doesn't take up poker. I can see the new thought zinging through her mind as clear as if it's in a bubble over her head. "Why?"

"Pen's sister was supposed to drive us to Oak Copse on her way to meet her friends at the water park, but she's grounded forever, so Pen and I don't have a way to get to the barn."

"Yes."

Charlotte bats her eyelashes. "Yes, what?"

"Yes, I'll drive you and Pen to Oak Copse."

"Oh, I wasn't trying ..."

"Come on — don't pretend."

Charlotte giggles. "OK. I won't." She runs out of the kitchen yelling, "Pen! Hey, Pen! Wake up — we have a ride to the barn!"

***

This place is starting to feel like my second home.

The girls bounce out of the car at Oak Copse without interrupting the flow of chit-chat they kept up all the way to the barn.

"Hi, Rose!" they chorus.

"Hey, you two. You're just in time! The vet's here to do herd vaccinations and if you help, I'll give you a lesson after."

"Wow, you didn't have to tell them twice." Rose and I watch as the girls bolt off to the barn, then I turn to her. "Is Nate around today, by any chance?"

Rose snaps her fingers. "Yes. You should definitely talk to him since he was the one who found — or didn't find — Wren. He's out in the tractor on the cross-country course."

"Is it OK if I walk out there?"

"Absolutely. And meanwhile, I should go make sure those two are helping the vet more than hindering her."

I'm getting to know this trail. I know exactly where to avoid a rut in the path, and where to be careful not to trip on an old tree root.

There are signs of the horse trials everywhere. The flat-trodden areas around the edge of the warm-up areas. A single glove propped on a fencepost. A granola bar wrapper caught in a clump of long grass.

The way humans mark the landscape makes it even harder for me to understand how there could be no trace of Wren at all.

As I walk, I'm trying to decide how to question Nate without getting his guard up. I'm distracted so, when I turn the corner into the wide warm-up area at the beginning of the cross-country course, I'm taken aback by the size and power of the tractor which is less than a hundred feet away from me and moving closer.

Nate raises the hydraulic lift with a jump balanced at the end of it. It comes so close to me, the shadow it casts falls across my face.

For just a moment I think, *what if he doesn't see me?*

Then I think, *what if he didn't see Wren?*

It would be so easy to hurt or kill somebody with that powerful piece of equipment. You wouldn't have to mean to. You might not even know you had, at first.

He waves at me as he passes by with the jump, so at least right now I know he sees me, but what if there was an accident on the day of the horse trials? What if he covered it up instead of coming clean?

Except, of course, Nate wasn't driving the noisy, hulking tractor around the course in the middle of the horse trials. Honestly, if that's the kind of theory I'm going to come up with, maybe I'm not up to writing this story.

"Hey!" Nate yells over the idling engine. "You wanna help me?"

I cup my hands around my mouth. "I can't drive a tractor!" Halfway through my sentence, he cuts the engine, which leaves me yelling so loudly they can probably hear me at the barn.

"No need for wheels. This is a job we need to do on foot."

***

We're scanning the ground, looking for groundhog holes, or big rocks, or tree roots — "Anything that could trip up a horse going thirty kilometres an hour," Nate instructs me.

"I'm surprised you don't have a machine to do this," I say.

"In some ways, eventing has changed a lot, but there are also areas where the old basic ways of doing things are the best."

"Like paper score sheets."

Nate laughs. "Ah ... you're one of those. I can get behind the switch to the scoring app. What I don't like is all the money involved in the sport these days. Eventing used to be full of backyard horses and weekend warriors."

"I was amazed when I found out some of the horses competing on the weekend had come from halfway around the world," I say. "I didn't even know you could do that."

"It's a self-perpetuating thing — everybody wants to 'discover' a horse from far away, but they also want it to be proven at certain levels. The more people will pay for that, the more it becomes normalized." Nate picks up a rock and tosses it into the bushes. "This will make me sound old — probably just about as old as I am — but I got my first eventing horse thirty-two years ago from a trail riding place that was shut down by the humane society."

"Thirty-two years ago! Did you start eventing before you could walk?"

"You're a charmer!" He grins. "I'm fifty. I'm guessing you're the same age as my son."

At first I'm shocked. I wouldn't have said Nate looks fifty. Then again, I wouldn't have said he looks forty, either. He has the type of lean, wind-and-sun-tempered looks that make him attractive, but hard to pin an age on. "Charlotte told me you and Rose have kids at university, but I didn't know you had an adult son."

"Well, I'll admit I had him fairly young — too young for his mother and I to know how to make things work. Colin grew up with her in Toronto and we used to have almost nothing in common. Now he comes here as a break from the city."

It's my turn to bend over to pick up a rock. Somehow, it's easier to bring up the subject I've been worried about when I don't have to make eye contact. "Did Rose tell you I'm writing a story about Wren's disappearance?"

"She mentioned it." The downside of not making eye contact is I can't gauge his reaction.

Now that I've introduced the topic, I straighten, throw the rock into the woods, and look at Nate as I ask, "Do you think she could have left on her own? Or somehow gotten lost?"

He goes out of his way to pick up a rock that isn't in the path any horse would take to the next jump. For a minute, I wonder if he's going to answer. Then he does.

"No."

"OK. Why not?"

"Probably mostly for the same reasons you've already heard from Rose. She and I have similar opinions. There are the things Wren left behind — essentially, her whole life. There's the timing — why on earth would she go in the middle of a division at the horse trials? And there's the motivation — I don't think she had any."

"As to getting lost or having an accident, I don't buy either one. Not without somebody finding some trace of her." He stops walking and sighs. "There's something I haven't told anybody."

Here we go.

I'm hopeful, nervous, excited, and breathless, and the completely inappropriate words that pop into my head are, *Let me guess, you'd like to tell me, but then you'd have to kill me.*

For god's sake, Paige. I'm alone in the woods with one of my main suspects and I want to joke about him killing me? *Don't give him any ideas.*

I wait for him to tell me he was sleeping with Wren. That has to be it. I can't think of anything else.

"I looked for her with a drone."

"You ... I'm sorry?"

He rubs his forehead. "I'm not supposed to have the drone. I wanted one — a nice one with a quality camera. It was in the off-season when we have less cash coming in and we needed a new school horse. I went to a friend's sale barn to check out a bunch of horses he had and instead of buying the best horse, I bought the second-best one and I used the rest of the money to buy the drone which, I know was stupid, not least because I can never use it when Rose is around."

"OK." I'm still catching up to this admission that sounds so tame, and a little silly after what I was imagining.

"Anyway, I feel so guilty about the goddamn drone, I don't even enjoy having it. Then, when Wren went missing, I thought the least I could do was use it for something good, so I drove off the property, and hiked in along the Trans-National trail and flew it from there." He gives a short, sharp laugh. "Rose had brought some students out here to school on the course and later that night she complained she'd seen a drone and she wanted to figure out who to report it to because it violated their privacy and spooked one of the horses."

"I'm assuming you didn't see anything?"

"What? No. Nothing. Well, I mean, I saw plenty of things — the resolution is amazing — but nothing that would suggest anything about what happened to Wren."

"So, is that why you hesitated when I asked you? Because you didn't want to tell me about the drone? Or was there something else?"

"Did I hesitate?"

"You moved a rock that didn't need moving."

"Right. Yeah. That was about the other thing."

"What other thing?"

"The time I went to pick up takeout wings from The Mule and I saw Wren there."

The Mule again. I picture the restaurant / bar on the highway, with its false-fronted exterior and fake hitching posts.

With the image comes a flash of memory from the time I told Xander about — the time Leila took me there.

I remember a short skirt with fringes — despite me never liking skirts, it was one I'd always coveted and Leila knew it. "You can wear this skirt," she said. "Just keep your back straight and look cool, and nobody will ask you for ID."

"What if Mom's there?" I asked.

"Mom's with Wayne, in Wide River."

"Why do I have to go? Why can't I stay at home?"

"I've got us a ride and it will be fun."

"I'm hungry."

"You can have wings."

Wings. At The Crazy Mule. "They're good," I tell Nate.

"Rose thinks so. She was teaching a jumping clinic that ran late, so I went over to pick up our order. Wren was at the bar. There was this guy there playing pool, and he kept coming over between shots and putting his arm around Wren's shoulder, yanking her against him. In the few minutes I was there, he pounded down two shots, all while he was drinking a beer."

"Sounds like an over-indulgent drinker ..."

"Mmm-hmm, I wasn't impressed, but the real thing that bugged me was right before he went back to the pool table, he pushed his face against Wren's neck. She yelled, 'Ow!' and pushed him away. He was laughing and there were tooth marks on her neck."

I shudder, remembering a time back when I worked for Rowan that I had to push a drunk guy off me. "Ick ... what did you do?"

"I asked if she wanted a lift back with me. She said she wasn't ready to leave. So I said to call us if she needed a ride later. He gave me bad vibes — he didn't strike me as the kind of guy who would take no for an answer."

"Weren't you worried she'd bring him back with her?"

He answers with no hesitation this time. "No. Definitely not."

"Why not?"

"Because Wren didn't mix her personal life with her life here. She never brought anyone home. And she definitely wouldn't have brought him — when I left, he was outside having a cigarette. She wouldn't have let anyone who smoked anywhere near the barn."

Nineteen

Rose has Pen and Charlotte working their horses over a set of poles in the middle of the ring. They start out ragged and uneven, but soon they're flowing through with a steady rhythm that's almost hypnotic to watch.

I cant my head to one side, then the other, and there's no corresponding tug of pain running down my neck. I open my jaw wide, then close it again and find no tension hiding there.

Despite my looming story deadline and a barrage of new family emotions popping up every day, it's possible I've relaxed.

It might be the absence of the low-level background *everything* of the city. The sound of traffic, the smell of exhaust and hot asphalt, and the knowledge that people are around all the time — swarming the sidewalks, filling the parks, even downstairs in the pub when I'm upstairs sleeping.

Charlotte rides her horse by me, with his hoofs beating out a steady two-beat tattoo, and I nod in time.

Maybe when this is all over — when I've submitted the story — I can spend some time out here camping on Rowan's property, hiking, biking, and using his paddleboards. My mind drifts to a perfect day of outdoor activities — the kind that leaves you tired and satisfied — capped with an evening bonfire, and the person I want there with me is Dave.

The thought of Dave brings an extra activity to mind — zipping ourselves into a tent lit by the late-afternoon sun glowing through the canvas. Him helping me take my clothes off. Us giggling as we move together on our thin camping mattresses, trying to be quiet even though all I want is to scream with happiness and release.

Charlotte's horse sends a ringing whinny across the property and snaps me back to reality. That's my dream — there's no saying it's Dave's. And, anyway, I've let my daydreams skip ahead to a perfect post-story time without considering the need to explain my involvement in the story to Dave. How I came to be writing a story about a missing woman. How I never told him about the person missing from my own life.

I shake my head. I'm not here for relaxation — I'm here to write a story so I'd better keep my focus on that.

Rose calls the girls into the middle of the ring, which gives me the opportunity to check up on something I thought of while driving Charlotte and Pen out here today. This morning I did an x-ray search on Wren's name. What I didn't do was search under "VersMarais."

I do it now and, sure enough, I get a hit in the "Buy and Sell" thread. I suppose that's to be expected. Most people in this forum would have something to buy or sell at some point. I sigh. It's probably a dead end.

Still. *Don't assume. Keep looking.*

As soon as I do, my sigh turns to a gasp. Because not only is VersMarais' name (or, at least, username) there — so is Jeb Dixon's. In fact, she's recommending him.

> PonyMom: My daughter's outgrown her first horse and is hoping to find a show-ready horse she can compete on for the rest of the summer. We're new to the area and don't know where to look.

VersMarais: You couldn't do better than Jeb Dixon. If he doesn't have what you need, he'll find it for you. Your daughter could be showing by next weekend.

The cynic in me thinks, *If he doesn't have what you need, he'll steal it for you.*

UnicornSeeker: Just getting back into riding after twenty years. Need something sound, good-tempered, bombproof — bonus points for pretty.

VersMarais: Contact Jeb Dixon. The last time I was at his place he had exactly what you're describing. He won't sell a horse if it's not sound.

They're peppered throughout the thread, to the point where I read somebody else responding to a horse seeker, writing, "I saw somebody recommend Jeb Dixon — you might want to try him."

Another coincidence I'm sure isn't coincidental. Xander tells me there's something — or someone — rotten in the local horse community: Jeb Dixon. I track another person stirring trouble in equine circles — specifically commenting on Wren's case: VersMarais. Now it seems they know each other — or at least have some kind of connection.

What does it mean?

It means I have to keep looking — I need to let "curiosity be my compass."

It would be helpful if the compass needle would point me straight to the information I need.

A notification prompts me to check my messages. It's Maddy: I can give you today off, but tomorrow I need you to cover the unveiling of the new piano at City Hall.

She's also replied to the draft introduction to Wren's story I sent her this morning: I've never met her, but this made me cry. Paigey, this is the kind of work I knew you were capable of.

Now I'm the one who might cry.

Twenty

While they're still fresh in my mind I scribble a few things down on my makeshift back-of-score-sheet notebook. I should put these things in a binder. Or, at least, staple them together.

I start a new page to highlight that Nate said exactly the same thing as Rose about Wren not bringing partners home to her apartment — right down to her fear of fire. I chew on my pen. What does that mean?

My first inclination is to believe them — more precisely, to believe that's what they both believe. However, I'm trying to keep my mind open, so I jot down three options:

> *1) They're both right and some random person came into Wren's apartment and disposed of a condom.*
> *2) They're both wrong, but they both think they're right.*
> *3) They've colluded on a story and they're both lying as a cover-up.*

The last one leaves me wondering — a cover-up for what? That Nate really was having an affair with Wren, but neither of them want anyone to know?

I leave a row of question marks on the sheet as a sign to myself to come back later. I sigh. There are a lot of question marks on these sheets ...

Next, there's Nate's story about the unsavoury character he saw with Wren. When Nate was telling me, it took me so off-guard I didn't ask the most obvious question — has he ever heard of Jeb Dixon?

Because, again, going back to our old friend coincidence, what are the odds of there being two shady guys hanging around Oak Junction, both with some kind of tie to the horse world, or people in it?

I write another long line of question marks. Then I add two action items:

1) Ask Nate.
2) Go to the Mule.

I welcome the distraction from my note-taking as Addison walks one of her horses up to the sand ring gate.

I may have figured out how to identify a few horses during my jump judge volunteering, but I have no hope when it comes to telling Addison's two apart. They're both tall, long-legged, and a uniform deep brown all over. I know horses can have black or white markings — Addison's horses have neither.

Rose has added a small jump to either end of the poles and while Charlotte and Pen keep working over those, Addison rides in the background.

When Rose calls, "Great work! Let them walk," the two girls ride up and down along the fence, chit-chatting back and forth, occasionally ribbing one-another, always getting out of it with a laugh. A stranger could believe they're sisters. The thought gives me a sharp pang of missing Leila, then I think of my reconnection with Faye and the pain eases.

Addison moves into the area where the girls were riding — first making tight circles around and through the poles, then jumping her horse. Charlotte and Pen stop their horses to stand and watch. I move up to lean on the fence and get a better view.

When Addison takes a break, Charlotte calls over to her. "He looks amazing! Definitely ready for Vermont."

"I hope so," Addison says before turning back to the jump.

"Vermont?" I ask.

"Yup." Charlotte nods. "Since they've moved up to Intermediate, they have to travel farther to find competitions."

"Can you just take a horse across the border?" I ask.

"They have passports," Pen says.

"Really? What's on a horse passport?"

"The horse's colour," Pen says. "So, in Auckland's case, brown. Height — I think he's 16.3hh. Any distinctive marks — that could include hair whorls or markings on his face or legs. You can see that Auckland doesn't have any white markings, but I'm sure he has a whorl somewhere or other — I just don't know him well enough to say where."

Charlotte picks up. "Any unusual pigment in his hooves — again, Auckland doesn't have any. Also, any scars or standout features like a wall-eye, which Oreo has" — she strokes the neck of the horse she's on — "or a nick in the ear like the horse Pen's riding. That's where the slaughter ear tag was before Rose rescued her."

Addison gives her horse a pat and lets him walk with long reins and his head low. As she passes near us, Pen says, "Paige was just asking about horse passports — I guess you don't have much to mark in Auckland's."

"What do you mean?" Addison's voice is sharp.

"Just that he doesn't have many markings — come to think of it, neither does Paris."

"Ever heard of coincidence?" Addison snaps.

Coincidence. It's interesting how much it's coming up these days.

"Chill, Addison," Charlotte says. "Pen was just finding an excuse to talk to you so she could ask whether you got those new riding visors in at the tack shop."

"Right. Sorry." Addison gives a weak smile. "I'm just stressed about getting everything done before I have to leave for Vermont. Tell you what, Pen, come in anytime I'm working and I'll give you my staff discount."

I could learn a thing or two from my niece. The way she stuck up for Pen and put Addison in her place, then diffused the situation so they can all walk to the barn in harmony. I'm twice her age and I wouldn't have been able to manage that.

There's also the fact that Charlotte talks about things — about Leila and Wren — and about her feelings.

She's ahead of me on that, too.

Maybe I should get her to talk to Dave for me.

Twenty-One

"You're sure this is OK?" I'm standing with Rose, watching Nate hand paint brushes to Charlotte and Pen, then point from a series of buckets to a line of poles which are propped along the bottom fence rail. "Having them here the rest of the day?"

Rose laughs. "Why would I say no to free labour? I should ask if you're sure it's OK with your sister. They're going to come home covered in paint."

"She said it was fine. She also said she keeps an old bedsheet in the trunk so she can spread it over the back seat for occasions just like this."

"Your sister is a smart woman." She pauses, then says, "Nate says you two had a good talk yesterday." I can't deduce anything from her tone. It seems neutral to me.

"Yes. He told me about the guy he saw Wren with at The Mule. Do you know anything about him?"

She shakes her head. "No idea. Yesterday was the first I heard about it. That night I was still teaching when Nate got home. He left the food in the kitchen, then headed out to work on the tractor engine. Since he didn't tell me then, the encounter got lost to the sands of time."

I file her explanation under "maybe" in my head. I know a lot of people would have trouble believing it. However, I live under the same roof with Dave, but because of the different hours we work, sometimes something big happens to him, or me, and we can't tell each other right away, and eventually it just doesn't seem worth mentioning.

Or, in the case of me not telling him about Leila or my current story, it seems harder and harder to bring it up.

"Have you ever heard of a guy named Jeb Dixon?"

I believe her swift and decisive, "No."

Before she can ask who he is, and why I'm asking, I continue, "How do you identify horses? For example, how do you know Shine is Shine?"

"How do *I* know, or how do you identify a horse in general?"

"In general. The girls were telling me about passports, but they seem a little … I don't know … maybe I just don't understand, but it seems weird that you identify a horse by writing down things about the colour of their coat and the way their hair grows."

"I know what you mean. The descriptive aspect of a passport is as thorough as they can make it, but still, what's written on paper doesn't always translate well visually. I can see a horse and know it's them — like Shine — because I work with them every day, but I might not easily recognize them from their passport. I guess that's where tattoos come in."

"Tattoos?"

"Sure, tattoos and even brands, it's mostly Western horses that have brands. Racing horses — like Thoroughbreds, Standardbreds, and Quarter horses — are tattooed inside their lips. There's a system for assigning tattoo IDs and they're registered with the breed associations."

"I had no idea."

"They're not perfect, of course. They can fade over time, and not all breeds are tattooed. Also, not surprisingly, people have found ways to alter tattoos more and less successfully. And I guess *that's* where microchips come in."

"Of course," I say. "Microchips."

"So, you know about them?"

"No!" I laugh. "I don't know anything. I thought you knew that by now."

"Well, if you think about it, we microchip dogs and cats, so why not horses?"

"Makes sense."

"The technology is newer, and horse breed and sport associations are nothing if not traditional, so it's still not widely required, but it's coming."

With the girls enthusiastically slapping bright-coloured paint on poles in more-or-less even blocks, Nate wanders over.

"I'm just explaining microchipping to Paige."

He grins, lifts Rose's hair off her shoulder, and kisses it. "I'd microchip you if I could, so I'd never lose you."

On the surface, it's a goofy comment, but there's love in both their eyes and it sets off a pang deep in me. *I want somebody to want to microchip me.* Or, at least, something similarly romantic.

It also puts one more brick on my wall of believing that Nate wasn't having an affair.

Beliefs and gut feelings aren't fact or evidence ... but they're also not nothing.

"Hey," Rose says, "Paige asked me if I'd heard of some guy ... what's his name?"

"Jeb Dixon," I say.

Nate shakes his head. "Nope. But I don't get out much."

I leave the girls happily (if messily) painting and crawl along the driveway contemplating my Jeb Dixon questions. Neither Rose nor Nate know him — what does that mean? And is it even true?

I'm still mulling those questions over when I reach the end of the driveway and encounter a car turning in.

I stop and back up a few feet to give them more space to get by, then lift my hand in a wave to the driver and see it's Kimberly.

Oh, wow. Here's my chance. Better seize it.

I roll down my window. "Hi! How are you?"

She lowers hers as well. "Good to see you again! Did Rose charm you in? Are you going to start riding?"

"Well, she took me out on a trail ride yesterday, but today I was dropping Charlotte and Pen off. They're helping Nate paint."

"Right. I'd better get up there, then. My neighbour had lots of half-used tins of paint in their garage and I told Nate I'd drop them off."

"Um, before you go, I was thinking about what you told me — that Rose started the therapeutic riding program for your daughter and children like her. It's a great story. I'd like to write about it. I wonder if you'd be willing to let me interview you?" It's not untrue — I *would* like to write about it. I bet Maddy would even like me to write about it. And it keeps Kimberly from getting her guard up about Wren.

"How flexible are you? Avery's going to a birthday party later this afternoon at the old girl guide camp — they hold events there now. I'll take her there, then stay on the property, just in case she needs me. If you can meet me there, I could talk then."

"Yes. That would be perfect. What time?"

"The party starts at 4:00, so if you meet me at 4:15, the kids should be occupied."

"I'll see you then!"

***

With time to kill before my meeting with Kimberly, I head toward the old girl guide camp by way of my brother Rowan's place.

First, I hit the turnoff to the Ultimate fields, clearly marked with a big arrow declaring **Oak Junction Ultimate** above a stern warning **No parking on the road — you will be towed!**

Streams of city-dwellers turn off here every weekend for tournaments, but I keep driving for another couple of hundred metres until I reach the narrow driveway that serves both the tiny cabin I used to live in when I worked for my brother, and Rowan and Sophie's comparatively large two-bedroom house.

There's a bright new **Sold** sticker on the faded **For Sale** sign in front of the cabin.

What the ...?

The cabin has been for sale for so long it's a running joke. People use it as a signpost: "If you get to the 'for sale' sign, you've missed the turn. You need to go back and head toward the river."

I never believed it would sell. I wasn't sure Rowan would ever find somebody he and Sophie would like enough to accept as a neighbour — who would also have to be someone willing to put up with having one or two windows broken every season by stray discs.

There's also the fact that Rowan built the cabin off-grid before off-grid was trendy, and before the technology was as advanced as it is today. There's mostly enough warm water, and light, and heat ... but not always. The kitchen grey water needs to be dumped regularly down a pit behind the house. There is a bath ... outdoors, on the porch. In the winter it's a fingers-crossed-for-warm-water shower in a cubicle the size of an upright coffin.

I tell people I left to go to journalism school, but having electricity on demand was also a big pull.

I get out of the car, as though the **Sold** sticker is some kind of optical illusion that will shimmer and return to **For Sale** if I get closer.

Nope. Still sold.

As I'm staring at it, I hear a familiar whir that reels me right back to the weekend. To Nate navigating near-noiselessly around the cross-country course. Only this time it's my brother, Rowan, and he's coming from the Ultimate fields.

"Oh my goodness! If it isn't my favourite little sister."

I know the comment's meant to be lighthearted, and a lot of people would think I'm his only little sister, but I'm not. Because of Leila, it hits me wrong. I also know I'm hyper-sensitive right now, so I smile and step forward. "It's my favourite hippy brother." Then I open my arms for a hug, because Xander has taught me it's worth doing.

Rowan hugs me back, saying, "Who are you calling a hippy?" He's all lean muscle, and smells of the outdoors, and patchouli, with maybe a hint of cannabis. It's true he's one of the smartest small — or even not-so-small —

business owners I know, but his outward appearance, complete with undercut man-bun and t-shirt that reads This is how I roll with an image of a rainbow Ultimate disc, definitely gives him a laid-back vibe.

"You have a golf cart and the cabin's sold. Next thing I know, Macy will give up her dogs and start breeding cats."

"The cart's electric. I charge it off the solar panels I installed at the south end of the pitches. And I bought it used, from that horse farm where Charlotte rides. The guy was upgrading."

"Really?" I squint at it. One golf cart looks very much like another one to me, but I'm sure Nate could explain why his new one is superior.

"Mmm ... and that's also how I sold this place."

"Right — we need to talk about that — what do you mean that's how you sold it?"

"I met a woman who works there. She was asking me about the Ultimate club. Said she played a bit in high school. We got talking and she told me she likes it in Oak Junction. It has everything she needs. She'd like to buy her own place, but it's hard to find small, affordable places these days." He turns to look at the small cabin snugged under towering evergreens. "I invited her to come meet Sophie. Both Soph and I agreed she has the right energy. And she has a down payment, so ..." He shrugs, as though it hasn't been over a decade that he's been waiting to find someone with the "right energy."

I love the juxtaposition of good energy and a solid down payment. It's very Rowan. It sounds like a match made in heaven. And, if my concerns are right, I'm about to give my brother some very bad news.

"Is it Wren Sheedy?"

His brow furrows. "Do you know her? Is that why you came by today?"

"Row, I'm really sorry to tell you this, but Wren is missing."

"What do you mean, 'missing?'"

"I was at Oak Copse on the weekend, volunteering for a competition Charlotte was riding in. Wren was there, too, and partway through the day she just disappeared. Nobody's seen her since."

"But ... I haven't heard anything." I can see he doesn't want to believe me. I don't blame him. "I mean, shouldn't something like that be in the news?"

"I'm afraid it's true. And, in a way, that's why I'm here. I'm putting together a story about it. I didn't know you knew Wren — I'm on my way to interview someone who knew her and I had a few minutes, so I thought I'd stop in here."

He pushes back a strand of his hair that's fallen loose. "She gave me a deposit. She was excited. She was talking about paint colours ... she wouldn't just *leave*."

"I agree. Even though not everybody does. But I have a different perspective." I take a deep breath and do the thing I've so far done with Faye and Xander: I mention Leila's name. "*We* have a different perspective. Because of Leila."

Every time I say her name to one of my siblings, it feels like a big risk. Like an earthquake moment. It robs my breath and makes my heart beat faster. But every time so far, there's been an element of relief. Like they've been waiting for me to say something.

Rowan nods. "Definitely. You, in particular. And I'm sorry for what I said when I first saw you — about you being my favourite little sister. It probably makes it sound like I've forgotten Leila. It came out wrong. I made a mistake." He looks up toward the sky, then around the tree-ringed clearing. "I think about her more and more as I get older."

I step forward and touch his arm. "I've been thinking about her a lot lately, too."

"What can I do?" he asks. "To help with Wren, I mean."

"There's a Facebook group you could join. There have been rumours going around that she skipped town. If you told people she was buying this place — maybe even tell the police — that might help them believe they need to look for her."

"I could get the word out through the Ultimate community. Ask them to keep an eye out. Maybe we could help with a search?"

My heart swells. I haven't given my siblings enough credit. "It's a good idea, Row. You have Nate and Rose's contact info from buying the golf cart — I'd talk to them about it."

"Can you stick around for a while?" Rowan asks. "Stay for dinner?"

Flashing back to the last meal Rowan and Sophie cooked for me — a wild turkey Rowan salvaged for meat after one of the Ultimate players hit it on the road in front of the pitches, served on a bed of dandelion greens — makes me long to get back to the city for some of Dave's food. Having said that, if it wasn't for the interview with Kimberly, I'd probably stay.

"I wish, but I can't. I have to do that interview I told you about."

"Is that where you're heading now?"

"Yep. It's at the old girl guide camp. But there is another place I need to check out that I think is out that way. Do you know where Ed Cormier's place is?"

Rowan's shaking his head before I even finish saying Ed's name. "Nuh-uh. Cormier's super bad news. Why would you even think of going there?"

"It's not to see him. It's to check out a horse business working out of his place. Wren might have known them. Xander told me Cormier's in jail."

"No way did Xander tell you to go to Ed Cormier's place."

"He didn't tell me to go. He just told me the guy was someone he was keeping an eye on. But am I right? Is it out that way?"

"Since Xander's watching the guy, I don't think you need to know where it is."

"So you're really not going to tell me?"

"You're still my little sister, and I still want to look after you."

"Message received." I step forward for another hug. "I'd better be getting on to that interview — say hi to Soph for me!"

"Come by for dinner soon and say hi to her yourself."

I drive away thinking I'll come back for dinner, but I'll offer to bring the main dish. I also think I might have told Rowan I received his message, but I never told him I wouldn't go to Ed Cormier's.

Twenty-Two

THE OPEN SPACE OF the camp's parking lot is bright with strong afternoon sun, but as soon as I cross it, and step through the looped-back gate, memories press in along with the shade.

They're everywhere. In the lingering smell of campfire. On the big wooden sign with its layers and layers of age-oranged varnish slathered over the letters spelling out **Welcome to Camp Piney**. Underfoot, cushioned by the thick carpet of pine needles, piled so deep some of them were probably on the ground when Leila and I came here.

Because, yes, we did. It was a camp where everyone was supposed to be equal. Nobody would be turned away because they couldn't afford it. In practice, what that meant, though, was that the kids who could afford it went to posh camps nestled between multi-million-dollar family compounds in Ontario's cottage country.

Which left us a as part of a motley crew of kids with permanently runny noses, or hair knotted through with twigs, or raw-scratched mosquito bites, sleeping in heavy canvas tents with no floors, so puddles formed under our cots when it rained.

I hated it. The first day, I waited for my mom to show up and take us home. After a sleepless night listening to other kids toss, turn, and snore in the tent I wasn't even allowed to share with Leila, I cried until I threw up.

On the second day, after craft (the ugliest drip candles you've ever seen) when I discovered afternoon snack was warm apple juice and unsalted crackers, I found my sister and told her I was going home.

I stood with my hands on my hips and my bottom lip pushed out, waiting for her to tell me: *No way. Nuh-uh. You can't.* Instead, she said, "Change your socks and fill up your water bottle. I'll get us a bunch of crackers. It's a long walk."

My big sister. My hero.

Leila was right — it was a long way. We walked and walked and walked. Despite the fresh socks, I got a blister. On each heel. They burst, and they rubbed, and they stung, but it was still better than staying at Camp Piney.

We were walking by the school — a distance I know now is seven kilometres from the camp gates — when the caretaker, out on his ride-on mower keeping the weeds in check, spotted us.

He gave us freezies in the cool of his basement office until Faye showed up to take us to her place, which, at the time, was an apartment over the general store down by the beach.

Sitting at her two-person café table, sharing a box of Kraft Dinner, she warned us, "You can never, ever do anything like that again — do you understand? It's very dangerous."

"I took care of Paige," Leila said. "I made us walk on the side of the road facing the cars. And we moved over whenever a car came."

"That's not the kind of dangerous I'm talking about," Faye said.

Then, I didn't know what she meant. I wish I still didn't.

"Paige?"

I squint ahead. The sun is slightly behind the figure who just called my name, but logic tells me it's Kimberly. I lift my hand.

She waves. "There's a picnic table over here. I brought cupcakes for the party — there are extras, if you'd like one."

***

As Kimberly talks about the story she thinks I'm interested in, it all but writes itself. The way her daughter's life has changed thanks to horses. The friends she's met through the therapeutic riding group. The generosity of Rose and Nate in stepping up to support these families in the community.

I nod, check the recording app on my phone, and occasionally jot a time-stamp with a star or an exclamation point next to it. Maybe I'll find a way to pitch this story to Maddy.

I wouldn't even need to take photos — Kimberly tells me she has hundreds, any of which she could share. She props her phone up on the rough top of the picnic table and scrolls through her camera roll. Kids grinning on the backs of quiet-looking horses. Side-walkers, as I've learned they're called, walking alongside the small riders.

One photo makes me lean in more closely. I don't need a passport to identify Shine's bright gold coat. And the pink-streaked hair of his handler leaves no doubt.

Kimberly sighs. "Avery was so excited when Wren said they could use Shine in the program. She said riding him made her feel like a magical princess."

"I can see why. He's gorgeous."

Kimberly nods. "He's Wren's pride and joy. She has him trained so well I never worried once about Avery riding him."

I shift my gaze from the photo to meet Kimberly's eyes. "Rose said Wren would never have left him."

"Rose is right. But it's not just because of Shine. Wren wouldn't have left, period. She takes her students and her job seriously. She ..." Kimberly wrinkles her nose. "I'm not sure if I should say this."

I wonder if she's about to spill the beans about her husband and Wren. It's funny how even though this whole meeting with Kimberly is on false pretences, now that I have the chance to push her for information, I'm reluctant.

I've decided to use the same the line I did with Rose — "I'm happy to hear anything you have to say," — when Kimberly says, "I don't see how it can do any harm. Wren had no intention of leaving — she was buying a house here."

"You knew about that?" I ask.

"*You* knew about that?"

"It's my brother's house. Well, cabin. But how did you know?"

"I'm a real estate agent. I got licensed back when I lived in Alberta, got a different job for a while, but then when we moved here ten years ago and had Avery, going back to real estate gave me the flexibility I needed. Anyway, the purchase from your brother was a private sale, but Wren asked for my advice and I was more than happy to help."

I tilt my head back and take in the swaying treetops that surround us, the deep blue of the sky, and one scudding white cloud. I'm stalling while I gather my courage. "Now it's my turn to say something I'm not sure if I should."

"You want to ask about Ryan."

I nod. "Your husband."

"Former husband, please. I don't have divorce papers, but I don't want to call him my husband."

"Fair enough. I heard there was some tension between Ryan and Wren."

Kimberly laughs. "That's diplomatic, and I'm sure whoever told you that didn't say 'tension.' The truth is, he made a fool of himself over her. There was a time when I would have said he made a fool of me, as well, but I'm past that now. I live my life and do my best. I can't own what he does."

"When you say 'what he does ...'"

"Ryan has a long history of issues. It's hard to say which of those make him drink more than he should, and which are caused by him drinking too much, but one thing that's always been consistent is he feels misunderstood, and he latches onto people he thinks understand him." She pauses. "Even better if those people are attractive young women."

"And Wren was one of them?"

"Unfortunately for her. He met her at Oak Copse. I was working late one day, so he had to take Avery to her lesson. Wren got the kids warmed up while

Rose was finishing an online workshop. I knew something was up the minute Ryan came home. He was giddy. He insisted on barbecuing for us for dinner. It was the classic high he'd get on when he thought things were going his way."

"But they didn't?"

"They were never going to. Despite the stories the rumour mill circulated about Wren and her previous job, there are two good reasons she wouldn't sleep with Ryan."

"Which are?"

"One, she respected Rose and wouldn't let her personal life leak into Rose's business."

I fold the empty cupcake wrapper in half, then in half again. This wrapper makes me think of the condom wrapper. "Rose told me she was sure Wren had a sex life, but she didn't bring partners back to the apartment."

"I'm sure Rose is right. Wren was always aware that while they respected her privacy, the apartment was part of Rose and Nate's home. I think that was part of the reason she wanted to buy your brother's cabin. So she'd have a home that was truly hers, where she could do whatever she wanted."

"Hmm ..." I'm not about to tell Kimberly why I think she's wrong. Also, I think it's interesting that now Rose, Nate, and Kimberly have told me Wren wouldn't have brought a sexual partner back to her apartment.

Also, at the moment I'm more interested that, far from hating the woman her husband was pursuing, Kimberly seems to like and respect her. "So, nothing ever happened between Wren and Ryan?"

"She was nice to him. Kind. She had a way about her — I think it was the part of her that was good with animals. Kids also loved her, and I think that probably extended to damaged people like Ryan. But being nice to Ryan doesn't work out well for most people."

"As in?"

"He showed up at Oak Copse a few times on really thin excuses. Asking if Avery had left her gloves there. Asking if Wren could give him advice on a gift to buy Avery for her birthday. Rose told me, and I told him he couldn't go out there whenever he felt like it."

"By then he'd found out Wren often went to The Crazy Mule for Open Mic night on Thursday. He'd tell me he was going to AA and he'd go there instead."

Before I can ask, Kimberly says, "The reason I know is that they called me to come get him. He'd offered to drive Wren home and she told the bartender he shouldn't be driving, so they took away his keys and called me."

"I heard he looked for her in the café as well."

Kimberly shakes her head. "He looked for her everywhere. At first, when she was still humouring him, he was drinking more, but he was really up. Happy. High on life. Then, when she started avoiding him and told him to leave her alone, he started in on the angry drinking — coming home in the wee hours — he'd have injuries from picking fights with someone at a bar, or just from falling down. That's when I changed the locks."

"You did?" I think of everything this woman's been through — raising a child with a serious health condition, being married to a man publicly known as a non-functioning alcoholic and a woman-chaser — "You're a badass!"

Kimberly smiles. "Thanks, but it was Avery who gave me the strength to do it. I couldn't have her exposed to that."

I'm flooded with different memories now — yelling voices, tension in my gut, a much smaller version of myself lying in bed with my pillow over my head, just wanting a quiet house. "Avery's lucky to have a strong mom like you."

"She amazes me every day." Kimberly sighs. "There are days when I wish she had a different dad, but no matter what I think of Ryan's drinking, or his behaviour, I know he had nothing to do with Wren's disappearance."

"OK …" I'm ready to hear that it's not the kind of thing he'd do, or he might be a nasty drunk, but he'd never hurt anyone — aren't those the things people always say? I prepare myself to nod and show I've listened while not believing it for a second.

"That was the day we moved him into his apartment."

"Oh." It's more specific than I expected, but in my experience, moving days are pretty chaotic. By definition, people are moving from place to place and it's hard to say exactly where they were at any point in time.

"I was with him from noon until 8:00. I had to pick up the U-Haul and drive it because he had a cast on his right foot — a falling-down-drunk accident."

"Right ... that *is* a pretty darn good alibi."

"Yup. And it feels somewhat ironic that I'm the one to give it to him. Part of me feels like it would do him good to be dragged into the police station for questioning — might scare him off the booze for a while." She shrugs. "Of course, that would require the police to be doing any questioning at all ... sorry. Someone told me your other brother's a police officer. I shouldn't be saying this."

"Don't be sorry. He's already heard the same complaint from me."

"Speaking of which ..." Kimberly looks at her phone screen. "They'll be serving the kids pizza and cake under the gazebo in a few minutes. I should head over there."

"Absolutely," I say. "I just have one question. You said there were two reasons Wren would never have gotten involved with Ryan, but you only mentioned one."

Kimberly lifts her eyebrows. "I would have thought it was obvious — she's young, fun, and gorgeous and he's an aging, overweight, drunk."

"Oh, of course." I reach for my phone. Slot it into my bag.

"Wait, Paige. While that's true, I'm mostly joking. The main reason is that Wren doesn't break rules. Earlier, I said she wouldn't have an affair with Ryan because it could hurt Rose's business, but it's more than that. Wren knew he was married, so she wouldn't have slept with him. She has a strong view of right and wrong, and she isn't one to fall for excuses like 'my wife doesn't understand me.' It's one reason I've been glad Avery can learn from her. Wren tells the kids, you always try your hardest, your horse always comes first — she doesn't let them cut corners, literally or figuratively."

Kimberly slides another cupcake across the table, winks, and says, "It was nice chatting. Let me know if you have any questions."

I look at the treat, then at my laptop, and think, *Why not?*

I type steadily for half-an-hour. Using my notes and the recording as prompts. Making an outline from the therapeutic riding information Kimberly gave me while it's still fresh in my mind.

I dash off a quick email to Maddy — Just interviewed a woman about this attached outline. I have lots of quotes and there are tonnes of photos available. Any interest?

Then, I open an email to myself and type DON'T CUT CORNERS. It feels like a good reminder to me, and a good reminder of what Wren was like.

As I'm closing out of various tabs to prepare to fold my laptop into my bag, I come across the forum page, still open, now with a new post at the top.

> VersMarais: Hey, for anyone who's been around for a while, have you ever heard of Leila Turner?

My heart feels like it's beating right under my skin — like I could see it if I glanced down. *What the actual ...?*

There's only been one answer so far:

> AlwaysEventing: Why? Who's Leila Turner?

> VersMarais: A girl who went missing fifteen years ago. I heard she also used to ride at Oak Copse. I heard some other things about her, too. I wonder if anyone's asked Rose Newcomb about having two girls disappear from her place? I wonder if anyone's talked to Leila Turner's family to find out if any of them are still around Oak Copse? Just trying to do the responsible thing and get all the facts out in the open.

Twenty-Three

MY FINGERS GRIP THE steering wheel with white-knuckle strength. My jaw is clenched so hard it hurts when I open my mouth. I haven't taken a proper deep breath since pulling out of the camp parking lot.

That's my sister they're writing about. My sister, who never deserved what happened to her and never hurt VersMarais, whoever she is.

Whoever she is, she has no right to be even typing the letters that spell Leila's name.

I flex my fingers, open and close my mouth, breathe.

OK. That's better. I'm still angry, but at least now I can think.

How would anyone on the forum even know about Leila? She disappeared half a generation ago. The only coverage was in the OJJ, and the only copy of their old story is on microfilm. You have to know what you're looking for to find something on microfilm.

I think back to Faye's reasoning, "I think we're talking about an adult, but not an elderly one" — this new post backs that up. It seems like someone would need to be at least my age to remember when Leila went missing.

And they'd have to be from Oak Junction. Not only because there was no coverage of Leila's disappearance outside the OJJ, but also — that thing about her riding at Oak Copse. *I* didn't even know that until Rose told me.

What does this mean for the people I've been questioning? Rose obviously knows all the information in this latest post, but I still believe her alibi stands.

If Rose remembers Leila, it means Nate could, too. And Nate's more complicated — even if I don't think he did it, he can never really have an alibi. It's a reminder that I need to follow up on his Crazy Mule story — *Don't cut corners*.

Kimberly only came to Oak Junction ten years ago, and she has an alibi for Wren's disappearance ... it seems to rule her out.

Maybe the post is more reason to suspect Jeb Dixon? After all, he's living on Ed Cormier's land, and the Cormiers go way back. I remember things about their family, so maybe they remember things about my family, and maybe they've told Jeb? It's possible.

I sigh. That seems to be the theme of Wren's disappearance — so many things are possible, even if very few seem probable.

There's this thought that's been swirling around my brain as I run through the possible culprits. Rose, Nate, Kimberly, Jeb Dixon ... the fact is, there's one very strong candidate I haven't learned anything about. Someone who, at the very least, has a lot of opinions about Wren's disappearance and is spreading them around.

VersMarais.

If she's going to find out stuff about my sister, I need to find out about her.

***

The Oak Junction library seems like a good place to start. Especially since I'm almost there.

It's a tiny branch, and if somebody's been viewing microfilm there, the librarian's bound to remember. For that matter, the post just went up. Maybe the person would still be at the library.

My stomach flutters with butterflies and I stare down the road, watching every car that passes in case it contains the mysterious microfilm reader.

I pull into the parking lot across from the café, run up the stairs two at a time, and pull on the door to find it locked.

Which is when I read the sign on the door. The library is open Tuesday and Thursday afternoons, and a few hours on Saturday.

It hasn't been open today or yesterday.

So much for my brilliant theory.

I stand on the porch of the small building and look across at the café, which has a fair number of cars in the parking lot — early diners or takeout customers. The businesses in the strip are quiet during this hour when most people are getting their dinner.

I sweep my gaze across to the Oak Junction Journal building, and something catches my eye.

Whoa. That's the other way to view old copies of the OJJ — in old papers in the actual office.

I leave my car in the library parking lot and cross the road, then walk along the edge of the trees bordering the OJJ property line. The back door is ajar.

I stand beside a big evergreen and try to summon the anger I felt just a few minutes ago. Try to rekindle the determination to unmask whoever is dragging my sister's name into the forum. Realistically, my quickened heart rate and shortened breath are from nerves but, whatever, it'll have to do.

I dash across the weedy lawn as quickly and quietly as possible and slip inside the open door.

I'm standing in a linoleum-floored room with big windows that can be lifted to the ceiling and secured with hooks, leaving expanses of screen. There's a cast-iron woodstove on one wall, and a makeshift work area with a sink and shelves covered in contact paper on another.

The summer kitchen. Used to keep cooking heat out of the main house during the summer.

In its current neglected state, with the windows shut, it's stuffy and makes me think maybe the back door was ajar just because nobody cares about this place. And maybe the movement I saw was just a reflection in a window.

Maybe I've engaged in a spot of illegal entry for no good reason at all.

A bang comes from inside the house and my heart rate ratchets again.

Or maybe not.

It's one step up to the main kitchen, which looks like it was decorated back in the era when the summer kitchen would have been in full use. There's nobody there, and I cross it quickly, stepping on a floorboard so loose it squeals.

Shit.

I freeze. Wait until my breathing settles so it's not the only thing I can hear. Then I advance again, moving toward the half-open door which must lead into the main room that holds all the desks I saw when I peered in from the front porch.

I reach out for the door only to have it slam on my hand, hard and fast, with an extra oomph at the end that tells me somebody has leaned into the effort.

"Ow! Goddamn!" Even as I'm saying it, I'm yanking the door open and running after the footsteps I can hear pounding through the old house and up the stairs.

I dodge desks in the main room and take the stairs two-at-a-time, trying not to think about how old they are, and trying not to wonder how well they have — or haven't — been maintained.

When I get upstairs, there's nothing. No person. No sound. Emptiness.

Until I hear a gentle *bump-bang*. It guides me to the room at the back of the house where an ancient roller blind is being buffeted by the breeze from an open window.

I lean out to see a fire escape landing, a set of rusting stairs, and bushes swaying by the border of the woods I walked along earlier.

There's no sign of the person who ran into the trees, and with the pain in my hand I'm not sure I could hoist myself out of the window — much less catch somebody with such a long head start.

I do, and don't want to look at my hand. It's one of those things where it feels like looking at it will make whatever injury I've sustained real.

Instead, I pull the window closed and head back downstairs to what was once two rooms, knocked together to hold five desks.

When I looked through the window the other day, there were stacks of newspapers everywhere. Now, at one of the desks, there are copies spread around. I pick them up to find — no surprise — they're from October fifteen years ago and they contain that sparse, misleading story about Leila.

At the same time as I hate that story, it seems like a thread connecting me to my sister. I felt that way when I saw it on microfilm, but seeing it here, printed on paper right around the last time I ever saw my sister, tightens a vise in my chest.

Between that and the throbbing in my hand, I have to press my good hand hard against my chest to keep from crying.

I pick up one of the papers and backtrack through the dated kitchen, then through the summer kitchen, yanking hard on the back door to make sure it's closed behind me.

The parking lot at the café is nearly full as I cross back to my car. I think of going in to tell Marge somebody broke into the OJJ building.

I think of calling Xander to tell him.

Then I think of getting home to the security of my apartment, and the familiarity offered by Dave, and I go straight to the car.

Fortunately, I'm left-handed and the intruder caught my right hand in the door. Unfortunately, my car's a stick shift. I keep gear changes to a minimum and when I have to do them I use the heel of my hand.

Still, by the time I reach the merge ramp onto the highway, my hand is throbbing and radiating heat. How am I ever going to type like this?

Maybe it's a sign. Maybe I should give up the project. Maybe I should just go back to my old, normal life, and be a slightly better writer than I was before.

One thing I know for sure is that I shouldn't get on a divided highway with one functioning hand, and the other one in so much pain I can hardly think.

I'm not in any shape to make a decision about my entire future, but I am making a call about my next destination. I drive past the ramp and continue on the much quieter scenic route into the city.

***

"Hi?" *Not loud enough, Paige. Nobody's going to hear that.* I push the front door open, knock my uninjured hand against it, and try again. "Hey, Maddy? Hi!"

"Paige?" Maddy comes into the front hall, drying her hands on a tea towel. "What are you doing here? What happened to your hand? Oh my gosh, Jay! Come here!"

They fuss over me, which feels quite good. They sit me down at the table they just cleared. Jay — who's a medical resident — puts a bag of frozen peas on my hand, and Maddy boils the kettle and pours tea for all of us.

As my hand numbs, and the tea eases a thirst I didn't know I had, I explain. "... then I looked out the window and they were already in the bushes."

Maddy sets her mug on the table. "You weren't supposed to catch a kidnapper, or a killer, or whatever this person is — you were just supposed to write a story."

"To be fair ..." I start.

Maddy turns to Jay. "Now she's being fair to a criminal."

He puts his hand over hers. "Let her finish."

"To be fair," I repeat, "The person didn't come after me — I was the one who went into the OJJ office."

"Because they wrote about your sister!" Maddy says. "That's directed at you."

"What do you think, Jay?"

"Why are you asking him? He doesn't know anything about it."

"That's exactly why I'm asking him — he doesn't have preconceived notions."

"Why don't you let me read the actual post?" Jay asks.

"See? So sensible. I have a better idea — why don't you read all the threads?" I pull my laptop out of my bag, show him the different tabs I have open, and hand the machine to Jay.

Meanwhile, Maddy turns to me. "So, you don't have any idea who it was? You didn't see them at all?"

I shake my head. "I didn't see them, but they were quick. Also, light on their feet. I could hear them moving through the house, but they didn't clomp, if you know what I mean, and there was nothing distinguishing about how they moved."

"What do you mean?"

"Well, Rose has a slight limp. It couldn't have been her."

"Not Rose — which you already thought — still, I guess that's helpful. Could it have been a man?"

The peas have warmed slightly, so I turn them over while I think about it. "If he was athletic, and wearing running shoes, I think so."

"So, Nate?"

"On my way there I was already thinking I need to look more into the story he told me — I guess now I can also find out if he has an alibi for this afternoon."

"Good point — if it wasn't him, maybe you can rule him out. What about Kimberly?"

"I was at the camp with her when I read the post about Leila."

"Right with her?"

I wrinkle my nose. "Very close. She had just gone farther into the camp property to serve birthday cupcakes. And, when I left, her car was still in the parking lot, so even if she abandoned her kid at the birthday party, there's no way she could have gotten to the OJJ building ahead of me."

"And that bad guy of Xander's?"

I shrug. "I don't know anything about him. I guess that's next on my list."

"That's my point, Paige. It really isn't. This story is meant to be a lifestyle piece — to tie your experience losing someone with Wren's disappearance. Not an expose of what happened to Wren. The deadline's coming up and given what happened today" — she points at my pea-covered hand — "it's time for you to get writing it so you stop having to go to Oak Junction and you're in less danger."

For the second time in just a short while, I think about going back to my normal life. Not heading out to Oak Junction all the time. Maybe it's because I'm safe now, and not hungry, and my hand hurts less, but this time, the thought saddens me.

"Paige? Are you listening? Can you get stuck into writing the story based on the information you already have?"

"Kimberly told me something today," I say. "She said Wren always tells her students not to cut corners and not to take anything for granted. I think I can write a story about that — encompassing Wren and Leila — not taking your loved ones for granted, because look how fast they can be gone, but also how people took a lot of things for granted around both disappearances which led to them not being looked for properly. Maybe we'd know more about them if less things were taken for granted."

"I like it," Maddy says. "It's a solid framework. Maybe you should just take a quiet day and work on it tomorrow."

"Does that mean I don't have to go to the mayor's breakfast?"

Maddy arches her eyebrows. "Can you still hold a recorder?"

"Can I?" I turn to Jay, who's closed the lid of my laptop.

"Don't get me in the middle of this," he says. "How about I tell you what I think about those posts?"

"Yes, please!"

"This 'VersMarais' — whoever she is — is stirring things up. She drops distracting nuggets that misdirect people. So, somebody says maybe something bad happened to Wren, and she says, 'Maybe it was her own choice.' They say maybe we should search for her, and she says, 'She probably left on her own so there's no point.' She doesn't have to provide proof, or be definite, she just keeps people off-balance. So, in that way, it does seem like using your sister's name was directed at you, in that you showed up and started asking questions and suddenly she's asking, 'Hey, has anyone heard about this girl?' who happens to be your sister. Whether she means to distract you, or distract all of them — I'm not sure and I don't think it matters. I think she just wants chaos to continue, so nobody thinks logically and actually looks for Wren. But one obvious question is, who knows you're writing this story?"

I shake my head. "Not that many people — a handful at Oak Copse, my siblings, a couple of other members of the community — but the way gossip spreads around OJ, anybody could. I mean, just in the past couple of days, I've learned things about people I hardly know and didn't ask about, like Marge who runs the café wishes she could semi-retire, and Addison — a girl who rides with Charlotte — got her mother to mortgage her house to finance her riding. The information just kind of floats around out there."

"It doesn't matter anyway," Maddy says. "Because we've discussed the angle Paige is going to take on the story and she has enough to write it, so she doesn't need to poke around and ask any more questions, but she does need to get up early and get to the mayor's breakfast ... if you'll clear her, doctor."

She says "doctor" with a little quirk to her mouth, and Jay grins, leans in, and kisses the corner of her mouth, and once again I long for that — a shining moment of familiarity and love.

Jay turns to me and lifts the peas off my hand. "You might as well keep these now — just throw them in the freezer at home and put them on your hand at regular intervals. Now, can you move all your fingers?"

We both look at my hand, which has skin mottled from the pea treatment, and is losing distinguishing features due to swelling, but I can move each finger with a feeling closer to stiff achiness than acute pain.

Jay gives me an ibuprofen and rigs up a sling for me. "I recommend wearing that for the next little while, so nobody tries to shake your hand and to make you think twice before you use it. Take another painkiller in four hours and don't do anything strenuous tonight."

Twenty-Four

MADDY MANOEUVRES MY LITTLE car through the city streets, with Jay following behind us in their car.

"You didn't have to do this, you know."

She glances at my sling. "You shouldn't have even driven as far as our house. There's no way I was unleashing you on the streets again. Besides, it gives you a chance to tell me how things are with Dave."

"What do you mean?"

"When you told him about Leila — how did he react?"

"I haven't found the right time."

Maddy is silent for a few seconds and I put it down to concentration as she makes a left in a busy intersection, but when she sighs, I cringe. "Please don't tell me you're disappointed in me. When you get disappointed, I get defensive, and we both know that's not a good look for me."

"Oh, Paige," Maddy says. "I finally got you to take your writing seriously — when are you going to take Dave seriously?"

"What do you mean?"

She raises her voice. "He loves you, Paige."

I raise mine right back. "No, you've got that wrong — I love him." *Shit*. My body floods with adrenaline and the bottom drops out of my stomach the way it does when I miss the bottom stair on the fire escape. "I'm tired. Forget it. I didn't mean it."

She turns into the back lane behind the pub. "Why is it a problem to say that?"

"Because ..." I shake my head. I can't possibly explain that there's no easy outcome. If I love him, and he doesn't love me, that's a world of pain and rejection. If I love him, and he loves me too, that's a responsibility, something to live up to, something I'm not sure I can manage.

As Maddy pulls into my parking spot, Dave appears at the kitchen door. Reprieved by the appearance of the very person I was just too stressed to talk about. Whatever — I'll take it.

We step out of the car and Dave's gaze lands on my sling. "What's going on?"

"It's fine," I say. "I hurt my hand a bit. Jay gave me the sling for protection."

"It's true she will be fine," Maddy says. "But it's also true she needs to take it easy tonight. Can you do me a favour and look out for her?"

"Dave needs to work," I tell Maddy.

Rachel steps out of the kitchen behind Dave. "Oh my god, Paige. What happened?"

Dave turns to her. "I need to look after Paige. Can you take care of things down here?"

"Of course."

"There." Maddy smiles. "All set. My work here is done." She pulls me into a hug, hands me my keys, and whispers, "There's no reason at all not to love him." Then she walks down the lane to where Jay's waiting for her.

"Come on," Dave starts up the stairs and I follow him with my fingers throbbing again, and the familiar ache I get in my bones when I'm deeply tired.

***

It's amazing the difference a meal can make. A good meal, cooked by Dave, while I sit on the couch with ice on my elevated hand.

The pain has retreated, my stomach is full, and I feel gracious enough to say, "Thanks. I'm really sorry you had to do this, but I appreciate it."

"Paige, I'm not sure why you think I wouldn't willingly take care of you."

"You're right. I'm sorry. I do know that about you."

"How about you stop apologizing?"

While he clears the dishes, I think about what he said — why do I think he wouldn't willingly take care of me?

I used to be good at letting Leila take care of me. She was my big sister, and it felt natural, but since losing her, it's something I've found hard to accept from anybody — not just Dave.

Since that day Faye took me home, unplanned, to her busy household, I've felt like I was imposing everywhere I've lived. I babysat for Faye to earn my keep. My home with Rowan came as part of the job I did for him.

I moved in with Dave as a tenant, and that's kept things simple. I tell myself I want more with him. I've just told Maddy the same thing. I've blamed Dave for it not happening — because years ago he turned me down — but I've never tried since, because the thought of doing so is terrifying.

Right now, if he asked me to move out, I could tell myself it's because I don't pay enough in rent, and I could live with it. If we live together as a couple and he asks me to move out ... that's a failure I'm not sure I could face.

It's getting dark, and I gingerly rise from the table.

Dave hurries to my side. "Is it hurting badly?"

"Just being careful. It's much better, thanks." I glance out the back window and notice the flower box I planted on the railing of the stairs. "Could I ask you one more favour? Could you please water my flowers?"

He runs his hand through his hair. "What do you think I've been doing?"

"What do you mean?"

"You've hardly been here, Paige. Those flowers would have been dead days ago if I hadn't been watering them."

"Oh. OK, then. Thank you. I appreciate it."

"Really? 'I appreciate it?' What happened? When did we go from real, actual friends to two people who are polite but don't tell each other anything important?"

"I do appreciate it," I say. "I want you to know that. And I want to share things with you, but it's hard for me."

"Why?"

"I don't know where to start."

"How about starting with how you hurt your hand?" He shakes his head. "No, how about I take my own advice and ask what I really want to know — are you moving back to Oak Junction?"

"What? Of course not!"

"It's your home. Your siblings all live there. And you've been there so much lately. It's not such a crazy question. Or maybe that's not even where you've been at all, and you just don't want to tell me the truth."

"I am!" Wait, maybe that wasn't the right answer. "I mean, I'm not. Not lying. I have been in Oak Junction. But I'm not moving there ..."

"Maybe you should. Maybe you'd be happier."

The vice tightening around my chest hurts much more than my hand. "Is that what you want?"

"No, Paige. I want you!"

I wait for him to walk it back. Then I change my mind — why give him the chance? I step toward him. "Can you help me with something else?"

He sighs. "Of course. What is it?"

I use my uninjured hand to tug at the neck of my shirt. "I don't think I can get this off myself."

"Really? It looks pretty loose ..."

"Dave ..."

"Oh. *Oh!* Right," he says. "I can help with that."

Now he steps toward me, so close I can feel the warmth of his body. The ambient light washing through the windows into the dim apartment highlights the ancient white t-shirt covering his lean frame and accentuates the creases in the worn jeans which I've dreamed of easing off him so many times before.

He looks down at me and says, "I don't want to hurt you." His voice has that touch of gravel I love so much. I might hear it with my ears, but I feel it between my legs.

It's a moment. There's no denying it. It's a definite timestamp occasion.

That time we met, and he found out I had the same name as his pub.

That time he stopped me mid-kiss and broke my heart.

All those nights I didn't sleep because I was wishing away the wall between our bedrooms.

That moment we both stood in the dark, mostly undressed and held our breath while we thought about what might happen next.

What might happen next?

My heart's been through a workout today, but now it's pounding for the right reason. I want to feel the length of Dave's body against me. On top of me. I can't feel my hand at all.

"The only way you could hurt me is by not taking my shirt off right now."

He grabs the hem of my shirt and eases it up, his hands searing lines of desire along my skin as they go. He lifts it off over my head.

"Now yours." I pitch in with my good hand, to show him I mean it.

***

It's everything I imagined, but better. It's my skin against his. It's the lean muscle of his shoulders, and his back, and his butt under my hands. It's maintaining eye contact as we both come to climax.

It's how well I sleep afterwards, curled against him, with his arm canted over my body. No bad dreams. No tossing and turning. No worries. At least not for a few hours.

I sleep late. Too late, so when I focus on his bedside clock, I scramble upright.

"What is it?" he mumbles.

"I should be leaving now."

He sits up as well. "Don't go." He reaches for my hand. "You need to rest this." The skin has gone dark, and my fingers are puffy, but yesterday's throbbing has gone.

"It hurts a lot less, and I'll wear my sling."

"Paige ..."

"Dave, it's my job. Maddy was the first one to see my hand, and she still wants me to go."

I'm up, padding into the bathroom. Breezing through the one-handed job of brushing my teeth.

Dave stands in the doorway. "Tell Maddy you need more rest."

I spit and rinse. "I have to work, Dave. I have to pay my rent."

"I think your landlord might give you a break on the rent if you asked him."

This is where I should say something sweet. This is where I should kiss him and go back to bed with him. But his words revive all my panicky insecurities of needing to prove myself. I have no confidence I can offer him anything of value if I'm not his tenant.

So I say, "Sorry, I need a second to pee," and close the bathroom door.

When I come back out, he tries to catch my gaze, but I slide my eyes past his. "Now I'm really late."

He helps me tie my sling in place and says, "At least let me drive you."

"It's a ten-minute walk and you'll never get close to the building in the car. It's fine. I'm fine."

I thank him. I kiss him on the cheek.

It's something, I tell myself as I hurry down the staircase.

It's not enough.

It's all I know how to give right now.

Twenty-Five

THE MAYOR'S BREAKFAST IS dull. Still, I ferret out a couple of interesting side stories — a city staffer who started in the mailroom at age sixteen and is now retiring after serving under twelve mayors, as well as a rumour that the city's going to test-pilot an aqua-bus to give people an extra option to access one of the city's main festival sites during the summer.

Since I started working on Wren's story — realistically, since I started taking Maddy's feedback on board — I've gotten better at my job.

That's one positive.

The other is that my hand is much better today. It looks worse by the moment and that, plus the sling, keeps people from trying to shake my hand. I move my fingers gently now and then, and find I can use them as long as I'm careful.

Which is just as well, because as I walk home from the breakfast, I decide I need to head out to The Mule today.

I know what Maddy said, and I'm not saying she's wrong. I could write the story as we discussed, and it might even be good.

But it would feel unfinished to me.

It would feel like I cut corners.

And it was Maddy herself who encouraged me to dig deeper, so I have to give at least one more day to digging.

I ditch my mayor-breakfast clothes for visiting-a-dive-bar clothes, then head down to my car ... where I run into Dave coming out of the kitchen door.

"How did the breakfast go?"

"Too many speeches for so early in the day, but generally fine."

He looks at the car keys in my hand. "Where are you going?"

"There's something I need to check out in Oak Junction."

He freezes. Goes silent for several long seconds. "Are you serious?"

My instinct is to go on the defensive, but I know that's the wrong move. The right move would be to explain everything to him, but The Mule will get busier as the day goes on, and I want to get out there while it's quiet.

While I'm hesitating, he continues. "Even if you don't care about me as a ..." He throws up his hands. "Whatever I might be to you, you at least owe me an explanation as a landlord — do I need to make other plans for your room?"

"I already told you, it's not that. I'm not moving out. I can explain everything and I will explain everything, but it needs more time than I've got right now. Can we talk tonight?"

He bites his lip, then answers. "We'll see — I might be busy doing this little thing called running a business." He turns and heads back to the door and I call after him.

"Dave? I do care about you as a ... whatever you're willing to be to me. I really, really do."

He doesn't turn around, just lifts his hand in what might be acknowledgment, or might be dismissal.

And I get in my car and drive to The Mule.

***

When I step through the door, I'm flashed back twenty years or more. My mom used to say, "I just need to stop here a sec," and bring me, and sometimes Leila too, in with her to pay down her tab.

It's weirdly familiar to be here during the day. It smells of spilled beer and, lingeringly, of cigarettes — even though it was already illegal to smoke inside back in those days. One of the many cases against carpet in a drinking establishment.

I head to the bar, picturing the big man, beer-bellied and stubbled, who would greet my mom and count the bills she handed him. He'd slide them into the cash drawer, then wink and hold out a mason jar full of lollipops so my sister and I could choose one.

I knock on the wood of the bar — "Hello?" — then turn and do a full-circle assessment of the place.

It's dim back here, far from the front picture windows, but the glass is clean, all the surfaces shine, and there are pots full of blooms by the fake hitching posts outside.

I have the impression of a place making the best of what it has.

The creak of door hinges turns me back to the bar to face a tall, thin guy. Younger than me.

Time moves on, even at The Crazy Mule.

When he asks, "What can I get you?" I can't think of a natural segue into my question, so I simply show my media ID — the same one I used to get into the mayor's breakfast. I remember back in journalism school how proud I was to have press ID. For the first time in a long time, I feel that way again.

"I'm writing a story about Wren Sheedy's disappearance. I wonder if I can ask you a few questions."

"No." His tone is flat. Matter of fact. It doesn't invite the follow-up question I ask anyway.

"Why not?"

"I don't talk to cops or reporters."

Fantastic. I'm finally proud to show my press pass and it's to a guy who doesn't like reporters.

I need a new plan of attack. I'm just not sure what it should be.

A woman pushes through the saloon-style doors from the kitchen to the bar. She's curvy, pretty, freckled, and red-haired. Also, somehow familiar. "Hey hon, has Amos helped you?"

"No." I mimic his flat tone and shoot him a sideways glance.

In response to her raised eyebrows, he says, "She's askin' questions about the customers."

"I wasn't ..." I start. Then stop. I was about to protest I was asking about Wren — not about the customers — but maybe that's a clue in itself. Maybe, without meaning to, he's confirming Wren is a customer.

The woman narrows her eyes and studies my face. "You're that little Turner girl, aren't you?"

The woman doesn't look like she's old enough to call me "little" but being able to get a "yes" into the conversation seems like a step forward, so that's what I say.

"I'd recognize you anywhere. All you Turner girls have the same gorgeous eyes. Even that little Charlotte — she's friends with my daughter — and especially your sister Leila; a baby owl had nothing on her big, bright eyes." She pauses and laughs. "You don't recognize me — I was in your sister Macy's class. My family runs this place. I remember you coming in here with your ma and your sis way back when. I'm Jessie."

Jessie clearly has an amazing memory, which hopefully bodes well for my questions about Wren. I tell a white lie. "Now that you mention it, I remember you — it's just that I was so young. It took me a minute." It's not a full-on lie — I did think she looked familiar.

"Of course, hun. So what brings you here, now? I thought you moved to the city."

"I moved there to go to journalism school. Now I'm writing a story about Wren."

"Mmm-hmm ..." Jessie nods. "You're the perfect person to write about that, with your own sister going missing."

If I had pictured myself having this conversation, I would have imagined it would be uncomfortable, but there's something about Jessie's complete lack of filter that's actually quite refreshing.

"That's what my editor thought," I say. "Anyway, somebody told me Wren was in here with a rough guy."

Jessie nods. "She used to come in, alright. And, sure, sometimes I guess she was with a guy, but I can't say I noticed him much. Do you have a picture?"

"No. I don't know anything about him. I was hoping to find out by coming here."

"Well then, you need to look at the video, don't you?"

The bartender has been busy rearranging bottles, but now he stops and says, "You can't show her that."

"Of course I can. I'm the day manager. I decide."

"She needs a warrant," he says.

"Nope. She needs my permission." She points to a sign behind the bar saying Smile! You're on camera. "People know they're being videoed when they're in here and I can show the footage to anyone I like." She turns to me. "Now, what day do you need to see?"

That is a very good question.

***

Not only is Jessie unfiltered and no-nonsense, she's also very resourceful. With just a few clicks through social media feeds, she finds the date of the jumping clinic hosted at Oak Copse, complete with videos of riders splashing through water jumps with Rose shouting encouragement.

"There we go," she says. "And here you go — the footage for that day's uploaded to the cloud, but you can watch it here." Click, click, and one more click, and I watch the footage with bright eyes, pencil poised in my good hand, bruised hand hovering over the mouse.

It's so boring. There's so much of it. At first I think I'll watch the entire day, just to be thorough, but eventually I decide it's fair to skip ahead to late afternoon.

The watching gets slower the longer the recording wears on, because there are more and more people in the bar and every few minutes I pause it completely to scan all the faces and make sure I'm not missing Wren's.

I've just done that, and restarted when Amos comes in with a pint glass of Diet Coke clinking with ice cubes.

"Wow, thanks," I say.

"Jessie said I had to."

"Well, thanks anyway."

At least crunching the ice cubes gives me something to do while the faces blur in front of my eyes.

I watch a man pick his nose. Nice. I watch a woman adjust her bra. I watch a couple come in together then, when the man goes to the bathroom, the woman leans across the bar and kisses Amos.

Maybe that's why Amos didn't want me to see the video.

I gasp out loud when I recognize Nate. My first reaction is relief, which quickly morphs to dismay because I haven't seen Wren at all.

Have I missed her? Is it possible she could be out of camera range? But Nate specifically said Wren was at the bar.

My eyes are scratchy and my patience worn thin. I don't think I can go back and watch again … *wait* … there's someone I know …

It's not Wren, though. It's Addison. She's talking to a guy I don't recognize. I freeze the picture to take a screenshot and Jessie walks in. "If that's the guy you were talking about, he is bad news."

"Do you know who he is?"

"Unfortunately. Name's Jeb."

I straighten. "Jeb Dixon?"

"I thought you didn't know who you were looking for?"

"I don't. I mean, I know of him, but I don't know him. And I don't know if he's the one I'm looking for — do you remember seeing him with Wren?"

"There's only one thing I remember about him — it wasn't this night, though. Must have been a few nights later. He got in an argument with one of our regulars at the bar over something stupid like the guy got served when Jeb thought it was his turn. They got going at each other, disrupting the place. Amos told the regular to sit down and shut up, and he and one of the other staff members kicked Jeb out. Which would have been the end of it, except that guy Jeb waited in the parking lot for over an hour until the regular left. He jumped him when he was getting into his car, slammed him from behind, and broke his arm."

"Are you serious?" My hand hurts just thinking about it.

She nods. "We called the police and when they came he was stood there, cursing and swearing at the guy, saying nobody gets the better of him."

"The police came? Like Oak Junction?" I wonder why Xander didn't tell me about the incident.

Jessie shakes her head. "Since we're on the highway it's the provincial cops that come here. Anyway, don't ask me what happened to him. They took him away, and I haven't seen him since, which is fine with me. We wouldn't let him back in if he came anyway."

There was no way I was going to interrupt Jessie while she was telling her story, but my brain's stuck back on one thing. I point at Addison, frozen on the screen. "I know it was pretty common to let underage kids sneak in back in the day, but I'm surprised you let them in now."

"Who's underage? That girl is at least twenty."

"What? No ... she rides with Charlotte. There's a bunch of them. They're all young teenagers. She looks so sweet."

Jessie snorts. "She's a lot less sweet after a few drinks. I told her she'd had enough to drink, and she told me where to go. Come to think of it, maybe she and old Jeb there are a good match."

Wow. OK. So, yeah, that whole thing about being a better journalist, not cutting corners, digging into stories. Maybe the first thing would have been not to assume Addison was one of the teenagers just because I've seen her with them a few times. And what was she doing with Jeb Dixon?

As Jessie returns to work, I'm left thinking I suck at this.

I've watched hours of video, found out I've been making guesses and assumptions about people at Oak Copse, and I haven't seen Wren at all — except *there she is.*

Hallelujah.

The thing is, though, it's a good hour-and-a-half after Nate's brief three-minute appearance to pick up his wing order.

She's with a guy, but it's not Jeb Dixon. And whoever he is, he looks nice. They look happy. Although I guess I've just learned not to assume.

I freeze the screen again and call Jessie.

"You found her! Good job. Is that the guy?"

"I don't know. I thought you might."

"Nuh-uh. I have no idea. Amos!"

Amos comes in, looking even less happy than the last time he came back. "It's getting busy out there."

"If you didn't complain so much, you'd already be done. Just look here and tell us if you know this guy."

He squints at the screen. "I don't know who he is, but I've seen him a few times with her."

"Any idea what his name is?" Jessie asks. "Can you tell us anything else?"

"I have a feeling it might have always been on a weekend. I can't say that for sure, though."

"While we're asking questions, does 'VersMarais' mean anything to either of you?"

They both turn to me with furrowed brows. "I don't even know what you just said," Amos says.

"Like this." I write it down.

They each look at it and each shake their heads.

I shrug. "Thanks anyway." My research on this story has devolved into asking anybody I meet anything I can think of. It's what I'm supposed to do according to my journalism training, and Maddy, and even the annoying writer who won last year's lifestyle feature award — the one Maddy wants to enter my story for.

I remember her telling everybody, "I just kept asking questions, and it got me this terrific story."

Right now I just feel like it's getting me a terrific headache.

Or maybe that's all the quick transitions between slow-mo and fast-forward video viewing.

Whatever. Time to get back to it. I take a screenshot, then let the video advance until Wren and the unidentified guy drift out of the camera's view.

I keep watching until, eventually, through the crowd I can see a back view of a couple leaving, which I'm pretty sure is them.

I screenshot that as well, and skim the rest of the video with no further ah-ha moments.

As I leave with the screenshots emailed to myself and my head full of questions about Addison, and Jeb Dixon, and Wren and the mystery man, and Nate, Amos hands me a neatly wrapped sandwich.

The last food I saw was at the mayor's breakfast, and the sandwich is made of thick bread and full of cheese and veggies. My stomach rumbles. "What do I owe you?"

He shrugs. "Nothing. I'm sorry for giving you a hard time. Jessie told me you're local. Local press is OK by me. I just hate the big guys, you know."

The power of the local press. Faye and Marge would say I told you so.

As I open my car, my stomach contracts at the thought of the food, my brain whirrs with new information, and my hand throbs at the thought of what I'm going to do after I eat Amos's sandwich.

Because after what I've seen here, I don't see any other option except to go to Jeb Dixon's.

Twenty-Six

Since it's one of the afternoons that the library's open, that's where I head to eat my sandwich. I sit on the porch with my laptop connected to the public Wi-Fi and let the breeze ruffle my hair and carry the scent of the country to me. It contains cut hay, drifting in from a far-off field, pine needles from the nearby forest, and it's free of car exhaust, fryer oil from food trucks, and holds no cannabis, cigarette, or vape smoke.

I almost feel like I'm on holiday.

If I wasn't about to drive out to the property of a known con artist who breaks people's arms.

Of course, first I've got to find him.

The thing is, I don't know exactly where the Cormier place is. It's not like Julie Cormier used to invite the whole class out to birthday parties at her house.

Out past the ferry.

The phrase floats into my head. If you grew up in Oak Junction, "out past the ferry" means the same thing as "the wrong side of the tracks."

The ferry itself is fine, obviously. A means of transport for many people who need to cross between Quebec to the north, and Ontario to the south. And *way* past the ferry — like a couple of concession roads to the west — is the provincial park, bordered by a pretty country cemetery. In between though ... well, I can't say I've ever been to that area. I have a vague picture of a couple of narrow dirt roads and I know they curve along the shore, but I don't know exactly what's back there, other than places *out past the ferry*, where we weren't supposed to go.

I'm pretty sure Ed Cormier's place is one of them.

People think technology's made it easier to find people, but back when I was a teenager everybody had a landline, and most of them were listed on Canada411, just a quick search away, complete with address.

Now ... not so much.

Still, we didn't have Google Maps back then. I figure there are only so many houses in the area I've identified, and not many of those will have sufficient open space to keep horses.

I zoom in as closely as my screen will let me and find two properties that have what could be fields or paddocks around them, along with large roofs which might be barns.

It might not be either of them, but it's a start, and there's only one way to find out.

Go there.

Maybe I shouldn't. Maybe I should go back to the city and start writing like Maddy told me to. Maybe I should text either of my brothers, who would most definitely talk me out of this.

Or maybe I should just act like a real journalist and do the final bit of legwork on my story. All this "out past the ferry" and "Jeb Dixon breaks people's arms" and "Ed Cormier's in jail" is probably just Boo Radley stuff. Urban legends, except in the country.

Well, except I guess Ed really is in jail ... which means he won't be at his property, so one less thing to worry about.

Anyway, it's ridiculous that I've never been to a place that's less than twenty kilometres from where I grew up. I'm sure it's beautiful out there. The river by the ferry is a broad expanse of clear, blue water, framed on either side by dense mixed forests, and the nearby properties are probably gorgeous.

I guess I'll be finding out before long.

***

The first property I identified is interesting but a no. The building that could have been a barn appears to be a small airplane hangar and the open space is a long grass runway surrounded by windsocks. A private airstrip.

Very cool. Something I'd find out more about if the Oak Junction Journal was up-and-running and I was an OJJ reporter. But I'm not, and the property isn't what I'm looking for, so I move on.

Fortunately, the second one is the right place and there's no need to guess about it. An off-kilter mailbox covered in peeling camouflage vinyl sports six faded red stickers: C, R, M, I, E, R. The gap between the C and the R tells me this is Ed Cormier's mailbox.

A length of fence runs along the road with horses grazing behind it. I cruise past the mailbox and the grazing horses and pull into the next crossroad, which is very narrow, with rutted gravel that clearly hasn't been graded for years. I pull the car as far off the road as I can without getting it stuck, under some low-hanging branches that make me feel like I'm in a cave.

It's good that I changed out of my fancy breakfast clothes — cropped chinos and sneakers are definitely better for a spot of country walking than strappy sandals and wide-legged pants. Still ... I keep a stash of "emergency" supplies in the spare tire wheel well. There's an old hoodie in there which I pull on, relieved that it's green and should blend into the vegetation.

I snug my hair into a ponytail and pull the hood up. What I don't do is pause to ask myself why I'm doing all this. Why hide the car? Why disguise myself? What am I getting ready to do? How far am I willing to go?

I'm just being prepared. That's all. I won't do anything dangerous, but if what I've heard is true, and Jeb Dixon is as unpredictable as everybody says, it's best to be on my toes. This is me tiptoeing.

I want to see his horses. I should have brought horse treats. There's a tin of mints in the console of the car, which I slip into the hoodie's kangaroo pouch.

Then, I set out through the brush toward the horses' paddock. *Why aren't you going by the road?* I'm not sure if it's Rowan's or Xander's voice in my head, but my answer is quick — *He might have cameras by the road and you were the one who didn't want me to confront him.* This is me being careful.

This is also me wading through hip-high undergrowth, tripping on fallen logs, batting at bugs, and trying not to get scraped by low-hanging branches. A big tick-check will be in order tonight.

I'm using the overhead map image I looked up as a mental reference. I had the impression I could get to the paddock this way ... I just didn't think it would be such a long hike.

As I'm wondering whether I've been walking in circles without knowing it, the trees thin ahead and I can make out the lines of a wire fence.

The sun's come out and I stand for a moment, arms propped on the fence, blinking to adjust my shade-accustomed eyes to the brightness of the wide-open field. The cicadas are sawing for all they're worth. The horses' coats gleam under the sun's rays. I can imagine them hot under my palm.

Even in my hoodie, in the mid-afternoon sun, a chill runs through me. Maybe it's a poke from my subconscious reminding me of my brothers' warnings. It was a day like this one when Wren disappeared, and nobody thought it could happen then. Best be wary.

I pull out my phone and type out a message: If you get this, I need help. I leave it unsent, but ready to go. And, yes, I feel silly, but better silly than sorry.

This is me being careful.

I shake the mint tin.

Heads pop up, one after another. One horse immediately begins walking, head outstretched, straight for me.

I hope nobody's watching the field because there's no dismissing the herd's reaction.

I keep my eyes open, ready to run if I have to. Ready to press "send" on my message if I need to.

I slip a mint to the first horse to arrive. "Good boy. You're such a good boy. Aren't you a good boy?"

He crunches it, and a waft of peppermint hits my nostrils. Finding that he likes mints is a good first step.

Now for the second step, which is to see if he's tattooed and, if so, take a picture. After combining Xander's information about Jeb's past horse-related swindles with the horse identification information I gained at Oak Copse, determining the true identity of Jeb Dixon's horses could be very useful.

However, how to juggle the mints — which the horse wants immediately — while holding his halter and my phone? I could use one more hand.

Honestly, I don't even know how to read a tattoo on the inside of a horse's lip. It seems like a hard enough thing for a complete horse rookie like me to do without trying to take a photo at the same time.

So, OK. Don't try to take a photo. I switch my phone to the front camera, select video, press record, then put the phone grip in my mouth. If the horse minds being approached by a pair of eyes, fronted by a cell phone, he doesn't show it. I offer him another mint and he noses eagerly toward me.

While he crunches, I take hold of either side of his halter and rub the soft skin around his mouth. He seems to like it. I slide my hands forward and maybe they have mint residue on them, or maybe it's just good, old-fashioned salty sweat, but he licks at my fingers.

It's now or never. The horse might pull away. Jeb might show up. I slide my thumbs under his top lip, leaving my fingers behind it as leverage and, taking a deep breath, flip the lip.

I'm surprised how easily it flips right up. I can clearly see the tattoo — I just hope my camera's pointing in the right direction. I'm also surprised at the horse's reaction. He seems to think it's a game. He pushes into my hand and, when I release the lip, instead of backing away from me, he nuzzles me.

While he's doing that, I switch my phone to photo and take as many pictures of him as I can, from different angles, trying to show all the markings on his legs and face.

Then I try for another horse.

Three more of Jeb's horses are happy to play along with my mints-in-exchange-for-photos game. I figure any who don't approach the fence are less amenable, and I probably don't want to be messing around with their mouths anyway.

It's actually good that they stay a ways out in the paddock, heads down, grazing. It makes what I'm doing at the fence less obvious.

With my phone full of horsey photos and videos, and my mints gone, I begin to walk along the fence line, just inside the trees, hoping the horses won't follow me. No mints, no interest — they drop their heads and graze with their friends.

I'm not sure where I'm going, but Maps showed me the driveway — and the buildings strung along it — are on the opposite side of the paddock. Ahead, I can see the end of the cleared field. I'm assuming when I get to the corner, I'll be able to turn right and continue walking along the fence, in the shelter of the trees, except this time I'll be walking toward the buildings.

Sure enough, when I reach the corner, the fence stretches off along the edge of the forest. I set off that way, looking to my right across the field to the group of horses slowly drifting away from the fence where I stood. When I look to the left, there are occasional spots where the trees are thinner and I can glimpse openness and the river through them.

I'm not really thinking beyond staying in the shade of the trees, not stepping on anything that will trip me, hoping that my photos and videos turn out.

Then I hit the far corner. The one closest to the farm buildings. Now I need to make a decision. Now I need to figure out what I'm doing here.

Now, I should really turn around and go back to the car.

The buildings are right in front of me, though — about fifty feet away. A line of them, running along the gravel drive. They look interesting. They look like they could hide any number of intriguing things. They look to be a reasonable distance from the house — given that there's no house in sight.

I'm still hidden, but if I step out any further, I won't be. Then again, anybody out and about also wouldn't be hidden from me. I stand as still as I can for five minutes, keeping my breath shallow, keeping my eyes open, listening.

Beyond the rustling of something small in the leaf litter by my feet and the light breeze touching a branch here and rustling a leaf there, I swear I'm alone.

I won't have another chance like this.

So, I'll just be careful. I check my phone — make sure my SOS message is still ready to be sent — then I take my first step out from the tree trunk I'm sheltering beside.

Twenty-Seven

I RUN. I STAY on my tiptoes — quick, but quiet. At least that's the aim.

The first building is a proper, classic barn like the ones scattered across fields and farms in this valley and throughout Eastern Ontario.

It's clapboard sided with a fieldstone foundation and topped with a central-ridge pitched roof. The double doors at the end are rolled wide open and when I peer in, I see the entire inside has been gutted. There would have been stalls in here once, but now all that's left are regularly spaced load-bearing posts, leading up to structural beams, and a loft covering about half of the overhead space. There are hay bales stacked high in the loft. The floor is a loamy mix of dirt and sand, and there are haynets strung from the walls.

A loafing barn. Just about the right size for the herd of horses in the field.

Because it's wide open, with nowhere to hide, I don't feel comfortable going in. However, for the same reason, I don't think there's anything of interest hidden in there.

Time to move on. I hug the non-driveway side of the barn until I get to the corner. Here, a lane divides this building from the next one, which is a large quonset hut. Looking right, the lane leads to a gate, which leads into the field

I just walked around. It all makes sense for bringing the horses in during bad weather.

I force myself to wait for another long, quiet interlude and again, not hearing or seeing anything, I scamper across the lane — once again going as quickly as I can, once again trying not to make any sounds.

In just a few seconds, I'm hugging the side of the quonset.

I've already seen a barn big enough to hold all the horses. Peering ahead, I can just make out the back of the house with several sheds dividing it from the quonset hut. Those are big enough to hold any equipment needed on the farm.

So, what's in this hut?

I think of what Maddy would say — *It doesn't matter what's in the hut.* It has nothing to do with the story I'm supposed to write ... supposed to be at home, in the city, writing right now.

But I've come this far.

There are double doors on the hut, just like on the barn, but these ones are closed. I roll from my heels to my toes, taking the few silent steps needed to reach the doors. There's a hasp, with a padlock threaded through it, and I have to admit relief floods through me at the sight of it.

That's it — investigating over — nothing more I can do. I'm not a lock-picker, nor do I have bolt-cutters.

I give the padlock a casual tug ... and it opens in my hand.

Shit.

I don't want to look inside.

What if Wren's in there?

The possibility makes me want to look even less.

I open my phone one more time and override my privacy settings to allow tracking. Double-check my emergency message. Cautiously crack the door open.

If there's someone inside, they'll see the door moving. I stand, poised to run, and wait for a yell.

Nothing.

Right. OK, then. *Am I really going to do this? Am I going in?*

I pull the door open just enough to slip in, then shut it behind me. Unfortunately, there's no way to replace the padlock in the hasp, so I'll just have to hope nobody strolls casually by and wonders why the padlock is missing.

Unlike the loafing barn, which was dim and cool, the top part of the quonset is canvas so the area is bright, and the air is warm. It makes me feel ridiculously exposed, but it also means I can see everything.

Massive shelves line each of the long walls, and a row of vehicles occupies the open space down the middle — a couple of trucks, a tractor, an ATV. I start taking video.

I walk the entire long side, recording the contents of the shelves, which mostly seem to be bags of horse feed. I cross in front of the other set of double doors at the far end of the hut and walk back along the other set of shelves. At one end is a variety of equipment — buckets, ropes, and other equipment, in the middle are stacks of bags that say "shavings," and back at the end where I entered, are plain old boring cardboard boxes. Except for the labels on them that say **Equine Pharma** and read **Warning. For delivery to veterinary offices only. Not for resale.** and **Ketamine, Banamine, Bute.**

Even though it's not my thing, I've heard of Ketamine. And the other two ... Banamine and Bute ... they're familiar. For some reason, I think of bananas. Not *bananas, Banamine,* I tell myself. Then, like a lightbulb it all comes together. The smell of bananas. Ruth telling me about Banamine. A sachet of Bute in Wren's medicine cabinet.

I open the nearest box and find rows and rows of the little wet-wipe-looking sachets. My brain is racing. It's too much to figure out right now, so I scoop a few out and stuff them in my pocket, then I stop the video and take pictures of each of the different labels on the boxes.

I've just captured **Ketamine** when the doors at the far end of the hut roll open and somebody yells, "Hey!"

Run. It's all I can think. I don't even take time to consider that another person could be waiting for me right outside. It's my good luck that nobody is, but that's the end of my good luck because I still have to get out of here.

I can't run along the drive toward the road since the person who yelled at me is at that end of the hut. The route back to my car is long and circuitous, and the most direct path — straight across the field leaves me wide open to observation, not to mention being chased down on an ATV.

My instinct is to get to the river, but I also don't want to run straight there — I don't want the person chasing me to know where I've gone. So I run across the drive and push between two bushes into the woods on the far side.

The forest here is as dense as the thickest patch I pushed through between the car and the paddock, and it's impossible to run quickly.

My heart's pounding high and thready in my chest and I recognize the cause is fear rather than exertion.

Calm down, I tell myself. *Nobody coming behind can run quickly either.*

All I need to do is leave them unsure which way I've gone, then make my way to the river.

Then what?

Worry about that then. For now, just keep pressing forward.

Only seconds later I hear the first cracklings and snappings of branches telling me my pursuer has entered the woods. "I'm going to get you!" he yells.

I drop to my knees and crawl, hoping to stay below his radar. I turn toward the river, knowing it's hard to see any distance in the thick undergrowth, counting on the green of my hoodie to help camouflage me.

My hand's hurting. *It'll hurt more if you get caught.*

I know the water's not far ahead. If I'm lucky, I'll find a friendly fishing boat right at the shore.

Behind me, the person I assume is Jeb yells, "You can't come onto my property, you little thief! Nobody steals from me — you won't get away with this!"

I don't think he's that close. I don't think he turned when I did. But I'm not looking back to find out.

I can see the water now — *Stay low, stay low* — there's a downhill slope to the shore and I duck and let myself roll down it.

There's no fishing boat. In fact, there isn't really a shoreline, just a scrubby, rocky strip separating the trees from the water. The stretch of river in front of me is empty, but I know the ferry is ahead. A quick consultation of my mental map tells me it has to be less than a kilometre.

So I go.

I scamper along, half in the water, slipping, getting wet. I remember Maddy telling me about going out with a group to do an activity like this when she took a trip to Wales. She called it coasteering, and she paid to do it. You couldn't pay me enough to ever do this again.

I'm still breathing hard, mostly because the terror hasn't left me, but I don't think there's anybody behind me and the woods alongside me seem as difficult to penetrate as the ones I ran through, so even though I'm slow, anyone trying to push through them would be slower.

It's only when I round a sharp bend and see the ferry dock jutting out a couple of hundred metres ahead that I take a second to pull my phone out of my pocket. It's miraculously unbroken, and unsoaked by any of my splashing. I pull up my earlier message and add **I'm at the Oak Junction ferry dock.** before hitting send.

Then I push forward toward the dock.

Twenty-Eight

WHEN I ARRIVE AT the dock, I expect to find a couple of cyclists, two or three pickup trucks, at least one family with a car stuffed full of beach toys, and, of course, one or two staff members.

Instead, the dock is deserted. No line-up, no boat, no ferry crew.

Just a hand-scrawled sign saying the boat needs an unexpected repair and is on the Quebec side waiting for a part to arrive. *We'll be back when we get back.*

So helpful.

I peer across the river just in case the boat's on its way back. I use the zoom on my camera to help my tired eyes, but there's no bow wave making its way toward me.

The rush of energy supplied by adrenaline and straight-up fear has drained away. My knees are shaky and my chest is tight. I have to battle an irrational urge to cry — as if that's going to help anything.

The quietness of a place that should have a constant stream of people coming and going is eerie. I came here to be safe, but I feel unsettled and exposed.

The road is visible from where I'm standing and I know, for sure, if I found an intruder on my property, then wanted to cruise around looking for them, I'd definitely drive down here.

What am I going to do? I don't want to be a sitting duck — just waiting here for Jeb to find me — but I don't know where else to go.

There's no other busy public place nearby. Plus, I sent a message saying I'd be here. Plus, my hand is throbbing again, I have a gash on my leg, and I'm tired.

I hear an engine slowing up on the road and retreat behind the building, which serves as office and ticket booth. It's tiny, and there's a mowed expanse of grass around it on all sides. If Jeb's in that car, and he comes looking around the building, I can either make a run for the trees again — and restart this whole chase sequence, except with no destination in mind — or I can keep scuttling around the building trying to stay out of his sight.

Gravel crunches under tires, which roll to a stop. A car door opens, then another, and there are voices — more than one, including a woman. I peek out to see a family.

As the tension drains from my body, I pull out my phone. Six missed calls and one text which reads **Coming!** I look at the timestamp and calculate how long it will take before help arrives.

I need to find a better hiding spot.

I listen to the family react to the sign. "Bummer!" "What a pain!" "Let's go get dinner and come back."

As they leave, I think maybe there's somewhere to hide on the other side of the road, so I'll see help when it arrives, but won't be seen by anybody — by Jeb — if he pulls into the ferry parking area.

Just as I'm about to head up to see, I hear another engine and retreat with no time to spare.

This time it's Jeb.

He stops the truck far enough back that from my spot behind the building I can see him get out, leaving it running. He walks toward the dock. By moving to the other end of the building, I can watch him read the sign and hear him say, "Not this way."

He paces back and forth, then stops, bends down and picks something up.

Oh. No.

It's one of the sachets of Bute I stuffed in my pocket alongside my phone. It must have fallen out when I used my phone to look for the boat.

"Shit!" Jeb yells.

I couldn't agree more.

He turns back to face the parking area and the building I'm hiding behind and raises his voice. "Thought stealing from me would be easy money, huh? Just skim off some of the stuff your crooked uncle delivered to my place? You'll be sorry, you little shit!"

Poor Jeb. It sounds like his life is complicated. What's the world coming to when a criminal can't trust the family of his crooked suppliers?

It's good he thinks it's an inside job, connected to stolen goods. If he has Wren, or did something to Wren, I don't want him to know I suspect him.

He walks right out onto the dock and peers over the end, then looks out toward Quebec. What does he think the person he's chasing did? Swim for it?

Whatever he thinks, he's given me a chance, if only I can talk myself into taking it.

Run to his truck. Drive it away.

My insides are liquid, my legs are weak.

What if I'm not fast enough? What if I trip? What if he catches me?

If he looks behind this building, and I have to run from here, he'll catch me.

I move to the other end of the building, closest to the truck, and count down — *Five, four, three, two…*

Sit tight. The word is a whisper in my ear, distracting me, robbing me of the focus I need.

I start again — *Five, four, three, two…* — I'm tensed to go, about to run, when a new noise hums in the background, prompting an exclamation from Jeb, who runs back to the truck, double-beeping it to unlock it as he goes.

It was locked.

I wouldn't have been able to get in.

I would have been out in the open, exposed, with running from him my only option.

I'm shivering as he spins his tires and speeds out, throwing gravel, past the car driving in.

An Oak Junction police SUV.

Suddenly my legs are working. I sprint to the car, but before I can run to the driver's side, where my brother's sitting, Dave gets out of the passenger door. I hurl myself against him and hug him as tightly as I can. "Thank you," I whisper in his ear. Then I pull back, kiss him full on the lips, and whisper in his other ear, "I love you."

Twenty-Nine

XANDER GOT ON THE phone as soon as I spluttered out, "Jeb Dixon. Quonset hut full of stolen stuff. Chased me."

He's been saying, "Out past the ferry," "Cormier's place," "Vehicles, equipment, medication" — this last as he held up one of the sachets I'd handed him.

"Did you say you saw an animal in distress?" Xander turns away from his phone to ask me.

"Excuse me?"

"Animals," he says. "There were animals there?"

"Yes."

"Were you concerned about their welfare?"

I look at the sachet of Bute in his hand, then think of the Banamine also on the premises. Rose said they shouldn't be combined. "Yes."

He turns back to the phone. "Sounds like we should get the animal welfare inspector over there and give her some backup."

When he finishes the call, he says, "Let's get you out of here. We'll talk in the car."

As Xander follows my directions back to my parked car, he and Dave explain why they came to get me together.

"I freaked out when I got your text," Dave says. "I jumped in the car and started driving to Oak Junction, but I didn't know how to get to the ferry, and I was already on the highway so I couldn't start messing around with maps, then I remembered your brother was on the police force …"

Xander takes over. "Good thing I was in the station. The duty officer took the call and said, 'I have someone on the line asking for Paige Turner's brother.'"

"I couldn't remember his name and it was the only way I could think of to find him," Dave says. "He told me to come to the station, and he was waiting when I got there and drove us straight to the ferry. It would have taken me ages to find it on my own."

"I've never been so happy to see two people in my life." Just ahead is Ed Cormier's mailbox. Where this all started. I shiver, and Xander catches my eye in the rearview mirror. "What were you thinking?"

"I know. I owe you an explanation. A long one … both of you."

"Yes, well, you can give me that explanation at Faye's. She's hosting dinner. You can take your car and I'll come there after I meet up with my colleagues when they do their animal welfare check."

"Yeah, what's that all about?"

"A way to get onto the property. Animal welfare has the right to follow up on a concern. We can provide backup. If we see anything in plain sight while providing that backup …" He shrugs.

"Everything I saw was in the quonset."

He nods. "Some people keep animals in quonset huts. It would only be prudent to check it out."

"When did Faye organize dinner?" I ask.

"When I called her to see if she knew what the heck was going on."

"She does!" I say.

He lifts his eyebrows.

I squirm. "Well, she doesn't know about just now — today — but in general, she knows."

"All part of your explaining. Which probably starts with Dave while he drives you to Faye's." Xander stops the SUV behind my car and I'm thankful to be with Dave and Xander in the official car. I would have been terrified to come back here on my own — afraid Jeb had found the car, and was waiting for me.

It seems almost impossible that the scene should be so peaceful — the little car tucked under the low-hanging branches, birds twittering overhead, a gentle breeze blowing, me as safe as can be with two people who love me.

I'm fortunate that the whole interlude at Ed Cormier's place and the ferry dock remained a blip in the middle of a summer afternoon instead of ballooning into a newsworthy story.

Dave gets behind the wheel, adjusting the seat to its maximum settings to allow for his long legs, and Xander follows us back as far as the Cormier driveway, and I know this is it. This is the long-overdue moment. This is when I have to explain everything to Dave.

I start with, "Thank you for coming."

"Really?" he says. "We're really going to make polite conversation? Because I'm not in the mood, and if that's what this drive is about, I'll just drive to the police station so I can get my car and you can go on to your sister's."

"It's not!" I shake my head. "I'm going to tell you everything, but I thought it was important to at least say thank you."

He sighs. "You're welcome. I'm listening. The kilometres are ticking away."

It's such a familiar feeling. Knowing I have to start. Wanting to start. But battling a massive current of hesitation. Like when I was a kid standing on a dock so hot it burned my feet. Wanting off the hot dock. Wanting in the cold river. The inner battle raging inside me:

— *It's cold.*

— *That's the point.*

— *I want to jump.*

— *Nothing's stopping you.*

More than once, Leila came up behind me and pushed me in and, far from being mad, I was relieved.

I wish she was here now to push the words out of me.

Go.

It's the voice from Maddy's office. From the ferry dock — except that time saying "no" instead of "go." This time, though, the "go" is unmistakable.

I blurt it out. "I had a sister ..."

I can't blame Dave for the puzzled look he turns my way. He knows I have a sister. We're going to her house right now — if he doesn't decide to ditch me on the way.

"Not Faye," I say. "And not Macy either — you might meet Macy at Faye's tonight. I'm talking about my sister whose name was ... is ... Leila."

Thank goodness he doesn't say anything because I've managed to jump off the dock — or Leila pushed me off — and I'm swimming.

"I know I've never told you much about my family, but I have four older siblings — Faye, Xander, Macy, and Rowan — who are all close in age to each other, then there was a big gap down to Leila and me. She and I lived with my mom" — I lift my hand — "don't ask about my dad because I don't even remember him — so, as you can imagine, Leila and I were very close. Especially because my mom had issues with drinking, and with not-great boyfriends, and it also turns out she was sick. Anyway, Leila was my big sister, and my best friend, and she disappeared fifteen years ago. She went to school — I saw her at lunch — and she never came home." I look out the window while I take a deep breath, because I'm not ready to face Dave yet.

"Of course I've thought about her all this time — but in a foggy way, if that makes any sense." I shake my head. "I realize it probably doesn't, but that's the best way I can describe it. Then, recently, Faye told me about this missing woman here in Oak Junction — Wren — and Maddy assigned me to write a story about her, and it's brought it all back. Sharp and real. And it turns out, not only do I not know what happened to my sister, I'm not over it at all. I know it was wrong to never tell you, but once I hadn't, I didn't know how to bring it up. And I wasn't worried about you somehow finding out because nobody wrote about her when she went missing, which is why I've been coming out here, and doing my best, so at least somebody will write about Wren." I take another shaky breath, and say, "Of course, there's more, which I'll explain later when we're with Xander and Faye, but that's the important part, and ... are you furious? Why are you stopping the car? What ...?"

We're on the shoulder now, in a spot that's about halfway to Faye's, but isn't familiar to me at all. No memories of Leila, or any of my siblings, or being on the school bus, or being chased by Jeb. Nothing.

Dave gets out of the driver's seat and walks around to my side of the car. He opens my door. Stepping out seems like the only logical thing to do.

He's so tall and I'm standing so close to him there's no chance of me seeing his expression. "Are you dropping me off here?" I ask. "Are you that angry? Or do you want me to leave you here? Because I'm not going to, even if you ask me ..."

"Paige."

"Yes?"

He opens his arms, and I step into them, and he hugs me, and rocks me, and says, "I'm so relieved. Everything makes sense now."

"Everything?" I mumble against his chest.

"No. Not everything. I doubt everything with you will ever make sense, but, oh my god, Paige, it's actually miraculous how normal you are considering everything you've been through."

"You think I'm normal?"

"Absolutely not," he says. "But I love you, so it doesn't matter."

Thirty

DAVE IS A HIT. Which is no surprise.

Xander's young kids love him because he stands chest-deep in Faye's swimming pool, hoisting them through the air in elaborate flips until I notice his lips are turning blue and order him out of the water.

Charlotte and Pen love him because he shows them how to make his famous nachos, then they get to eat them.

Rowan loves him because Dave has a beer and discusses Ultimate with him, and Macy's dogs follow him around and lean against his legs every time he stands still.

Macy sits next to me at dinner, and halfway through she leans over and whispers, "God, could he be any hotter?"

"I didn't think he was your type." Macy's the sibling I know least, but I know she's gay. At least, I've met her girlfriend, but maybe ...

"I didn't say I wanted him for me. In fact, I definitely don't — I want him for you. Take it from me — I know bloodlines, and you two will give me gorgeous nieces and nephews."

I choke, gasp, and make a squeaking noise at the same time and Dave, sitting on my other side, puts his hand on my back. "What? What did I miss?"

"You so don't want to know," I say.

"Actually, for a change, it would be nice to know things."

"Don't worry, I'll tell you later." Macy winks, and I make a mental note not to leave Dave alone with her.

I take the first dishwashing shift, and when Rowan bumps me out of the way, I find Dave standing in front of Faye's family photo wall. The photos are a mix of Faye, Brian, and their three kids, and various ones of us siblings. Xander with his family, Macy with her dogs, Rowan playing Ultimate. There aren't many of me, but there's a copy of the one Faye has on her desk at work and, beneath it, one of all six of us, much younger, standing in the same order, only with Leila there this time. I never noticed the parallels before.

I've spent a long time not noticing — or acknowledging — many things.

"So, that's her," Dave says.

I nod. "I have a more recent one, though." I pull up the scan of the photo from the microfilm OJJ story.

He studies it. "She's so young." He *gets* it.

"I know, right?" I swipe to show him the next photo in my gallery, which is the main one of Wren from the Facebook group.

"Whoa. No wonder this is hard on you. They're alike."

"Who's alike?" Charlotte has come into the room. I show her Leila's photo right after Wren's. She lets out a long breath. "They are." She turns to me. "It makes me so sad and she wasn't even my sister. I'm really sorry, Auntie Paige."

"It's OK, sweetie. It was a long time ago." I stop, rethink, and rephrase. "Well, obviously it's not OK, and it isn't really over, but your words help."

The pictures we're looking at give me an idea. "Hey, Charlotte, can you please look at these photos and tell me if you know anybody in them?"

She stares at my screen as I swipe through the stills from The Mule's surveillance footage. "That's Addison!" she says right away. She turns to Dave. "I ride her horse sometimes, and Addison let me compete on her last weekend, which is a huge deal because she buys green horses and trains them so she can sell them for a profit, and she's never let anyone compete any of her other project horses."

"So, she does it for a living?" Dave asks.

Charlotte shrugs. "That, and working at the tack shop. I don't know how much she makes, but her main aim is to get to the Olympics, so at least her jobs get her deals on her equipment, and let her work with high-end horses."

I was so surprised when Jessie told me Addison was much older than I thought — turns out I could have just asked my niece. *That's what happens when you assume ...* I scold myself.

I point at Jeb Dixon, suppressing a shiver. "What about the guy she's with — ever seen him?"

She shakes her head. "No." It doesn't mean he wasn't at Oak Copse on the day Wren went missing, but it makes it less likely.

Next, I show her the picture of Wren with the mystery guy. "Oh! That's Colin!"

Colin. Where have I heard that name before? "Nate's son?"

"Yup. He's around sometimes — he helps Nate build jumps and he runs the show-jump crew if he's here when there are horse trials on. He's funny."

"Was he here the weekend Wren disappeared?"

She grins. "Oh, yeah. Jocelyn got Rose to switch her from dressage scribe to jump crew because she thinks Colin's cute."

"So he would have been there all day?"

Charlotte nods. "Pen and I walked into the show-jump ring for our lunch break, to see Jocelyn, and Wren was there, too, talking to Colin. We told Jocelyn to forget Colin — you could tell he was head-over-heels for Wren. The show jumping started a few minutes before we had to be back out on the cross-country course, so Wren walked back with Pen and me. That was the division when she stopped answering her radio."

Right. All the things that didn't add up are starting to. Colin in town for the weekend. Colin head-over-heels for Wren. Wren entertaining a secret sexual partner in her apartment. And Nate, trying to protect the son he's just started building a relationship with, not wanting anyone to put two-and-two — or Wren-and-Colin — together. Offering a story about Wren with an unsavoury mystery man. Throwing the scent off his son.

Not counting on anyone reviewing the video footage.

Nate lied, and now I'm pretty sure I understand why he lied. And, if what Charlotte says is right, he didn't even need to. Colin was sitting next to Jocelyn in the middle of the show-jump ring when Wren disappeared, so he couldn't have taken her.

People are funny, though. They assume things, and they keep secrets, and they lie. I told myself to look for lies, but I should have told myself to look for lies with no explanation.

Pen sticks her head into the room. "Wanna swim?" she asks Charlotte.

As Charlotte leaves, Rowan comes in. "Tell me I heard wrong. Tell me you didn't go to Ed Cormier's place after both Xander and I told you not to."

"She did," Dave says at the exact moment as I say, "I didn't mean to," which earns me sideways looks from Rowan, Dave, and Xander, who's entered the room.

"How can you possibly argue you didn't mean to?" Xander asks.

I sigh. "Get Faye in here, too, why don't you? I only want to explain this once."

And I do. Explain, that is. How I didn't *mean* to go all the way onto Ed / Jeb's property. I didn't mean to explore the buildings. I definitely didn't mean for Jeb to catch me.

"It was just one step at a time, one photo, then another, then another, one foot after the other. Literally, once he was chasing me."

Faye leans forward. "Paige Turner, are you telling me some criminal was chasing you?" She turns to our brother. "And Xander Turner, why didn't you tell me she was *chased*?"

I reach out and lay my hand on her arm. "It's OK. I'm here now. It's over. I'm fine."

She shakes her head. "One minute I'm persuading you to write this story and the next you're trespassing in criminal lairs and nearly getting killed."

"I wasn't nearly killed." I don't tell her I was scared enough that it felt that way.

"Speaking of one photo after another ..." Xander asks.

"I can forward them to you. I have videos, too."

He nods. "Not that we can use them as evidence — since you're a civilian who was trespassing. However, my colleague just happened to see the boxes of medication when he was escorting the animal welfare officer, and noticed the labels say 'not for sale outside Alberta,' so we're going through all the items in the hut and your photos might be helpful to see if anything was removed before we got there." He pauses. "Even though you shouldn't have been there."

I rub my forehead. Pinch my temples. Then I look around the room at my four brothers and sisters, Dave, and two of Macy's dogs sprawled on the floor. "I know it was a bad idea. I know I put myself in danger. I know I was lucky. The thing is, though ..." I pause and give my head a tiny shake. "... I wondered if I'd find Wren somewhere on the property."

With that, they all shift in their seats. "Yeah," Macy says. "OK. Fair enough. I would have looked, too."

"I didn't want to find her. But I also didn't want to not find her if she was there. If that makes any sense."

Rowan exhales loudly. "It does. I don't approve, but I get it."

Faye nods. "You know we don't want to lose you in the process, though?"

I lay my hand over my heart. "I'm just going to write the story now. Promise."

***

The night noises sing us into the car.

I leave the passenger window rolled down to feel the caress of the late-summer air on my skin. When we emerge from the tree-lined section of the road, I tilt my head back and watch through the moon roof as the last rays of sun retreat and the stars pop in their wake.

After we told Faye we couldn't stay overnight, she packed us multiple containers of food. "At least take this with you." My stomach's full, my aches and pains are muted thanks to an extra-strength ibuprofen, and all the touchpoints where my family hugged me — where their hands gripped me, or their lips brushed my cheek — linger on my skin like tactile tattoos.

"You were amazing." My voice comes out lazy, languid, happy.

"It was fun. I like them all."

"That's not what I meant. Although you were a great guest, as well."

"What did you mean, then?"

"The way I dumped the Leila thing on you. The way you reacted. How you just went with it, even though it had to be a shock. And telling me how pretty she is, and how much we look alike, was icing on the cake."

Dave indicates and turns onto the highway heading back toward the city. "I have a confession to make."

"I know, I know. She's actually way prettier than me, and I don't look that much like her."

"Ha! Never. You're my favourite, but you two look a lot alike."

"You're on a roll today. Just gathering in the brownie points." I watch his fingers flex and release on the steering wheel. I've always liked his hands, but today I love them more.

Make sure those hands end up somewhere good tonight. That's what Macy would say. It's the first time I've heard Macy's voice instead of Leila's. I had fun with Macy today — with my sister who's still here.

I've been missing out. On so many things. I need to stop that.

"... Paige?"

"What, yes, sorry?"

"You just tailed off," Dave says.

"Mmm ... yes, daydreaming." I roll my shoulders back into the seat. "You were about to confess."

"I knew."

"You knew what ... *oh* ..."

Dave nods. "I knew about your sister."

"But, I never said. You never said ... *Maddy*."

"Yep."

"I can't believe she told you. I only told her a few days ago ... *no* ..."

He nods. "She's an editor who checks facts for a living. She can find out anything about anyone."

"I do know that," I say. "I just didn't expect she'd find out anything about me — how did she even know to go looking?"

"It was a while ago," he says. "When you were both in journalism school. Maddy did a project with somebody who lived close to Oak Junction — who went to your high school — something like that. They mentioned about a girl who'd gone missing and Maddy eventually put it all together."

"But she didn't ... you didn't ..."

Dave manoeuvres through the streets leading to the bar. "It felt like something you needed to bring up."

I sigh. "It's something I think everyone's been waiting for somebody else to bring up. I thought my brothers and sisters didn't want to talk about it, but I've sure been proven wrong about that these last few days. I guess I was waiting for them to take the lead, and they were waiting for me?"

He pulls into the parking spot behind the bar. "We're probably all guilty of that sometimes ... waiting for somebody else to take the lead."

Whoa. Something in his voice fills the car with a humming tension — fills my stomach with butterflies.

He turns to me, and as soon as he does, there's no question whether one of us will take the lead. We both lean in, closing the space between us.

Our lips touch and I want to simultaneously dive right in, kiss him hard, push my mouth against his — shortly to be followed by the rest of my body — while also waiting forever, holding this position, breathing his breath, and savouring his presence.

While I dither, he takes charge, giving me a kiss that makes me think of fireworks, sunsets, hot afternoons lying on a dock, and late nights sweating on a dance floor. It carries me from bliss to joy, before setting off a pop of happiness that bubbles all through my limbs and my core.

The only place he touches is my mouth, but I feel that kiss in the tips of my ears, in the curl of my toes, and the clench of my core.

A tiny giggle escapes me, and he stops. We're both breathing hard.

I want more. I want everything. I want all of him.

So take him! Macy's voice again. "Back seat or bedroom?" I ask.

Thirty-One

AT LUNCH ON THE first day of my story-writing marathon, Dave comes upstairs to find that I've pushed the kitchen table against the window and have littered it with my makeshift score sheet notebook, pens, books, my laptop, a coffee mug, a pint glass of water, and a can of Diet Coke.

As he stares, I apologize. "I'm so sorry. I know it's a huge mess. It's just until I power through this story, then I'll put it back."

He shakes his head. "That's not why I'm staring."

"Then, why?"

"Because we could have done this years ago."

I lift my eyebrows.

"Or, OK, not *this* ... but we could have gotten a desk, put it in the window, given you a place to work, if you'd just asked."

"You're thinking we wasted time," I say.

"I am, kind of."

"We didn't."

It's his turn to raise his eyebrows. "You say that with authority."

"I didn't tell you about Leila before, because I wasn't ready to. I didn't move the table here earlier because I wasn't taking my writing seriously enough. So, if we'd started something earlier, when I wasn't ready, I would have just screwed it up and we'd probably be over already, and you'd probably hate me."

"That's quite the extrapolation."

"Oh, that big word is quite exciting." I take his hand and tug him toward my bedroom. "It makes me think that right now I'm ready for a break from writing if you can take one too ..."

***

At dinner, Xander calls with an update. Dave and I squish into a big chair in the living room so we can both be in frame as he explains, "Everything at Jeb Dixon's place was stolen."

"Everything?" I ask.

"Well, everything in the quonset hut. We contacted the biggest tack supplier in the country — EquiEssentials — and they did an inventory check on their main warehouse and found all the equipment was from there, although they hadn't missed it until we asked." He shakes his head. "The shavings were from a producer just across the border in Quebec, and the medication was diverted from a shipment in Alberta."

I snap my fingers. "That's why the packaging was different."

"Different from what?" Xander asks.

"I found one of those sachets of Bute in Wren's apartment at Oak Copse. When I showed it to Rose, she said it's not the brand they use — she thought Wren must have brought it from her last job. But ..."

Xander clears his throat. "But maybe not."

"It's a connection, right? Wren's last job was outside the GTA, not in Alberta. That sachet must be from Jeb's stolen batch."

"Jeb's a criminal," Xander says. "There's no doubt about that. All the vehicles parked in the hut were stolen, and we think the hay was, too — from a farmer nearby who went to his loft one day and found it empty. However, we've searched the entire place and there's no sign of Wren, or of anything belonging to her."

"You were the one who said it couldn't be a coincidence that he's a bad guy who knows horses and Wren was in the horse business. Now she had a sachet of the medication he stole. She probably confronted him. He probably came after her to shut her up ..."

"He has an alibi for when she went missing."

"He, what?"

"He was delivering a horse he'd sold to somebody on the other side of the city. They confirm he arrived at 2:00 because the horse was a gift for their daughter, and her birthday party started at 2:00."

"Really?" I squeeze Dave's leg in frustration and he flinches.

"Ouch, tiger!"

"Well, now, there is good news," Xander says. "Or good news if you want Mr. Dixon to go to jail — maybe less good news for the horse purchasers."

"What is it?"

"He lied about the horse. Told them he was a registered quarter horse. Brought them papers and showed them the horse's tattoo. Everything was made up."

"Everything? Even the tattoo?"

Xander nods. "Not only did the registration number not sync up with anything registered with the American Quarter Horse registry, the tattoo doesn't even look right."

"That's terrible." Something about forcing a fake tattoo onto a horse feels a step too far to me. I shudder, which makes Dave hug me, which makes me feel a little better.

"It was the same with the rest of the horses. He had a binder full of histories for them, which was a total work of fiction. Of course, just finding those at his place doesn't mean much. He can say he was just doing it for fun. But by giving us his alibi, he introduced us to people who can testify that he perpetrated a fraud on them. So Mr. Dixon's going to be in some trouble."

We're still jammed in the chair, talking over Xander's call, when there are three sharp raps on the back door and Maddy walks in. "Hi, you two ..." She waggles her eyebrows at me as I struggle to get up, elbowing Dave a couple of times in the process.

"I was just coming by to give Paige some moral support writing her story, but it looks like she has lots of support."

"I'm just here to find out what she wants for dinner. Put your order in and I'll bring food for you, too." Dave gives his very best innocent smile and heads down to the pub.

As the door handle is clicking behind him, Maddy says, "I see things have changed with Dave."

I wave toward my work table, now holding two more Diet Coke cans. "I'm too busy writing this story to fixate on that."

"I hope you're enjoying it," Maddy says.

"I mostly am. I haven't hit too many snags."

"Not the writing ... the *Dave* ... but you knew what I meant."

I wink. "I'm enjoying it at night. Oh, and at lunch."

"Ah, the honeymoon phase. Long may it last. Now update me on the story ... after you update me on that hand." I've gotten used to its shades of yellow, purple, black, and blue, but I can see how they'd be a shock to Maddy. "I won't be getting a manicure anytime soon, but it actually doesn't hurt at all when I type. Thank goodness, because I've been doing a lot of typing — let me give you a walk-through ..."

After we review it together, Maddy says, "You've struck a balance. It's moving without being depressing. And you've brought both Wren and Leila to life for the reader."

"That's what they deserve," I say.

"To live their lives?" Maddy nods. "I agree."

"Anyway, there are obviously a lot of gaps to fill in, and I've tried not to commit to the ending yet. When you came in, Xander was giving us an update on their search of Jeb Dixon's place. They found a tonne of stolen goods, and faked horse tattoos, but so far nothing about Wren." I sigh. "I keep hoping I'll be able to have a triumphant conclusion to the story, but not yet."

"Honestly, Paige, I'm just glad that guy didn't conclude your story. I told you not to go all investigative journalist on me ..."

I hold up my hand. "Yes, you did already tell me that. And I hear you. But I was just telling Dave I finally feel ready."

"Ready for what?"

"Ready for so many things I wasn't ready for before."

"Which is great, Paige. Really. But don't take it too far. Now, tell me more about what the police found at Jeb's. I'm confused about these tattoos and horse passports ..."

***

It's been a good day. And it's going to be a good night. Since all I'm doing for the next couple of days is staying in and writing, I've made my hours fit Dave's. So I wrote until just a few minutes ago, and now I'm scrolling through my phone in search of mindless social media content to keep me awake until he comes up.

I intend to stick to mindless social media ... but I can't resist a quick side trip to the forum.

Bingo. New activity on the post on the "Out of the Country" thread. The one where I cheered RedRibbons for telling VersMarais to come back with proof of Wren being in Upstate New York.

She has.

She's posted a photo. It looks harmless enough. It's been taken in some kind of indoor market or vendor area with products on tables on either side of the frame. There are quite a few people in the picture, but the focus is on a slightly built woman with her back to the camera. There are pink streaks in the brown hair falling over her shoulders. She's wearing a fitted t-shirt, breeches, and paddock boots.

My entire body is on high alert. Stomach, jaw, and fingers clenched.

What is VersMarais pulling?

RedRibbons, bless her inquisitive little heart, wants to know the same thing.

RedRibbons: Sorry, not sure what this is? Am I missing something?

VersMarais: Wren, at the Rolling Hills vendor village.

RedRibbons: Are you sure? Because that could be a lot of people.

VersMarais: Except not that many people have Oak Copse fanny packs, and how many of those also have forest-green Elegant Equestrian breeches with jeweled back pocket detailing that were discontinued three years ago?

She's included a super close-up showing just the woman's waist and backside, which, indeed, has both the fanny pack and the fancy-back-pocketed breeches.

ChestnutMare: How do you know Wren had those breeches?

In response VersMarais has posted the picture I've seen on the Find Wren Sheedy Facebook page where Wren's wearing forest green breeches.

ChestnutMare: How do you know the photo's from Rolling Hills?

RedRibbons: Yeah, and how do you know it's new?

VersMarais is a whiz at cropping. She posts a close-up of a different part of the photo — this time showing a booth behind the person who might be Wren. On the table are hoodies and t-shirts saying **Rolling Hills — New York's Biggest Horse Show** with this year's date.

ChestnutMare: Were you there?

RedRibbons: Also, how do you know so much about those breeches? Like, how do you know they were discontinued three years ago?

There's a post labeled "VersMarais" that says "**post withdrawn by author**" and that's it.

I straighten in my chair and wonder if that really will be it. Now that VersMarais' little following is questioning her, will she stop posting?

I feel a surge of pride at the two other posters on the forum. When gossip is questioned, or pulled into the light of day, it loses its power.

I wish somebody had done that for my sister way back when. Fingers crossed that the story I'm writing now will go a small way toward repairing that wrong.

I think for another few seconds, then search **Rolling Hills Horse Show**. Sure enough, the show was last weekend. I don't blame the forum participants for their Upstate New York debate — I wouldn't call its location "Upstate New York" — more like borderline Quebec. I'm about to click out of the map when a name catches my eye. Ironwood. Where Addison competed with Auckland last weekend.

Just the thickness of my pinky finger from Rolling Hills in New York.

Next I search **Elegant Equestrian**. I select the "breeches" dropdown. I can't find any in forest green. So it's true they don't currently sell the pair in the photo.

I click the "Where to Buy" tab and select "Ontario." The list of tack shops means nothing to me, so I take a screenshot and forward it to Charlotte — Any of these tack shops mean anything to you?

After messaging Charlotte, I send Xander the link to the latest forum posts. Have you heard about this supposed Wren sighting? Do you give it any weight?

A message pings in from Maddy. Great work so far on the story. Can you send me what you've got so far? I'll start tackling the fact-checking. Also, we're going to need photos. The weather looks beautiful tomorrow, but the photographer's booked with other assignments. Any chance you can go out and take some? We can look over what you get and I can still send the photographer if needs be.

There's a telltale creak from the staircase that leads up from the pub. *Dave.* Finally.

I shoot Maddy a quick reply with my story file attached. You know I'm not a pro photographer, but I'll go tomorrow and see what I get. Entire file attached. Story is in there along with anything else I've collected. Go crazy.

Then I close my laptop.

Thirty-Two

It wasn't exactly an ulterior motive that made me agree to come out and take photos. It was more like killing two birds with one stone — I want to get into Wren's apartment again and see if those famous green breeches are there. Because if they are, then Wren wasn't wearing them somewhere in New York on the weekend.

Unless she has two pairs.

I sigh. My head is full of information — of possibilities, and probabilities, of facts, opinions, and rumours. I've tried to harness them, with my scribbles on the score sheets, but those have just become messy and unwieldy, filling page after page. Not really helping.

If I'd asked Faye, she probably could have created a spreadsheet complete with a formula that would magically spit out the details of exactly what happened to Wren and who was involved.

Maybe I should still ask her to do that. But for now, I'm here, where Wren lived, and the breeches might be in the apartment, and they might not. And if they are ... or aren't ... that might prove something, or it might not.

Still, I want to see for myself. I may be feeling around in the dark, but I have to trust that eventually I'll put my hand on something that I'll recognize, and it will be important.

It was something that was drummed into us in journalism school — do interviews in person whenever possible because you never know what you're going to see, hear, smell, or touch that will make your story.

It's why Maddy kept sending me out, waiting for me to use my senses and write better stories.

At least that's one mission accomplished — or, at least, a work in progress. And, in the meantime, on this story, I'm still seeking a miraculous conclusion, so I'll keep looking.

Except there's nobody around to let me into Wren's apartment.

I've never been here when it's so quiet. Strike that: now and then tractor engine noise drifts across to my ears, but right here, in the stable area, my car is the only one in the parking area, there's nobody riding, and when I knock on the farmhouse door, there's no answer.

This is important. This is important, and Rose has already shown me through Wren's apartment, so I decide I can at least try the door and see if it's open. If it's open, I'll have to decide whether it's OK to go in.

No decision to make — it's not open.

Great.

I turn around at the top of the landing, catching sight of Shine and Pudding grazing together in the nearby paddock. I notice a car parked by the side of the barn — I don't recognize it, but since it's not in the public parking area, maybe it belongs to Rose. Maybe she's around somewhere after all, and she can let me into the apartment.

I'm just about to descend the staircase when my phone pings. It's Charlotte answering the question I sent her last night asking if any of the tack shops mean anything to her.

> Not really, unless you count that I can use Addison's staff dis-
> count at Super Saddlery, so I'd probably shop at that one first :)

Addison ... I don't have time to think about that before another message pops up:

> Hey Paige, It's Jessie, from The Mule. The weirdest thing just happened. My nephew kayaks for Canada. He just got back from an international competition and he was telling me he hopes he'll go to Maraisville — it's a small village an hour away from the main site, where quite a few of next year's summer Olympic events are being held. There's probably no connection, but I remembered you were asking about Marais, so I thought I'd mention it just in case.

I sink to the top step and reread the message. Maraisville. The Olympics. Oh, my goodness.

Just in case.

Be curious. Go out and talk to people. Ask everybody every question you can think of, just in case.

Because sometimes it pays off. Sometimes it makes everything clear.

Or, at least, parts the fog.

I'm still working through it, still getting there, but the mist in my brain is definitely swirling. Revealing clear patches. Helping me think things through.

I'd really like to find Rose and get into Wren's apartment.

First, though, I rifle through my bag, finding a pen and the second-last score sheet, which is already half-filled with scribbles. *Maraisville*, I write. *Olympics*. Then I type into the search bar on my phone **Equestrian event venue next summer Olympics.**

The answer fills my screen. **Maraisville.**

I ask it to translate "VersMarais." No hesitation — **Towards Marais.**

I underline "Maraisville" and "Olympics" in my notes and put a big star beside them. Then I descend the stairs.

Might as well take another look through the windows of Wren's car just in case I missed seeing a pair of forest-green breeches sitting on the back seat the last time I looked. After all, I wasn't looking for them then.

Nothing. But I didn't check the trunk. Maybe it's open. I step around to the back to try the hatch, and my foot catches on something. After determining the hatch is locked, I crouch down, reach under the car, and close my hands on a camp chair.

I remember Charlotte doing the same thing with my chair when she carried it back for me. I remember in her reenactment she said she picked up Wren's abandoned chair.

Then she scooted off into the woods and I thought she was lost. In my panic, I forgot to ask the follow-up question — what happened to Wren's chair?

I guess I know now.

Then I remember something else — everybody saying, just like me, Wren used paper score sheets. I wonder if, just like me, she kept them in the pocket of her chair?

I plunge my hand into the deep side pocket and … sure enough … come out grasping a sheaf of paper.

Oh, wow. It feels strange to be holding the very last things that Wren held before she vanished. Speaking of which … it's probably too much to expect that her phone is in the pocket as well.

A deep root-around confirms that, yes, it was too much to expect.

Still, I have the sheets.

I lower my bum onto the grass and leaf through them.

Her check marks are backward. Or, at least, backward to me. I think that means she's left-handed. Hours and hours spent learning about her, a day spent sitting in her spot on the cross-country course, a couple of thousand words written about her, and I didn't know Wren was left-handed until now.

The realization feels strangely intimate. It gives me a pang.

Other than the left-handed check marks, Wren's score sheets look very much like mine. Like the front of mine, anyway. Page after page with straight rows of checks in the "clear" column.

Until there's one that isn't.

It's in the Preliminary division which, as Charlotte mentioned, was ranked as an international one-star event which riders could count toward their MERs (I've learned so much). There were only fourteen riders in the division that day, and thirteen went clear over the big tree trunk.

Rider twenty-six didn't.

Wren's put a big X in the box that says "Refusal, run-out, or circle" and in the "Remarks" box, noted, *Cut corner, bad approach*. None of that is what makes me gasp. The part of the comment that makes the breath whistle out of me is the second part of the explanation, *Auckland slammed on the brakes. Addison circled away, re-approached, over on second try.*

Auckland. Addison. Oh my goodness.

Thirty-Three

BECAUSE, OF COURSE, TWO different people — or was it three? Charlotte, Rose, and Nate, I think — told me it was essential that Addison went clear that day. That it was posting a clear on the cross-country that secured her MER and let her move up a level. Which is what let her qualify for Ironwood where she competed at the Intermediate level last weekend.

Except, she didn't go clear that day.

I lock the sheets in my glove compartment, take out my camera, then lock the car. I beep it twice to make sure. Those score sheets feel like a burning beacon that prove something — I just have to figure out exactly what. And for that, I need to walk.

Slowly. My brain has a lot of churning to do.

What questions have I not asked? I'm writing a story about a woman who didn't cut corners, about not taking things at face value — *where have I fallen down?*

I thought Addison was just one of the riders — more motivated, sure — but I lumped her in with Charlotte, and Pen, and Justine, and Rose's other "girls."

That was a big mistake. When Faye and I worked through who could have been responsible for Wren's disappearance, we discounted the teenage riders. I discounted Addison because of my assumptions about her.

Not only did I get her age wrong, which means I didn't realize she could drive and probably has her own car, I also didn't fully understand what riding means to her. Unlike Charlotte, who rides as a fulfilling extra-curricular activity which will probably go on the back burner when she moves on to university, for Addison riding is the thing she's moved onto. It's her purpose, it's how she makes her living. Faye told me her mother mortgaged her house to supplement Addison's career, for goodness' sake — that takes on a whole new level of meaning now that I know the true role of horses in Addison's life.

Right. So I missed all that, but I know it now. So how do I put it together with the other stuff I know?

I pause, lean on the fence next to me and snap a couple of photos of the two horses grazing there to get a feel for the light. Also, might as well give Maddy a bunch of options for background photos.

Going back to the score sheets, I now realize that it's more important than I ever thought for Addison to move up a level in eventing. A refusal at Wren's jump would have derailed that. A single refusal.

How upset would that have made Addison?

Not at all, if everybody thought she went clear — which they did.

Why? How?

Because it must have been entered in the app as clear. Why would Wren do that? Why would she write out, in detail, how Auckland refused the jump, then mark Addison clear on her phone?

I'm reminded of the snippet of conversation I heard at the duck race, where one competitor told the other the only way he could win was to cheat and get away with it.

What if that's exactly what Addison decided to do? To cheat and to get away with it by changing Wren's entry on the app?

I know Addison was at the hut during the turmoil after Nate went to check on Wren and found her missing. I know that because Rose sent her out to cover for Wren.

I also know Addison knew the scoring software intimately. Faye told me she was a technology whiz.

How hard would it have been for Addison to come in through the back of the hut, change her refusal to a clear in the software, then be there, ready to help, when Rose needed to send her out as a replacement?

Not hard. Especially because nobody would expect it. In the hive of activity around the horse trials, nobody has time to worry about other people's jobs — Rose reminded us of that at our volunteer pep talk.

That would also explain away the radio evidence.

Because Wren would have marked the refusal in the app, and on the score sheets, and she would have radioed it in. It would have been one of about two-thousand radio calls that day. Even if somebody had noted it, known Addison was number twenty-six, and thought *Oh, she had a refusal* — if she, herself, then said she went clear, and if the software said she went clear, they would have shrugged and figured they got it wrong.

In fact, Charlotte did say that — I just didn't realize it at the time. She said she was worried Addison had a refusal, but when she found out she went clear, she put it down to distraction.

Oh my goodness.

So far, this has all been theoretical thinking. *What could have happened. What isn't impossible.*

But I'm starting to believe Addison did it — she changed her score to a clear. And she would have gotten away with it ... except for Wren's paper sheets.

The sheets that Kimberly told me aren't required, but if they exist would be definitive in case of a dispute.

The sheets that lots of people knew Wren used — it was a running joke I heard several times when I used them.

So, to be sure of her refusal being erased, Addison would have to get Wren's sheets.

I imagine her walking out across the field just the way I am now, heading for Wren's post to get those sheets.

But that's where the story breaks down, because there are actually *four* sources of information about each rider's attempt at each jump: the score sheets, the app, the radio ... *and the jump judge.*

Do I remember every single rider who went through my station when I jump judged? No ... but I remember more of the preliminary-level riders, because they jumped the big trunk, and there were fewer of them. I remember that they all went over clear, but if one of them hadn't, I think I would have remembered it.

In Wren's case, she knew Addison and Auckland. Like everyone at Oak Copse, she would have known they needed a clear to achieve their MER. And, based on what everyone's told me about her, she would have noted their refusal anyway, and even if Addison asked her to, she wouldn't have lied about it.

Which means ...

Before I can go there, my phone pings, offering my thoughts a welcome break. It's a message from Maddy:

> I've been fact-checking your story. You have a line saying, "Competitors came from as far away as California, with one horse imported from New Zealand." After you explained about horse tattoos and passports, I looked up Auckland's — it says he's never traveled outside Ontario. While you're at Oak Copse, you might want to clarify.

I stand still for a minute. I hear the tractor engine again. I watch a fox slink across the edge of the field. Two lies. Auckland isn't from Auckland, and he didn't jump clear.

Unlike Nate's lies about his son, I can't think of any innocent way to explain Addison's lies away.

I resume walking, entering the cross-country course where Nate and I scoured the footing for groundhog holes. The tractor noise recedes, replaced by insects and birdsong.

Just like the day I jump judged. Probably just like the day Wren did.

I automatically look for divots and rocks on the path while still scanning for anything that's out of place in the trees on either side. I don't haul my thoughts back to the subject of Addison — I let my subconscious work away.

Coming up to Wren's station — my station — I purposely approach on a tight line, cutting the corner. The tree trunk jump comes into view, but at an awkward angle. I can see how it could make even a brave horse stop — just like Wren wrote that it did. I snap a photo.

As I step closer and closer to the big jump, taking photos as I advance, I'm vaguely aware the insect and bird song has stopped — probably because of my intrusion.

I decide to climb up on the jump and take a photo from that viewpoint. I may not be a professional photographer, but that angle should be a good one.

I'm stopped mid-climb by something closing around my ankle. Before I can twist to see what it is, a yank thuds me onto my back on the ground, my camera rolling out under the jump.

Addison's standing above me. With a shovel.

Before I can say anything, she slashes it toward me.

"You were on Jeb's security footage." She states it flatly. Like a simple explanation.

I roll under the overhang of the trunk, feeling the camera press against my back, and pull my hands in just in time to keep them from being sliced off by the down-chopping shovel blade.

"He caught you on camera at the quonset hut. He told me somebody tried to rob us, but when I saw the footage, I told him it wasn't a robbery." As she speaks, she's lifting the shovel for another stab.

This time I don't feel any of the frozen indecisiveness I felt at the ferry terminal about running for Jeb's truck. This time it's clear I have to move.

Also, I'm really mad.

I thrust my legs out and connect with Addison's. She falls sideways, dropping the shovel, and I scramble up. "Yeah? Well, I saw you two together on The Mule security footage and the police know about it."

Addison reaches for the shovel. "So what? I was at a bar at the same time as somebody else." She jumps up and thrusts the shovel at me, but I step sideways so the shovel hits the jump.

"And you're VersMarais. You were sending horse buyers to Jeb for what? A kickback?"

"It's called a commission." While she's answering she's not actively trying to kill me, so I keep talking.

"You were in the States at the same time as the photograph of 'Wren' was taken, except it wasn't Wren at all. It was you, wearing Wren's breeches, which you either stole, or sourced through your job at the tack shop. Did you bully your mother into taking that picture for you as well? Did she have to try three times to get it right for you?"

Addison lifts the shovel high over her head. "You need to shut up." As she scythes it down, I grab the shaft using my damaged right hand. Obviously, it's not quite healed — the pain makes me wince, but I'd be in more pain if I let her slice through my skull.

"You need to stop making things up so you can get ahead," I spit back at her.

She growls, "Aarrgghh!" Now we each have a firm hold on the shovel — tugging it back and forth. Addison trips over a root and loses her grip and I launch it into the trees, yelling, "Ha!"

My triumph is fleeting because by the time I turn back, she's wielding a knife — the very definition of "out of the frying pan, into the fire."

"You're nuts!" I leave my camera, drop my bag, and run.

"I'm determined!" Based on how close her voice is, I have about two strides on her. There's no way I'm looking back to double-check.

I keep going, one foot in front of the other, but my hand is hurting all over again, and the sore muscles and cuts I got when Jeb chased me the other day are twinging. I thought adrenaline was supposed to make me impervious to pain, but obviously not.

Also, based on Addison's grunts as she follows me, I'd say she has her fair share of adrenaline.

I remember how the path splits before Charlotte and Pen's jump, and I hurl myself down the left fork, my feet pounding the ground, seeing the jump right in front of me with the bright, open hayfield on the other side. I count down *three-two-one* strides and leap over the jump, stumbling but not falling, and immediately fixing the tractor in my sights and belting toward it, yelling "Stop!" as I wave my arms.

Nate stops the tractor, sticks his head out the door, and looks confused. I turn to see Addison isn't following me. Rather, she's a heap on the ground at the landing of the jump.

While part of me thinks, *Do* not *go back there*, she looks … not right. Plus, Nate's following me.

He catches up to me and the two of us arrive at the same time to find Addison — and her knife — on the ground, with a huge gash pumping bright red blood out of her arm in sharp contrast to her very white face.

"What on earth …?" Nate starts.

"Tourniquet," I say. "What can we use?"

"There's binder twine in the tractor." He's already turning back toward it.

"Wait!" I pick up the knife and hand it to him. "Take this with you. Put it somewhere safe."

Addison's eyes meet mine. "I don't give up."

I look back at her. Part of me is tempted to prove her wrong. For me to force her to give up by not tying the tourniquet as tightly as I should.

I guess I fall somewhere between Addison and Wren, though — I don't make my own rules, but I also don't think you always have to stick to every rule.

Which is why, as I rip the sleeve off my t-shirt to wrap around the cut, I give a sharp press of my thumb into the cut. "That's for dragging my sister into your dirty forum rumour-spreading."

"I overheard some information, then researched it. Maybe I'm a better journalist than you." She holds my eye contact, which is good, because when I add my other thumb to her cut and put my body weight into the pressure, I get to witness the pain that hits her face.

Addison curses as Nate returns. "Putting pressure on it?"

"Exactly," I nod. "Now you can add the twine on top."

"Has she hit an artery?" he asks.

"I have no idea."

"Why was she running around with a knife?"

"That I do know, but I think we should focus on getting her back to the stable."

Together, we manoeuvre her into the tractor cabin. She's gone silent. I'm not sure whether that's from blood loss or the general realization that it might be better not to say anything.

"She can't get at the knife, can she?"

Nate raises his eyebrows. "She's barely conscious."

"She's determined," I say, grimly. "Better safe than sorry."

"It's in the glove compartment, which is on my side of the cabin."

I nod. "I'll call the paramedics while you drive her back. Hopefully, they'll get to the stable yard around the same time you do."

***

Nate, Rose, and I stand in a row and watch the ambulance bump down the driveway. It's breaking Nate's twenty-kilometre-an-hour speed limit, but not by much. "I always leave a few potholes on purpose to slow people down," he says. "Now I feel a little guilty about it."

"Don't," I shake my head. "There's only one person who should feel guilty, and she's in the ambulance."

"Yeah," Nate turns to me. "You said you'd explain once we got her taken care of."

"That'll come," I say. "But first I'm going to need your help. I figured out where Wren is."

Thirty-Four

At first I thought I'd get Nate to use the tractor to move the tree trunk, but now, looking at it in the late afternoon sun, that seems wrong.

"Are you up for a spot of digging?" I ask.

"Are you sure about this?"

I sigh. "Pretty sure."

"In that case, of course."

I retrieve the shovel I tossed into the bushes earlier. Nate lifts a second one from the cargo bed of the golf cart we bumped out in.

Then I take him to the far side of the jump. The side nobody looks at, or pays attention to. The side that gets jumped clean over. I look down at it. I replay Charlotte stomping down churned-up footing on the take-off side of this jump on the day of the horse trials, saying, "If we compact this down, the weeds and grass will grow in by the next trials."

There are weeds and grass growing here now. It's been quite a few weeks since Wren disappeared.

I hesitate. I don't want to dig, but I don't want not to.

"I don't think it will be deep," I tell Nate. "So maybe just go gently."

"You really think she's buried here?"

"Tell me this. If this area had been raked over and tamped down at the end of the horse trials when Wren went missing, would you have noticed?"

His answer is immediate. "Not until we were preparing for the next horse trials. First, since this jump is permanent, I would have had no reason to come near it in the days after the trials. Second, when I'm going around the property, I only ever approach this jump from the other side. Third, even if I did notice something, there are spots all over the course that get churned up and smoothed over in the course of a horse trial."

"So here's what I think, and if you think it's ridiculous, we won't dig — we'll wait for Xander to arrive and see what he says. But if it sounds like it could be true — well, then I don't want her left out here alone for any longer than she needs to be."

He directs us both a step sideways to get the low-slanting rays of the late-day sun out of our eyes, then says, "I'm listening."

"Right. Stop me if I say anything wrong." I take a deep breath, trying to figure out where to start. Wanting to make sure I say everything without going off-topic. "That was a big day for Addison. She needed to complete the trials with a clear cross-country to achieve her MER and move up a level."

Nate nods.

"Not only was Addison determined, she also had big financial motivation. She makes her living training and re-selling horses she buys, and her mother has taken out a mortgage on their home to support her."

"Really?"

I nod. "Really. Her mother told Faye."

"Continue," Nate says.

"Addison goes on course, has a bad approach to jump six, gets a refusal, makes it over and continues on her way. It all happens quickly. Wren radios it in, marks it in the app, and makes a more detailed entry on her paper score sheets, then goes on to score the next competitor."

Another nod from Nate.

"Addison can't just move on like Wren does. Everything she's been working for — her careful timeline — is scuppered if she doesn't move up that day. She decides the only thing to do is to record a clear ..."

"But ..."

I hold up my hand to stop him. "First she has to act like she got a clear. If anybody asks how her round went, say, 'Amazing — not a single problem.' That way, even if somebody heard Wren radio the refusal in, they'll think they heard wrong. After all, riders don't lie about stuff like that, do they?"

"Not normally."

Not normal ones, I think. "Next is to change the score in the software. That's incredibly easy. Nobody questions Addison being in the hut and everybody knows she's a whiz with the software — she often helps fix glitches and run reports."

"OK. True. But ..."

"But — you're right — Wren always uses paper score sheets. Maybe Wren already knows that, or maybe somebody mentions it while she's in the hut. Steps one and two were easy, but as soon as Wren hands in that score sheet with the refusal on it, Addison's sunk. She decides to talk to Wren."

"To *talk* to her." Nate pokes the ground with his shovel.

"I'm giving her the benefit of the doubt. Addison heads out to the jump where she knows Wren's stationed. She knows all the little shortcut trails, so can get there quickly and nobody would ever question her being anywhere on the property. Once there, she explains the situation to Wren. Wren understands ... but she won't change the score."

"Right." Nate nods. "Wren never would."

"So Addison kills her."

"Whoa ..."

"Too fast? I know. I'm sorry. Lots of things could have happened, but for the sake of moving forward, let's say, for some reason, Addison had picked up one of these shovels you have around. Or, maybe, Wren had used one earlier, and it was still here. Or maybe it wasn't a shovel — maybe they were fighting and Wren hit her head." I think of the irate competitor I heard over the radio. Imagine Addison fueled by that same anger.

"Addison *was* chasing you with a knife," Nate says.

"Yes. Good point. Maybe she got knifey with Wren. I suspect we'll find out when ..." I look at the ground by the jump. "Also, there's another thing."

"What you've already told me is a lot."

"Agreed. However, I think Wren also knew that Addison was giving Auckland Bute."

Nate doesn't even hesitate. "She wasn't." I don't contradict him as he continues. "She couldn't. Auckland reacts strongly to bug bites. We keep him on a low-level dose of Banamine during bug season to avoid swelling when he gets bitten. He can't compete with Bute and Banamine in his system ... *oh* ..."

"Oh." I nod. "Wren had a sachet of Bute in her medicine cabinet. Rose saw it, and it's not the brand you use here. I found an identical sachet in Addison's tack locker when Charlotte asked me to get some tape out for her."

"So, you're thinking ..."

"I'm thinking Wren knew two reasons Addison wouldn't get her MER and move up a level. One was the refusal at this jump. The second was Auckland having both Bute and Banamine in his system. Do you do drug tests here?"

"No. Not routinely. Not unless ..."

"Not unless somebody says you should?"

"Wow." Nate shakes his head. "It's not that I'm saying it couldn't have happened, but what about the body? If this happened, I was here ten minutes or less, afterwards."

"Where did you look?" I ask.

"Well ... where she was sitting. I mean, it was obvious her chair was empty, but still I went over and looked around it." He gives a little snort-laugh. "Silly, really. Like she'd be hiding under it, or something. And I had to keep listening to the radio, because I was supposed to be helping somebody start their truck — and they were blocking the exit — and Rose was trying to figure out what to do about Wren's jump."

"So, you didn't walk across from the chair — for example, to this spot right here, beside the jump, where the bushes are really thick, and look for a body?"

"Of course not! I wasn't thinking of looking for a body."

I nod. "I suspect that's where it was."

"But after — we all walked the course. People brought dogs."

"Addison was the one Rose sent to cover this jump. Or ..." I pause. "Did Addison volunteer? If she dragged Wren into the bushes, then cut through the shortest trails, she'd be at the hut before you even got here to check up on Wren. Then she could put her hand up and say, 'I'll take over,' and not only would it seem like she had an alibi, because she was in the hut when you found out Wren was gone, but she had a perfect excuse for being back out where the body was."

"But the event was still running. She couldn't very well dig a grave between riders."

"No, but when Charlotte and Pen came through on their way back to the stables, they didn't see her. So, what if she just waited until everybody went in to clean up, and for the barbecue, and she dug a hole then? Would anybody notice?"

He rubs his temples. "I doubt it. Once the cross-country's over the course empties. There's lots to do around the rings and the stables, and at the barbecue, and nobody keeps track of who's where at that point."

"I know it sounds far-fetched, Nate, but I think that's what happened. There's more, too. Like Auckland isn't from Auckland at all. And I think I can prove Addison was the one posting all the rumours about Wren on the forum. I can also prove she was involved with Jeb Dixon."

"You asked me about him before."

I nod. "Xander's been watching him, and the police have charged him with theft of horse equipment, medication, and feed. He has a long history of ripping people off when he sells them horses — Addison has been recommending him as a horse dealer, and I'm pretty sure he gave her a kickback. Also, possibly, found her horses. I won't be surprised if we find out Auckland and Paris came through Jeb Dixon."

"Enough," Nate says.

"I know it's hard to hear these things about somebody you know ..."

"No, I mean enough information. I believe you enough to dig. Just ... do you think we should wait until the police get here?"

The tree trunk is casting a long shadow across the grass, as are Nate and I as we stand with our shovels. "If she's here, I don't want to leave her here overnight."

Nate nods. "OK. Carefully, then."

I'm right. She's not buried deeply. She wouldn't be, though. It's a lot of digging for one person — even a person as determined as Addison.

It's Nate who uncovers, not something horrible, like I was afraid we would, but a phone with a distinctive case that glitters even through the dirt that coats it. "That's her phone." He chokes and turns away.

I'm sorry for Nate that he found her, but I'm glad for Wren that it was somebody who knew her, and who cares. I sink to the grass and flatten my palm on the ground.

"I'm so sorry," I whisper.

I mean her, and more than her.

I mean Nate, and Rose, and all the people who are going to miss her, including my own sister and niece. And I mean Leila, and me, and my brother, Xander, who's on his way now — I can hear the rumble of the golf cart driven by Rose, who was waiting for him at the house.

I take one more look at the sparkly case in the earth in the last few seconds when it's just Nate, and Wren, and me, then I stand to meet the cart, to explain my reasoning, to tell what I think is Wren's story.

Thirty-Five

THE DAYS AND WEEKS that follow are a whirlwind.

There's a funeral for Wren with a barbecue at Oak Copse afterward — the barbecue Wren didn't get to attend the day she died. The people who cared about Wren are there, including Nate's son Colin. When I find a few minutes to talk to him, he says, "We kept our relationship a secret, and now I'm not even sure why. I miss her."

It's one of those late-summer evenings where the cool air presses in early and the blue of the sky is deep and crisp. People take turns getting up on Rose's porch to say a few words about Wren and how she affected them. The final speaker is Rose, who announces that Shine will always have a home at Oak Copse — "Into retirement and beyond."

It's a sad day, but these poignant moments give it depth.

Dave comes to the funeral, and just having him standing beside me makes everything better.

These days I often invite him when I go to Oak Junction, and he always comes. He's getting to know my brothers and sisters, in some ways better than I know them. I listen to them tell him things I didn't know about, like Faye saying she always wanted to learn to mix cocktails, or Xander saying he worked in a pub in Australia for six months and nearly stayed.

I learn things about Dave, too. At the dinner Faye organizes to celebrate the publication of my story, I hear him talking to Rowan's wife, Sophie, about running the pub. Sophie, a small business accountant, nods in understanding as he explains how hard the pandemic hit his business and how difficult it's been since, with the ballooning costs of food, utilities, and wages. "It's so tough. I love what I do, but I don't see any way it's sustainable to keep doing it where I'm doing it with the property taxes as high as they are."

I'm hit with a rush of guilt at my blindness. I had no idea. But I should have. I've been working on asking questions, finding answers, being curious, and digging out stories, and I haven't done it on my own doorstep.

Also, why didn't Dave tell me? Does he not want me to know? Or does he just think I don't care? I think about that as I drive home from a meeting at the Oak Junction police station where Xander and his colleagues wanted information from me, but I spent most of my time asking about the status of the murder (Wren) and attempted murder (me) charges against Addison, along with whether they believed Jeb Dixon knew Addison killed Wren (leaning toward no, but still investigating).

A bold, bright **For Sale** sign attached to the porch of the OJJ building catches my eye. Just like that, the same way the pieces came together in my head to tell me Addison had killed Wren, all the opinions, thoughts, and ideas I've had about community journalism come together and I know what I have to do.

I pull into the café parking lot and dial Maddy's number while I stare at the sign across the street. She answers, "Hey, what's up?"

"What would you say if I was thinking of reopening the Oak Junction Journal?"

"I'd say, do you need an editor?"

"Really? You don't think it's a crazy idea?"

"Of course it is. But you're already in journalism, so the 'sensible' job ship has sailed. Also, crazy can be good."

"I'm going to think about it."

"Keep me posted."

Marge has come out to hand a white takeout box to somebody waiting in the parking lot and I catch her eye as I end the call. She steps to my car. "Did I see you staring at my building?"

"Your building? You own it?"

"Not for much longer."

"Can we talk?"

Thirty-Six

Marge leads us up the wooden stairs.

"It has a porch." Dave turns to look out toward the road and I follow suit. We're at the heart of the junction. The late-summer foliage is so thick it nearly blocks out the view to the low strip mall to the right. "There's a mini-grocery, pharmacy, and butcher's over there," I tell him.

Straight across the road is the café, where we left our car and where we've just walked from with Marge.

Turning left, the view is of the long, straight, tree-lined highway, stretching off toward the bungalow where I grew up and, much farther away, the city and our lives there.

"It's so green," he says.

He's right. This time of year everything's growing in Oak Junction. The trees are incredibly thick, even here, at what's supposed to be the commercial heart of the community.

"I apologize in advance — it will be dusty as all heck in here," Marge is saying as she pushes the door open. "And the newspaper people didn't clear out properly."

I suppose it's dusty, but the dust sits on wooden floors and deep trim, and floats through the sunshine that floods in through the big windows.

"Bones …" Dave whispers. He's right. The bones are there.

"Now." Marge's voice is muffled — she's already disappeared through a door toward the back of the building. "The kitchen is old, but the water runs, and the electricity is hooked up."

All I can see when I enter the square room is the sink with a view out the window and into the sun-dappled shade of the green trees growing to within a few feet of the building. I tap the sink. "I have what I need." I look at Dave. "This would be your call."

"I can see it," he says.

For a flash, so can I. I see the old wooden floors the same. I see the high tin-stamped ceiling unchanged — although with the addition of a vintage-style ceiling fan.

I see stainless steel — on the appliances and the work surfaces — offsetting the rustic trim around the doors and windows.

I see Dave prepping vegetables on an island that would fit perfectly in the centre of the room. I see me at a much deeper sink, with the dishwashing faucet of my dreams.

I see this place churning out late lunches and evening meals, so people have somewhere to eat after Marge closes the café mid-afternoon and goes home to relax. Finally.

Again Marge goes ahead, through the doorway at the back of this room and down a few stairs into the room I first stepped into the last time I was here. During my "unauthorized" visit.

Dave takes in the cast-iron wood cookstove sitting on the brick floor, the rough-and-ready sink and shelves, and the screened windows offering three sides of ventilation.

"A summer kitchen." Dave's whispered words are the sounds of him falling in love with this place.

I'm falling too — I must be — it's the best explanation for my giddiness.

As we follow Marge back through the wide-open area that was the offices of the Oak Junction Journal, Dave nudges a stack of decade-old newspapers. "Page Turners."

I nod. "Just a different kind of pages."

"Perfect." It's another one of his whispered words.

The stairs creak under Marge's steps, and ours as we follow her to the second floor. Up here is a large living space that runs front to back and takes about half the width of the building. Along the rear wall are cabinets, with a sink and small stove interrupting the stretch of counter. "Kitchenette," Marge says.

Sweet, I think.

"All we need," Dave whispers.

There are two doors leading out of this space. The one at the front is open, revealing a bathroom with a proper bathtub. "I'm afraid it's dated," Marge says.

"Vintage." Now I'm the one whispering.

Marge opens the door into the final room at the back. When I was in here before, I was stressed and in pain, and it was getting dark. Now I take in a bright space with windows on the side wall and the one out to the back, leading onto the fire escape.

During this happier visit, I have a vision of this room with breeze-blown curtains at the windows, area rugs softening the wide-planked floors, and a big bed, right in the middle. A bed with me in it. A bed with Dave in it.

"There's just the one bedroom." Marge wrinkles her nose. "I'm not sure whether that would be a problem."

"Oh," I say. "We have a two-bedroom now, but I think we've outgrown it."

Marge furrows her brow, while Dave laughs. "I think you're right. It's time for us to upgrade to a one-bedroom."

"You two are silly, but you're cute." Marge grins. "Make me an offer, and I'll accept it."

"I'm pretty sure that's not how negotiation works," I say.

"I'm pretty sure I want you to buy this building," she answers.

"I'm pretty sure we can make a deal," Dave says.

***

Even though Marge has locked the door and gone back to the café, Dave and I linger on the porch. There's nothing like the laziness of late summer afternoons, when cicadas buzz and crickets chirp, and the air is still warm but with the promising hint of a temperature drop later in the evening.

Good sleeping weather.

I could live here.

It's probably not surprising, or a stretch, for me to think so. After all, this place is in my bones — a part of it has always held me, even when I resisted.

Dave, though. He's a city boy. And even if he's finding the central location of the pub difficult to maintain, does that mean he wants to move this far out? Surrounded by farmers rather than farmer's markets?

It would be a huge change.

While I'm trying to muster the courage to do that thing I've been working on — to just say the first sentence and ask Dave how he feels — a car slows and turns into the drive, gravel crunching under its tires.

A man hops out and comes over to the porch, looking up at us. "I'm so glad to see you."

I don't recognize him, but this is Oak Junction. Chances are he knows somebody I know, so I nod and say, "Great. Glad you found us."

"Yeah. I was searching online just last night, but I couldn't find anything. Is your site down?" I can't figure out what he's talking about, but it doesn't matter because he doesn't wait for an answer. "Anyway, I saw you here, so I just pulled in to ask. We're having an estate auction and I want to buy an ad. How can I do that?"

Fortunately, customer-service-guru Dave is several steps ahead of me. "Do you have it written out now?"

"No. We're still finalizing the details."

"That's fine." Dave says, "Just email 'ads@oakjunctionjournal' and we'll get it in."

I open my mouth to protest, but the man's already talking. "Great. And you'll invoice me?"

"Actually, today is Free Classified Tuesday. Everybody who brings in a classified ad on Tuesday gets it free. Even if you don't send the text today, we'll honour that."

"Do I need a code or something? You must get a lot of ads. How will you remember mine was a Tuesday ad?"

"Just put 'Tuesday free' in the subject line."

The man nods. "Thanks." He steps back, then furrows his brow. "You don't have your sign up, either."

Dave nods. "We have a new logo, so we're redoing the sign and the website. They'll be up soon."

"Cool." he says, "Good to see the local newspaper flourishing."

"Absolutely!" Dave agrees.

I'm a beat behind, "Yes. Absolutely. Thanks."

As the car pulls away, I turn to Dave. "What did you just do?"

"I just sold your first ad."

"For a paper that doesn't exist. And, also, you actually gave it away."

Dave shrugs. "It exists now. And that ad is a loss leader — just like the free dessert I give customers on their birthdays."

"Dave! We don't even own this place. I don't even know if you want to move to Oak Junction. And what if I can't get the paper running? What if it's too much for me?"

"Paige."

"Yes?"

He opens his arms and, when I step in, folds them tight around me. When he talks, I hear his voice through my ears, but also feel it as a rumble in my chest. "We're buying this place. I want to live here. You can get the paper running. And all those things are true because I'll be right here with you, and we'll do it together."

It sounds right. It feels right. I press my cheek tight to him and speak back into his chest. "Thanks for helping me come home."

Reviews mean everything ...

Reviews help me sell books. More sales let me write more books. A simple star rating and a few quick words are all it takes to help other readers decide if they want to read my books.

To write a short review, please go to this link – www.amzn.com/1990802338 – or, use this QR code:

And, if you liked this book, and want to make sure you don't miss my next release, follow me on BookBub, or sign up for my newsletter.

... learn about Paige's back story in *She's Out There*, the prequel to the Paige Turner Mystery series – free when you sign up to my newsletter.

Prologue — *She's Out There*

The world's gone green and wet. After two days of steady rain, the driveway's more puddles than gravel and the trees have closed in around the property, their branches low-bowed from the constant stream of rain drops along their leaves.

Despite my raincoat and umbrella, a rivulet of water is snaking its way down my back.

The dogs are happy, though. Their silky topcoats shed much of the rain, and they rarely lift their noses from the ground, following the moisture-amplified scents.

I don't want to get any wetter, but I also don't want to take the dogs in where, water-resistant coats or not, they'll waft wet-dog smell throughout the house.

While I hesitate, an SUV comes bouncing and splashing down the potholed drive.

Its paint is sun-faded and specks of rust rim the wheels, but the bold decal on the driver's side door pulls my eye away from those features. Oak Junction Journal — Telling the whole story.

I glance over to the dogs, but they're fine. The woman getting out of the vehicle isn't nearly as interesting as whatever critter died in the spot where they're taking turns rolling.

So, wet-*and* carcass-smelling dog later. Great.

I step forward. "Hi?" I don't particularly want to chat as the watercourse down my back widens to a stream. Then again, if the OJJ wants to feature the business, that's free advertising we can use. "Can I help you?"

"Yes, my name is Annelise Silver. I write for the Oak Junction Journal." She holds out a card which I take and shove into the back pocket of my cut-off shorts before the rain can pulp it.

"I've seen your name in the paper."

She smiles. "Great. Perhaps you've also seen the news about Cassidy Winthrop?"

The smile I was about to give her in return freezes. As does the blood in my veins. Cassidy Winthrop. A thirteen-year-old girl missing from the city.

"Yes." I swallow before I can continue. "I heard the story on the news yesterday." On the car radio, to be precise. Two words — *missing girl* — stopping my breath as I drove to the grocery store. I arrived with my knuckles white from gripping the steering wheel and no recollection of the turns I took to get to the parking lot.

Annelise nods. "I'm going door-to-door asking people if they're seen something out of place. For example, is there somewhere on your property a young girl could be hiding, or trapped?"

A dozen questions bounce around my brain, and an equal number of emotions squeeze my heart, but I answer on auto-pilot. "Well, of course, we have the tents — they're the A-frame style army surplus ones — we use them for our outdoor adventure clients. Although we don't have any clients right now, because ..." I lift my hand to the rain. "Nobody wants to mountain bike in a deluge. Or whitewater raft, although you're already wet, so what's the big deal? But I just checked the tents while I was walking the dogs, to make sure they weren't leaking. And I looked in the office, too — the old cowshed —" *Paige, you're babbling*, I warn myself.

It's the nerves. And the inner turmoil.

If you liked the first part of She's Out There, *why not read the rest of the story? You can get it by signing up for my newsletter using the above QR code, or with this link — https://BookHip.com/QVPSFBL.*

About the Author

I've spent my whole life writing - I wrote my first novel in a spiral-bound notebook when I was twelve.

Even that very early novel was inspired by (maybe stolen from?) my favourite childhood books. I loved mysteries with a strong sense of setting. I always wanted to write myself a part in those stories and work and play alongside the characters.

I still love books that can pull me in and make me feel, "that's a place I'd like to live," "those are people I'd like to spend time with." Writers like Louise Penny, Dick Francis, Kathy Reichs, and Sara Rosett give me that feeling, and when not reading books by these, and other talented authors, I write my own.

I write immersive, page-turning mysteries about ordinary people who have complicated histories.

To help generate ideas for my writing, I hike, run, ride horses, and volunteer with my local food centre, and my best times are doing just about anything with my two university-aged children, my husband, and our sweet rescue potcake.

I'd love to hear from you at tudor@tudorrobins.com!

www.ingramcontent.com/pod-product-compliance
Lightning Source LLC
Chambersburg PA
CBHW061616190726